Other Books by
George W. Clever

Dancing with Grandfather (Time line of one life in Poetry)

Bear Lake Monster and Other Clever Stories (Short Stories)

Lenape Animal Tales (Oral stories of the Lenape Indians)

7 Twisted Mysteries to Die For (Short mystery stories)

No Longer Needed: Robotic Short Stories (Human vs robot stories)

Bright Colored Beads (Poems with an American Indian flavor)

Words Can Kill

A Mystery Novel by

George W. Clever

Published by:

Words Can Kill

A Mystery Novel by

George W. Clever

Printed in the United States of America

First Printing, 2017

ISBN-13:
978-0692985120 (George W. Clever)

ISBN-10:
0692985123
8108 Bear Lake Rd., Stockton, NY 14784

www.Cleverartandbooks.com

<u>Dedication</u>

To my grandmothers, grandfathers and all my relations

Acknowledgements

I am indebted to four very special women for their assistance with my first novel. Niece Jessie Clever-McQuaid, a successful author of historical romance novels, for sharing her writing experiences. She recommending Alicia Dean for manuscript editing when I sought professional help. Alicia kindly dealt with my rough grammatical and punctuation writing style, offering excellent suggestions for necessary improvements in the story line and composition. My prayers go with Autumn Fisher. She shared information on her work in Nevada rescuing Mexican and Central American children who have been sold into slavery. What I learned from her made this book more than a novel of my imagination. Once again, my wife, Jennifer, propped up my flagging motivation throughout the last three years, as she encouraged me to finish the novel.

Words Can Kill

1

Write Forever

"Nothing! Nothing! Staring at this damn monitor screen for an hour and all I get is...

NOTHING! Why did I ever think I could be a writer?" Fred yelled out loud. "All I want is to write something of any value, something publishers will buy. Write about what, the mess my life has become, no job, Myrna on a rant since her mother came to stay with us? I know I'm just hiding out here in the basement pretending to be a writer. Everything has already been written, said, and done before, by talented writers the world over. I can't even come up with a piece of crap to take to my Write Circle meeting on Friday. Hell, I avoided every college class that required a term paper. I should have known better. Got to write about something. Maybe a magic prompt waits for me in the bowels of a web search. There is a bunch of writer groups that post prompts, most of which really suck. What is this one? Trouble getting started with your writing? Click on this picture of a pen and you will be on your way. Caution!

George W. Clever

Once you do, you may not be able to stop writing. Now that is a cool prompt, a continual flow of ideas to write each day. Might even be a best seller novel in this thing. But what does it mean, you may not be able to stop writing? Ah! The warning is probably just a hook for some commercial ad covering any writing directions from the stupid prompt. Oh, why not. My brain is empty. Finger, do your mouse dance. A blue flashing monitor is not what I expected. That's weird. What kind of prompt is this? All it says is Write Now."

No instant thought about the next great novel appeared in writer Fred's head or on the screen. *Maybe a story prompt would come if I had a cup of coffee first*. He thought. The words Have a cup of coffee first, slowly became visible on the blank monitor screen. A steaming hot cup of coffee was placed at his elbow. Feeling the burning heat from the cup, Fred jerked his arm away, turning with a fake surprise on his face as his wife Myrna entered the room. He had not heard her footsteps, but the smell of her Night Shade perfume preceded her like a queen's herald trumpets.

Words Can Kill

"Thought you might like to have coffee as you do your weekly writing assignment for the Write Circle," she said. "Having any luck with the next great novel?"

"No, just looking for a place to start," he replied.

"Are you going to do anything around here today beside stare at your computer? Fred, am I to do all the housework, and still keep my job at the candy factory now that you have been fired from the call center? You have never made any money from your writing or books."

Myrna left the room without a reply, and Fred was alone again staring at the bright blinking eye. Words began to scrawl across the screen. *Write again*. *Who was it at this website wanting me to start my writing again, and how did they know I was going for coffee?* Fred considered. He set the steaming hot coffee cup down on his desk blotter. *Was it just a coincidence my wife arrived at that moment with my morning brew? The same words I was thinking appeared on the screen. Is this website reading my thoughts? How can it do that? Impossible. I must be imagining things, and yet this is happening. Just a bit too spooky for me.* Random thoughts ran through Fred's mind on most occasions when he was thinking about a story, or in this case, the possibility he had stumbled on to a very amazing, but frightening website. One of these unexpected butterfly thoughts pushed its way into his mind. *It looks cloudy today with a breeze from the lake. I had better take a jacket when I go to the Write Circle meeting.* He called these thoughts mental butterflies. Some guys, at the neighborhood bar he occasionally visited, called the thoughts brain farts.

His exact thoughts about taking a jacket began to form on the big lighted TV eye. ***I had better take a jacket when I go to the Write Circle meeting.*** Moving closer to the screen, Fred intently studied the words that appeared. *This cannot be! How could my thoughts about the weather be written on my computer screen?* He hunched over the keyboard as the wonder of this website began to sink into his half-awake morning brain.

Fred's shoulders began to feel warmer in the cool basement computer room as the press of a jacket covered

Words Can Kill

his back, and its sleeves hung down by his arms. It was a shiny maroon sports jacket with the Indian on the pocket, a jacket his father had worn. Fred turned from the screen with a start expecting his wife Myrna nearby. She obviously had returned to the room with the jacket. *Myrna probably noticed it was a bit chilly here in the basement computer room,* he thought. She was not there. No one was in the room. This was way too weird for even a writer with Fred's imagination. *Could it really be that this website was able to read my thoughts? Even if it could read what I am thinking, how did it make my thoughts appear on the computer screen? And then it made them come true? All this must just be from my lack of sleep last night. Perhaps it is one of those memory lapses a guy my age could expect to experience in the early mental stages of Alzheimer's.*

He considered one more test of the site. But what kind of test? *No, this is just too much foolishness*, he said to himself. *I really need to get something ready for the Friday meeting of the Write Circle. There could be some danger in just any thought running through my head so early in the morning, especially if the unplanned thought would come true.* A little voice rattled a warning in Fred's head. *'Choose your test carefully.' Ok, just to end this foolishness I will start a nonsense story with a catchy line,* he said to himself.

He returned to writing the line in his detective story he had left when the coat mysteriously was placed on his cold shoulders. *Mike opened the door of the old Coldspot Sears refrigerator looking for something to eat after a long night of boozing with his buddies.* He paused studying the screen. Nothing appeared. Another butterfly thought popped into his mind. *It was empty with the exception of a small plate holding a chunk of moldy, blue, and fuzzy cheese.   It was empty with the exception of ....**a small plate holding a chunk of moldy, blue, and fuzzy cheese**; appeared on the screen. A little flowery plate of nasty looking blue cheese appeared on Fred's desk.*

"What the hell is this?' He shouted. "Things I think to write in my story happen here? Damn odd, but it sure looks like a good start to my short story." He mused.

Words Can Kill

Fred was beginning to realize at that moment it would no longer be necessary for him to pound out story lines on the keyboard. All he had to do was think a line and it would appear. This was better than his Dragon software where it was necessary to speak the line into the computer microphone for it to print on the screen, He did not consider two troubling side effects of the writing assist. His story thoughts were materializing not only in print on the computer screen, but in his real world. They were brain farts he could not control.

*****

2

A Classic burn

Fred continued thinking about a better first line hook to his new detective story. Was it a strong hook for the reader? He typed several lines. *It was time for Mike Dunmore Private Eye to have a fine celebration and pay his long overdue bill at Kelly's Bar. He had finished a case for a lovely female client with beautiful long legs, legs he admired one more time as she handed him a healthy check for his services. Finding a way for his client to ignore a prenuptial agreement required a smelly and messy dig through the dumpster behind the Casey house the couple seldom shared. Mike found evidence that would help his client, the respectable Helen Casey, wife of the Free Party candidate for Governor, Harlan Casey. In spite of the Casey's pre-nuptial agreement, it was Helen Casey's intent to squeeze every last divorce dollar from her trucking company owner husband, turned aspiring politician. The evidence Mike found for Helen Casey could put Mr. Casey in the slammer for a long time.*

Opening the door to Kelly's Bar, it took a moment for Mike's eyes to adjust from the bright daylight to the purposely subdued and recessed neon lighted room. The people Mike loosely called friends in Kelly's Bar and Barbeque previously were more than happy to help him spend his retainer money. Yes, it was a fine time until the owner of the bar, Kelly, ran in from the parking lot to pick up his cell phone on the bar calling 911 and the fire department. He reported a car was on fire in the bar's parking lot. But whose car would it be?

The answer to Fred's question popped into his head. *Mike's car is on fire, appeared on Fred's computer screen.*

Kelly dropped the phone yelling, "Mike, your car is on fire."

The bar emptied as its patrons rushed to the door eyeing the fire department suppression team in action as the bright yellow pumper truck rolled into the Bar parking lot. Patrons made bets when the car would explode, and lend a fireworks touch to their previously tame evening. Mike watched the firemen hose down his burning wreck with chemicals, and stayed until the AAA wrecker hauled the smoldering mess to the police impound yard before

Words Can Kill

*calling a cab for his ride home. It was a bad ending to his
expected celebration. So much for my big payoff from the
Casey case after losing his classic Dodge Charger car.
Mike thought. It was not much of a car, but the old '69
Dodge Charger with its rust patina would still bring a
pretty penny as a barn find on E Bay for all those car
collector guys who wanted to restore a real muscle car.
Mike doubted the angry wife client, Helen Casey, would
accept another expense sheet additional bill for his burned
classic muscle car replacement.*

*Odd how quickly the car burned. The fire
investigator said it looked like a spark had set off a leak
from the gas tank. That explanation did not make any sense
to Mike as he just had the original rusty gas tank replaced.
The price of a gallon of leaked gas was not something his
meager income would stand for very long. Nothing is ever
an accident in Mike's book. Someone had torched his car,
but who was it? He could think of too many possible
suspects from his line of work. Looks like it would be
another free-be case to add to his endless list of no money
payout deals. Finding out who torched his car would have*

to wait until the next morning. He needed a few winks to clear his head of one too many margaritas. Back in his efficiency apartment he was going to sleep hungry. Mike made it a habit never to eat anything blue and fuzzy, the only things found when he looked into his refrigerator.

Just as before, none of the lines Fred typed appeared on the screen by themselves. Nothing was made real as he wrote more of the detective story. He hit the file 'Save As' icon for his story, and pushed away from the keyboard. Fred looked again at the flowery plate holding a chunk of fuzzy blue cheese resting on the corner of his desk. In that same instance, a butterfly thought fluttered into his thinking. He remembered the file saved was not checked for grammar errors.

"I wish grammar errors could be corrected without my help." He mumbled.

The same words appeared on the computer screen. Fred opened the story file again, and re-read the story lines. Any error in grammar or spelling was corrected. Proper paragraphs were made and incomplete thoughts completed.

Words Can Kill

His eyes opened wide in amazement as he began to smile broadly. He thought, *this is truly a miracle website for writers.* At least it seemed that way to him until one of those rogue mental butterflies drifted into his thinking again. As he reached for another sip of the coffee his wife had provided, it was cold. *Sure would be nice if my coffee never was cold.* His thought words began to appear on the computer screen. **Coffee in cup is never cold.**

His cup on is desk began to boil the coffee until the steaming liquid overflowed, spilling onto the floor. "Oh No! That was not what I wanted to happen," he shouted. "My coffee was not to boil forever!" His thought words appeared on the screen again, ***The Coffee was not to boil forever***. *The coffee stopped boiling, and the mess on the floor was gone. Smoke began to drift under the basement door putting Fred's nose on alert. There was a fire in the neighborhood somewhere.*

Rising from his desk chair he could smell acrid smoke seeping under his basement office door. Fred opened the door to check on the source of the smoke, and heard fire sirens. Pumper fire trucks were arriving in his neighborhood. Across the street he could see smoke billowing from his neighbor, Mike Haskell's garage. Yes, neighbor Mike was a city detective, and owned a classic '69 Dodge Charger. It was now on fire.

Fred ran back to his computer and read the lines of his story again. *Kelly ran in to call the fire department and report a car in his parking lot was on fire. It was Mike's car. Was it just a weird coincidence his neighbor Mike's car was also burning? I did not want my neighbor Mike's car to burn, he thought returning to his desk.* The words appeared on the screen. ***I did not want Mike's car across the street to burn.***

Rushing back to the cellar door, he could see there were no fire trucks across the street. No smoke was pouring from neighbor Mike's garage. Fred returned again to the computer desk a bit shaken. He assured himself he would be very careful with his story writing thinking, especially if he received one of those damned butterfly thoughts.

Words Can Kill

Perhaps I should try repeating the mantra when I was hypnotized to stop smoking. He considered.

"I must keep focused. I must keep focused. I must keep focused. I must keep focused. I must keep focused." Fred repeated out loud.

A familiar feeling of panic raced up his spine creating a numbness he had felt before. *What if I write somewhere away from my computer where I will not be able to make a corrected thought? What if one of my brain farts has no inverse correction? Maybe I should stop writing and re-boot my computer to make this all go away. That would be silly. What harm can my writing do?*

*****

3

Mistaken Identity

A hammer was pounding in Mike's head from one too many margaritas the night of his car fire. It was almost as loud as the sound of someone's fist pounding on his apartment door. He gave up on his dreamtime of hitting the lottery, and forced his tired body into motion toward the vibrating door.

"Who is it?"

"It's Sergeant Keith Farrell, homicide. Open the door."

Farrell was well known as a bulldog that never let go of a case until it was solved. Mike had worked as Keith Farrell's partner during his first year as a cop. Being a police officer was all Mike's father ever wanted for his son's life work. Sliding the two door bolts and a chain from their security place, he opened the door a crack.

"Jeeze Keith, I just closed my eyes after a hard night celebrating at Kelly's Bar. What do you want?"

George W. Clever

Detective Farrell pushed his way to Mike's one room efficiency apartment, and slumped into a well- worn leather chair near the kitchen stove.

"They found a body in the trunk of your chard Charger this morning or at least what was left of it. The fire pretty much cremated anything that looked like a human. What do you know about that?"

Mike steadied himself by the door. "They found WHAT?"

"Our police impound wrecking yard found a badly burned body in the trunk of that piece of junk you called your car. Put on some clothes. I need to ask you some questions, and I don't like to do it to a friend while he is standing in front of me wearing only white boxer briefs."

*****

Fred paused to consider what he should have Mike say. His fingers rested on the keyboard leaving enough time in his brain for one of those dastardly butterfly thoughts to make its way forward. *What would I say if I were Mike in*

Words Can Kill

this early morning scenario? **What would I say if I were Mike?** *appeared on the big blue computer eye. There was a knock at the door and a voice said, "Open up the door Mike. It's Sergeant Keith Haskell. I need to ask you a few questions about last night."*

Fred cautiously opened his front door ready to tell who ever was there they had the wrong house. No Mike living here. An officer of the Marin County PD was standing there slightly stooped over from the weight of his heavy pistol and equipment belt. His belly overlap was evidence a few too many donuts had settled around his waist. Fred recognized the policeman to be his neighbor from across the street. He opened the basement door and Detective Sergeant Keith walked in without an invitation. He settled into the old leather chair by the cellar stairs, and looked disapprovingly at Fred.

"God Mike, get some clothes on or I will have to arrest you for indecent exposure. Got you out of your bed did I, and at one o'clock in the afternoon? I need to ask you a few questions."

George W. Clever

In a panic, Fred hurried back to his desk where the computer sat idly on the ready. Ignoring Sergeant Keith, he sat in the desk chair confused for a moment thinking, *I don't want to know what Sergeant Keith will ask or what I will say! My name is not Mike. Why doesn't my neighbor know that? What can I say to him? The computer clicked and blinked out the words,* **don't want to know or say***. Furniture in the efficiency bedroom fell away like a tower of cards blown by a ceiling fan. Fred was once again in his familiar basement writing room. No Sergeant Keith would be waiting for his answer that day.*

"Dam mental butterflies!!" Fred mumbled to himself as he returned to his typing.

*****

4

One More Question

Throwing on his old Corps sweat suit, Mike returned to face Sergeant Keith's questions.

"Ok Keith, what do you want from me? I was just in Kelly's Bar last night celebrating my big payoff from a client."

"What can you tell me about the fire that torched your car, and the body we found in its trunk?" Keith answered.

"What! You found a body in my car trunk?" The news cleared the cobwebs from Mike's brain.

Keith continued, "Yes sir, the guys at impound had quite a surprise this morning when they did an investigation teardown of the car to determine the cause of the fire."

"Who was the person in my trunk, Sergeant?"

"Well about the same time today, we had a missing person's report for one Helen Casey. Our lab guys may be able to determine if the body they found might be Mrs. Casey. Do you know her?"

George W. Clever

"Yes. Oh my God...., she was a client. I was paid by her yesterday for the snoop work she hired me to do. That is why I was celebrating at Kelly's Bar last night when my car was torched."

"I think you had better consider carefully what you tell me now, Mike. Perhaps, as a friend, I would tell you to call a lawyer."

"I've nothing to hide Keith. I will tell you what I know."

"Ok, let's begin again. Where were you last night, Mike?"

"I was in the Kelly's Bar about nine o'clock last night knocking a few down. I was celebrating being able to pay my rent and my bar bill when Kelly, the bar owner, ran into the taproom shouting, 'There's a car on fire in the parking lot.' Then he picked up his cell phone on the counter behind the bar and called 911 reporting the fire. We all ran out of the taproom and watched our local Hose Company #5 in action. It was then I realized the burning car was mine. I didn't know any person was in the trunk of my car. The fire was so hot no one wanted to get close enough to see if anyone was in the car. The damn thing could have

Words Can Kill

exploded. There was not a body in the trunk when I parked the old Charger as far as I know. Are you sure the body was a woman? Did she die from the fire?"

"Just let me ask the questions Mike. We are looking at a homicide here, and the body was in your car trunk. Tell me again. What time did you arrive at the bar?"

"Around nine or nine thirty that night I think."

"Anyone you know in the bar able and willing to back up your arrival time?"

"Well there's Kelly who served me my Black Label beer. That is if he remembers. He is not rowing with both oars lately. Some kind of personal problem I think."

"Anyone else see you come in?"

"Yes, Carmichael, my pawn shop friend told me he was there a few minutes after eight. He said Oscar, my old desk Sergeant, came in a few minutes later."

"Is that the best you can do?"

George W. Clever

"What's wrong with you Keith? Am I one of your suspects in this case?"

"You never were one to hold back your thoughts Mike. Words seem to fall out of your mouth before the thoughts roll around in your brain. Perhaps you should know the burned body we found in the trunk of your car, if it was Helen Casey, it would be the wife of Harlan Casey the trucking company mogul who is running for Governor on the Free Party. You admit knowing her."

Detective Sergeant Keith took a look around Mike's apartment checking for something useful in his case before continuing with his questioning.

"We checked with your part-time secretary girlfriend, Angel Offrey. She said you were working on a case involving Harlan and Helen Casey, and yes you unfortunately are listed as a known suspect in the murder investigation. Don't leave town. Just one more question. Any of that old P.T.S.D. grab you watching your car burn?"

*****

5

Good Thoughts

Fred paused his typing. He stared into one of those empty abysses writers encounter when creative juices fail. His story string had played out leaving no clear direction to send his main character Mike. The story was going well so far with a twenty-five-hundred-word count. *I am sure this novel will bring an offer of at least $5000 from some publisher,* he considered. *Yes, one first time author recently in the news even received $4,000,000 advance from Knopf Publishing.*

Myrna yelled down from the top of the stairs, "How long are you going to stay down there Fred? You know mother needs to have you move the furniture in her room. Her bed is in the wrong place."

If I could receive a four-million-dollar advance from Knoph, I could have moving company guys move her damn bed, he rationalized. His writing on the computer screen vanished, and these words replaced it. **Receive a**

novel advance from Knoph Publishers for $4,000,000.
The cell phone on his desk rang like an alarm bell. Staring at the computer screen, Fred flipped open the phone knowing the call and the words on the screen were connected for better or perhaps worse.

"Hello, this is Becky Wilson from Knoph Publishing. Is this Fred Fonsworth?"

"Yes, this is Fred Fonsworth. How can I help you?"

"Well, Mr. Fonsworth, we are interested in publishing your recent mystery novel about the Private Detective with the burning Dodge Charger. Our publishing company is willing to advance four million dollars to you for the rights to publish this exciting novel. If you agree to the terms of the contract I am faxing to you, sign it, and return it to me by tomorrow along with your final draft of the novel. We have reserved a Swiss bank account for you where the money will be deposited. Are you interested, Mr. Fonsworth?"

Fred's mouth hung like a castle drawbridge just opening. "You said, four-million-dollars for an advance?"

Words Can Kill

"Yes, Mr. Fonsworth, four million dollars as an advance, but we must hear from you by tomorrow, and receive your final edited story. An Email contract attachment is being sent to you at this moment. Remember now, it is critical we receive the manuscript by tomorrow. Goodbye now."

Fred knew there is no way he could produce a final edited story by the next day. He didn't even have a title. His novel was missing a middle and an ending. There was a buzz and a blinding flash from his computer when these new words appeared. **No title, no middle story, no ending, no $4,000,000 offer from Knoph**. Once again his butterfly thoughts seemed to have been read by the computer, and turned into on-time reality. Again to his relief, there was an inverse to one of his butterfly thoughts. There would be no further additions to his novel story line this day as he hit Save As, and shut the computer down.

As a writer, he began to realize there was great potential for a computer website with the ability to read his butterfly thoughts, and best of all, create a new improved reality. He began to consider the dark side danger of this wonderful writing prompt website. *What if one of those crazy ideas floating through my brain had dire consequences with no inverse? What if the brain fart received was an evil revenge? Yes, all humans, including me, are capable of thinking those black revenge ideas and worse. I know these types of thoughts have come to me when someone in the past caused me to experience something harmful physically or emotionally. What if I would accidently think about someone being killed in a fall? It could happen. And that kind of reality event would most likely not be reversible.*

It was time for lunch, and time for thinking about the possibilities this wondrous website contained for motivating writers. *What could it do for someone out of a job living on unemployment and his wife's paycheck? What if I just thought about a small prize from Publishers Clearing House? Would that be so wrong if money showed up in my mail or maybe a visit from Gilbert Gottfried holding a big cardboard check? If it appeared to have some scary consequence, I could just send it back in the mail.*

*****

6

Experiment with a Butterfly

Lunch was a quick rubber sandwich of stale lunch meat, a tall glass of water, and a few chip crumbs left in the bottom of the nearly empty bag. Fred had a pressing website experiment to do before the afternoon slipped away. Settling into his squeaky black desk chair, he logged in with his Star Wars Pod Racer prompt. His hand shook slightly as it moved the mouse to click the mysterious icon delivering those special writers prompts. Only then did he notice the title of the website, Writing is a Virus. *What could that mean?* he wondered.

Fred Googled the word virus. It read: A virus is a small infectious life form replicating inside living cells of host organisms. They can infect all life forms as an important transfer of horizontal genes creating increased diversity. Fred pondered the virus definition scrolling through several offerings. *Could this be an ultimate virus creating diversity in reality by manipulation of any writer's thoughts? Oh well, there is so much more for me to*

George W. Clever

worry about with our mortgage coming do next week, troubles in the Middle East, and terrorism in our airports. I will concentrate on making my experiment provide at least one economic solution for me.

He clicked on his documents file bringing up the unnamed story. *Now, what will Mike say to Sergeant Keith about his connection to the murder of his client Helen Casey if she is the body in the burned Charger trunk?* No magic words appeared on the screen. Fred continued to write.

*****

Some believe a writer's story really writes itself. Fred was sure his detective story was a good example of a story writing itself as he began to pound out the P.I.s interrogation by Homicide Detective Sergeant Keith.

"My dealings with Mrs. Casey were only business although she was quite a hot babe. Guess that is a bad joke now, what you might call 'Politically Incorrect', with her possibly being a crispy critter in my car trunk. Never could

Words Can Kill

figure out why that Casey guy would be in the mess he was with her at home," Mike said with a slightly twisted smile.

"Ok, Mike, tell me about the work you did for her."

"Keith, normally my client cases are very confidential. Considering she might have bitten the bullet, I will tell you all I learned in the three weeks she paid me to tail her husband. She was ready to divorce him and wanted out of their pre-nup agreement. The only way that was going to happen was if she could gather enough dirt on him to twist his arm into giving her a substantial block of change in their divorce."

"Well did you find what she needed?"

"Yes, he was shipping illegal immigrant children into New York in his trucks. He ran a slick business with the trucking hauls from the Mexican and Canadian border where over116 million vehicles cross each year. He played the numbers game moving kids the syndicate wanted for prostitution, sweatshop slavery, and as drug couriers in unmarked trucks driven by his mules. If the mule was caught they would never make the connection to Casey

fearing death would make a call to their families. Casey paid off judges and lawyers who would free any of those drivers caught. He made one big mistake as all in the crime game do."

"What was that Mike?"

"He was careless with his trash and talked in his sleep."

"What did you do to earn your pay from Mrs. Casey?"

"I turned one of his angry mistresses into a photographer. Then I turned his gardener into a dumpster diver with me. I gave Helen the bedroom pictures and some smelly papers connecting him to the child sex slave trade."

"You keep anything from that case in your office?"

"No. Helen Casey got all of it."

"You sure there is nothing in some file, Mike? I know you better."

"Nothing Keith."

Words Can Kill

"Ok Mike, that is all for now. One more thing, how did you know the body in your trunk was shot? I noticed you said she bit the bullet."

"Just a figure of speech Keith, just a figure of speech."

*****

Yes, I could really use a big prize like those offered by Publisher's Clearing House, Fred mused. *Maybe it is time to do a little experiment with this magic website.* He watching the computer screen intently, and was impatient when no words appeared. Nothing changed in his writing room. No doorbell or phone rang. *Maybe this kind of thing takes a bit longer,* he considered. Still no prize presenter appeared. No large check carried by Gilbert Gottfried with a balloon carrying girl. He waited for a knock at his door.

After an hour waiting for words to appear on the computer monitor, Fred began to understand the failure of his experiment. His prize thought was not one of those butterfly type thoughts that jump into a conscience brain. He realized this Publisher's Clearing House prize experiment thought was pre-meditated by him, and just like pre-meditated murder, it had a steep penalty. The jury's decision? Nothing would happen. There would be no planned riches from this site unless he accidently had a brain fart thought about receiving a fine reward. *But how could he control those pesky mental butterflies so that one of them would contain a fine reward?* He considered.

"Fred, are you coming up? I need you to fix the leaky kitchen faucet," Myrna yelled from the kitchen.

"Be up in a moment Myrna. I want to finish this section of my novel."

Feeling the pressure of yet one more marching order from Myrna interrupting his writing, Fred set his problem of controlling brain farts aside to finish the last line in the chapter.

*****

7

Hide the File

Mike closed his apartment front door as Sergeant Keith of Homicide opened his squad car passenger door. As the blue uniformed officer pulled the dark blue Ford away from the curb, Mike reached for his cell phone.

"Hello Angel, this is Mike."

Like most men, Mike hated to talk on the phone. He would make this as short a call as possible.

"I want you to find the file I taped to the underside of my desk. Stuff it in your blouse, and take it to the bus station on the corner of 54th and Owl Street."

Fred continued to type with untapped energy as Mike's phone conversation with his secretary Angel flowed onto the monitor screen.

"Take a side trip through the Maryvale Mall with some shopping stops. Make sure you are not followed. No I am not going to pay for your shopping spree. Maybe lunch

later on me? The bus station is at the end of the mall near the Sears store. Put the file in an empty locker. Bring the key to Carmichael's Pawn. He keeps stuff for me. Just say it is for Mike. Did anyone other than Sergeant Keith show up at the office today? No? Ok, no I will not tell you why. I don't want to throw away this cell phone I am using, at least not yet. There may be spooks monitoring it since I became a suspect in their case of the burned body in my car. Will see you tonight at Kelly's Bar. I have a few things to check out there and need a date cover. Ok, a real date. Yes, I will spring for the dinner tab. See you at 1900. Bye."

Mike grabbed a quick shower shedding his old Corps sweats for the kind of clothes that would make him less conspicuous at a truck stop. His thoughts tumbled out like a pocket full of business receipts when he was preparing some client's bill. Maybe one of his old Marine Corp buddies who worked for Purple Trucking might provide a lead on who would be interested in having Mrs. Casey knocked off. If the woman in my trunk was Helen Casey, it would seem too easy to hang her murder on the sleaze husband. Harlan did have a powerful motive, but

Words Can Kill

there were always more ants under the picnic table, ants that knew the husband would be the first suspect the cops would finger as the killer, and car torch. If it is the body of Helen Casey in the trunk of my car, the discovery would make me the second fall guy.

He paused to load his Browning nine-millimeter automatic pistol while doing a re-run in his mind of something Keith had said. The burned body's DNA normally used for identification was impaired by the heat of the burning car. Why were there not dental records or some other more definitive result from the coroner's autopsy?

*****

8

Eat a Horse

"Even writers get hungry. I'm so hungry I could eat a horse", Fred said out loud. **Eat a horse** *appeared on his screen.*

"Oh No!" He yelled with a scream strong enough to penetrate the cellar cement block walls.

His explosive shout volume would not be enough to halt what was expected next from an accidental mental butterfly.

On schedule, someone knocked at his front door.

A voice hollered "UPS Package for Fred Fonsworth."

He opened the door a crack to see a brown clad driver in short pants, clipboard in hand, standing beside a huge cardboard box with Keep Cold labels.

"Mr. Fonsworth? I need a signature."

George W. Clever

The driver thrust the pen and the clipboard through the crack in the door. He moved the box slightly away from the door so it could be easily moved inside. Fred could hear scraping sounds the cardboard box made sliding across loose cement stones.

"It's from Rolling Hills Stables. You expecting a saddle?" He said with a smirk.

To sign or not to sign? That is the question. Shakespeare could not have said it better, Fred thought. If I don't sign maybe the delivery box with go back in the truck with the man in the short pants. I certainly do not want to eat a horse! Pushing the clipboard back through the widening opening, the front door began to creak with the added strain the security chain. Fred slammed the door closed pressing his back hard against it. In panic, he turned and peered through the peep hole.

The UPS delivery man let a curse out as he lifted the large box back onto his dolly, and pulled it toward the street. Fred would not have to eat the horse. He was again relieved to know this mental butterflies had an inverse. His

Words Can Kill

lunch would be just peanut butter and strawberry jelly this day.

Pouring a tall glass of milk, Fred spoke aloud like Myrna was across the table. "I wish I had never opened that writers prompt website. I have so little control over #$% mental butterflies. They could get me into serious trouble. Oh well, who cares?"

He remembered there were only 75000 words to go, and his first novel would be completed. *Let's see, that is about 15 days if I pound out 5000 words a day. No time for a good TV western movie break today. I still have 2000 words to go,"* he concluded.

Fred put the milk carton back into the refrigerator, cleaned off the kitchen counter, and returned to his basement man cave. Rocking back in his chair, he thought about Mike's predicament. *Harlan was a dangerous enemy well versed in keeping himself off the front pages of the newspapers, except when the publicity would promote his campaign for Governor. He would not be passive if and when the cops got to close. Some other doper would be*

George W. Clever

found to take the fall. This time it might not be a doper, but a private eye. What could Mike learn from his visit with an old friend, Gunny Jackson? I know my best writing will have to wait. Myrna's endless "to do list" was growing longer and her demanding voice, shriller since I have been laid off at work. Maybe after doing a few of those irritating chores the remainder of the afternoon would be my writing time again.

It was long after lunch before Fred had enough chores checked off of Myrna's list to keep her happy. Eager to returned to his computer, he had plans for the important meeting of the P.I. and his mentor Gunny Jackson.

*****

Tom Jackson didn't answer his phone. Maybe he was on a run with one of the Purple Truck drivers solving truck troubles, or out in the yard checking in a stolen rig recovered by truck bounty hunters. Mike considered those possibilities. Still, even then he could be reached by the cell phone he always carried. Why wasn't he answering his phone? A quick call to Angel told him she had followed his

Words Can Kill

instructions, and was handling the phones in his office as her part-time secretary gig. No one called except a few local politicians asking for campaign donations.

Sergeant Keith did not return with more questions even after Angel had made a new pot of his favorite hazelnut coffee. Mike had one more job for her that afternoon.

"Angel, see if you can get a security video copy of the Kelly's Bar parking lot on the night someone torched my car. Kelly told me he was thinking about installing new motion CCTV digital cameras with night vision so the data could be sent directly to his computer at the bar. I don't think he had the extra cash to spend so the old video security camera tape system is probably still recording in his office. The original tape may have been taken by Sergeant Keith, but your roommate Karen, working in Precinct 81 properties department, can get it for us. She owes me a favor for paying her overzealous landlord a visit the night he climbed through her bedroom window to fix *the bathroom sink. Have Karen copy the tape if she has it, and see what information you can get from it. I want to know the numbers of visible license plates on cars parked there at the hour Mrs. Casey was at the bar. The tape may tell us how my car was burned. Take the license numbers down and see Amber in the DMV on 34th Street. She will provide license data if you tell her it is for me."*

"No, I did not sleep with her. We go back a long way. Her husband was my second patrol partner. That was just before the police shrinks chased me out of the cop business. Yes, I know she could lose her job for providing us information about license holders. See her during her noon lunch at the Golden Arches. She's a regular."

Mike hung up and called the Enterprise Car Rental agency for a rental vehicle until he could come up with enough scratch to replace his burned classic Charger. Twenty minutes later, he was picked up by a young rental agent who did not look old enough to hold a driver license. After completing some car rental paper shuffling, Mike drove to the office of the Purple Trucking Company on 79th

Words Can Kill

Street. Surely someone there would know if Gunny Jackson was on a truck run, and why he was not answering his phone.

*****

9

Killer Dog Vanishes

Myrna peered over the banister of the stairs leading down to Fred's man cave. She was holding a dog leash in one hand while petting a snarling, slobbering dog standing knee high at her side.

"Fred, Killer needs to go out and do his ShowTime."

"Can't you take him out Myrna? I'm just a hundred words from my 5000-word story target today."

"No I can't. I'm cleaning up the mess you made last night in the kitchen making spaghetti pie. You can take a few minutes from your writing to give Killer some outside time before he leaves another Baby Ruth candy bar deposit on my kitchen floor."

"All right!"

Reluctantly, Fred took the leash, clipped it onto Killer's collar, and opened the sliding door to their outside patio. The fuzz ball poodle cross Rottweiler darted through the partially opened door pulling Fred along with him. The move was not without face numbing pain as Fred squeezed through the door opening. His shoulder forced the sliding door wider to accommodate the rest of his body, allowing all to pass outside. Fred's arm was nearly twisted out of his shoulder socket as the dog ran to his favorite potty stop location in the back yard. Killer sniffed the corner of the garden fence before lifting his leg to decorate the post. The overgrown poodle then squatted leaving a giant poop for Fred or Myrna to shovel before the dog land mine was stepped in, and poop tracked into the house.

Returning to the kitchen, Fred watched as the dog slobbered down a drink of water from his bowl leaving rivulets of drool on the tile floor. There would be no point in returning to his computer that day. He realized his writing focus was gone. On his way down the cellar stairs where he planned to shut down the computer, he rubbed his aching arms reflecting on joys of dog ownership. *I always wanted a little dog. A little dog eats little food, and makes little poop. Why did Myrna pick this big dog from the pound?* His last thought was not anticipated. *Why didn't Killer have a Poodle and a Chihuahua for parents?*

Words Can Kill

Reaching for the mouse to close his computer for the day, the thin screen above the keyboard blinked. These words appeared. ***Killer's parents are a Poodle and a Chihuahua.***

A horrific scream came from the kitchen followed by a piano roll of shouts from Myrna as she through open the cellar stairs door and demanded an explanation.

"Fred, what have you done with Killer? Who is this tiny dog in my kitchen eating from Killer's bowl? Where is my dog?" She yelled.

Once again Fred climbed the stairs to the kitchen like a beaten dog himself, and stared at the tiny frightened animal partially hidden behind the counter chairs.

"What did you do with my big Killer dog?" Myrna shrieked again.

"#&% mental butterflies." Fred mumbled to himself.

"What did you do with my beautiful big Poodle Rottweiler?" She screamed at a pitch that made the collector plates hanging on the wall tremble.

George W. Clever

"I traded him," Fred said as he turned back toward the cellar stairs.

Looking down into his man cave, he could see the computer screen still blinking. Fred considered the disappearance of old Killer and smiled. This time he did not look for any inverse. *Maybe there was some good coming from this weird writer's prompt site after all*, he considered. It was time to 'Get out of Dodge' and let Myrna deal with her new pet. Returning to his desk chair, new sentences for his story seemed to pour out on the computer screen like rainwater from a gutter down spout.

*****

10

Men's Room Meeting

It took Mike a few minutes to find the trucking firm when his Rio rental car GPS gave him a route taxi cab drivers use when intent on a big fare. The Purple Trucking Company was located in the industrial section of town with rail tracks on one side and eight lanes of interstate on the other. No uniform stood in the guard shed at the gate. Mike drove in like he owned the place, and parked by a sign that read Trucking Manager.

The Purple Trucking office was stashed away at the back of a semi-truck filled yard. Some of the trucks were lined up at the loading dock while others were belching black diesel smoke from poor maintenance as they approached the exit gate. The truck compound was surrounded by a high chain link fence topped with concertina barbed wire. No one in the yard seemed to notice Mike as he climbed the stairs to the heavy metal office door painted a bilious green. As he pulled the heavy metal door open, it made a nail biting screeching sound that could have been silenced with a little maintenance oil.

There was no foyer. The door opened to one large room with a sea of office cubes cast in the blue white light of overhead neon. No company secretary was stationed by the front door. A few of the twenty or more heads, sticking above the sterile gray cube walls, turned to greet him with a 'Who are you?' stare.

Mike spotted one of the cubes who was cleaning his nails with a pen knife and asked, "Is Gunny Jackson here?"

The pen knife holder folded his nail cleaning tool with a puzzled look, and said, "No Gunny here."

"How about Tom Jackson," Mike replied.

"Last cube in the right corner." In a monotone, said the pen knife returning to the fingernail digging job at hand.

Mike picked the most direct path through the maze of cubes, and stood before its desk. The man sitting behind the desk had his feet propped high on the corner wall. Showing only his back to Mike, he was talking on a cell phone. When his call ended, the broad shouldered man

Words Can Kill

swiveled in his chair and dropped his cell phone on the metal desk. A huge voice rolled out from deep in the throat of the stocky man with a receding military haircut.

"Mike Dunmore! What the hell are you doing here?"

It was the DI Marine Corps voice Mike knew well.

"Hey Gunny, I came to see you."

Tom Jackson shook Mike's hand long and hard.

"It has been a while Mike. Last I knew you left the Corps after the first battle of Fallujah instead of re-upping. You sure were one devastating scout sniper. Hell I heard you snuffed over 100 of those rag heads, one with a shot just under 1000 yards. What are you really doing around here?"

"I need a favor Gunny. After Iraq I couldn't keep my head in the cop business. Internal Affairs said I was suffering from PTSD, so I quit the force and opened a private practice. Things are better now, but I need to talk with you about one of my cases. It turned me as a murder suspect. Can we go somewhere to talk?"

George W. Clever

"Sure Mike, follow me into my office." Gunny led Mike back across the cube maze to the men's john. "Stick this wood wedge under the closed door. It makes a cheap lock. We won't be bothered. Now what can I do for you?"

Mike gave Gunny Jackson a short brief on the Casey case, and laid out the questions he came to deliver.

"Last Thursday, I gave Mrs. Casey enough dope on her husband's child slave and prostitution trade to guarantee she would receive a healthy divorce settlement. She turned up missing the next day, and the police think she was dead on Friday. My Charger burned in the Kelly Bar parking lot that night. A burned body was found in the trunk of my car. It could be Helen Casey."

"Why didn't you take all that slimy information about Boss Casey to the police?" Tom asked.

"Well that thought crossed my mind, but PIs have to lean on confidentiality to stay in business. Then there was the possibility Helen Casey would have been tied up in legal court business with her husband for many years. If they went to trial I might not get paid," Mike replied.

Words Can Kill

"Did anyone else know what you found out about Mr. Harlan and his trucking company?"

"No, well only Angel, my secretary, and I keep most of the hot stuff from my cases in a hidden file. I might have told Orville Kelly, the owner of Kelly's Bar, I was wrapping up a case, and would pay off my bar bill on Friday. Never did I say anything about Helen Casey being my client."

Gunny Jackson slid the wooden wedge from the door, and opened it enough to see if anyone was standing outside trying to pull it open. No one was there. He replaced the wedge under the door, and turned to face Mike.

"Can't be too careful in this place. Even the furniture has ears. What do you want from me scout shooter?"

"I know you dispatchers don't miss much of the gossip in the trucking business. Is there anything you can tell me about the racket Harlan Casey was running through his company? I need to know who does his muscle and torch work."

George W. Clever

"I don't know much about all that Mike, but some of the truckers have joined a loose organization to stop the child prostitution infecting too many truck stops. The Truckers Against Trafficking Association, (TATA), regularly works to recruit truckers into their organization. They encourage other truckers to make calls to the National Human Trafficking Resource Center (NHTRC), if they see any lot lizards, or what these women, and some young boys, sometimes call themselves, 'dates'. Last year 3600 children were rescued from sex slavery by the FBI."

Gunny shook his head with a face grimace, and continued explaining the interest trucking companies had in the slave smuggling trade.

"It's a big problem nationally and internationally. All those thousands of children being smuggled across the Mexican border bring more than their little persons. They bring disease, drugs, and often act as a diversion so the really bad guys can skip across the borders. I don't know how any of this can help you Mike."

Words Can Kill

"See if you can find out who else might be hurt if the information I gave Mrs. Casey got out. I need to find out who is on Harlan's payroll that might have torched my car."

"Ok, I will do what I can, as discretely as I can. You are playing in a mine field. These guys have all the money they ever need to make my life and yours really short. We had better meet somewhere else in a week. Don't call me. Have Angel ask me out to dinner."

"She will call you in a week. I will owe you a steak dinner then."

Tom Jackson removed the wedge from the bottom of the men's john door, and returned to his cube. Mike followed him out of the john a few minutes later after giving all the urinals a flush for cover noise. He checked his mental list of people associated with the Casey's, and decided it was time pay Harlan Casey a visit. Mike considered this visit potentially dangerous, and not one he was not looking forward to make. He thought about the hairy times he experienced with the Corps in Fallujah,

George W. Clever

remembering it is often necessary to enter the lion's den to see what the lion is eating. Hopefully, he mused, it would not be him.

*****

11

Corvette Gift

Fred pushed away from his computer desk, and heard his knees pop. It was time to do more 'Myrna chores' for the day. She had gone to work leaving her mother alone with Fred. The last words he heard before Myrna closed the garage door ricocheted around in his head. 'Fred, as my unemployed husband, your time should be spent tending to mother's needs, and doing the housekeeping chores'.

He began to vacuum the living room carpet hoping a new surprise direction for his story would come to him in the boring repetition of pushing the carpet sweeper. Fred reviewed his progress with the story. *I need a surprise killer for this story. Harlan Casey or any of his muscle are all just too obvious suspects. There has to be a hook in my novel with a surprise that keeps readers from putting the book down till they read the very last page. Then there is the cursed 'gifts' produced by this odd writer prompt website, gifts delivered by my mental butterflies. This website has made these harmless thoughts now too dangerous for me to handle.*

George W. Clever

Fred placed his thoughts on pause, took a sip of his beer before finishing his review of the magic writer icon. *And yet they create the most exciting moments I have ever experienced. My life is at a standstill with mind numbing jobs, Myrna's constant nagging, and when her mother visits, well, she smells. I must be delusional to expect my mystery story will ever become a New York Times best-seller. What a lousy pipedream. How could I ever expect a million-dollar advance from some editor? Now with the internet there are millions of writers pounding out best seller novels.*

Wrapping the vacuum hose around the cleaner, he went back in the basement to find something to write with in his desk. Lifting a pile of bills from the roll-top desk, he found a pencil, and checked off the first of Myrna's 'honey do' items. Fred looked at the second job on her carefully worded list feeling the weight of Myrna's most dreaded assignment. The battery needed changed in the Ford Pinto car Myrna drove every day. This job was not a simple task. Even if the battery was to receive a charge, there was no assurance it would hold it for a long time. He was not much

Words Can Kill

of a mechanic, and hated to get his hands dirty. Searching for battery changing information online, Fred read the instructions he found, and watched a You-Tube video 'How to remove a Ford Pinto car battery'. It was clear Ford engineers designed the vehicle to be capable of becoming a rear-ended firebomb never needing a battery change. He was sure the car designers never intended Pinto owners to live long enough to replace the car's battery.

If I had one of those 2014 Vettes I saw in Motor Trend magazine I would not have to change this damn battery, he thought. The Vette brain fart crept into his mind like morning fog on speed. The screen saver at his elbow blinked. The Google 'battery change' site disappeared as new words rolled across the screen. **Not have to change this damn battery** words appeared in heavy black print on the monitor with a background of blue green, northern lights. *Now what have we here? Why does it say I don't have to change a battery when I know the battery in this piece of car junk is dead?*

George W. Clever

The garage door button opened with a grinding groan when Fred pressed the large white plastic button. He flicked on the light switch, and six banks of LED lamps flooded the dark garage. He was ready to take on the onerous chore of the battery removal. The old 1975 Pinto's usual space was sandwiched between the refrigerator, the rusty freezer, his work bench, the furnace, and the old 1953 Buick automobile. The Buick was given to Myrna by her mother Bertha Scone, when mother Bertha was no longer able to drive.

He could see immediately that *Myrna's Pinto car was not there. Something was hidden by a gray protective cloth car blanket cover. Fred reached down to a lower corner of the covering, lifted it high, and pulling the gray blanket away. A white metallic sports car with maroon stripes gleamed under overhead florescent lights. Blue light danced over the sports car's hood, and erased shadows from its windows. Where their old Pinto car was parked a day before, a 2014 Corvette now occupied its space.* A mental butterfly had struck again. This time it was the kind of gift any man could really appreciate. *His face broke into*

Words Can Kill

a wide smile as he opened the driver side door. Everything about this car smelled new. The deep tan leather seats were stitched in a perfectly matching maroon color. This beast was ready to rock and roll.

Unwelcome fear drifted into his thoughts. *How will I explain this beautiful car to my wife Myrna? There was no room in our tight budget for me to buy a new Vette, and hardly any money to even replace the dead battery in the old Pinto car. No this new car would not do at all. I can't keep this Corvette. There must be a way to get this beautiful machine out of my garage and back where it belonged. Just where did it belong?*

Fred staggered back to his computer chair and stared at the monitor thinking about the dilemma the gorgeous Corvette sports car presented. From my experiment I know if I think something good for me it does not happen, he whispered. The computer screen does not blink and write its own words. It has to receive a mental butterfly to work, and I have no control over those thoughts. If Myrna finds out about this car exchange she will go out to find a divorce lawyer. I know she will be convinced I have lost my mental library after the scare I first gave her with the dog exchange. The monitor flashed a piercing blue light twice. The computer screen danced with abstract patterns as this thought snapped to attention in Fred's mind. Why couldn't she take her mother to visit her sister for a long stay while I figure this out?

Myrna and her mother will visit her sister for a long stay, appeared on the monitor. *Wow! If only that was true. It would be days before she would return. Maybe by that time I can think of a way to get rid of this beautiful car, and get the old Pinto back into its stall. In the meantime, why not enjoy the new sports car? I can attend a few local cruise nights.* His desk phone rang.

"Fred, have mother ready to go and visit my sister. I want to drive there before dark. Have mother ready to go with her bag packed when I arrive."

No more frightening adventures were added to Fred's living after Myrna and her mother were on the road. It had been a long time since he received waves and smiles

Words Can Kill

from young girls like those he saw while driving the Corvette. No words were added to his novel for several days until he received a call from Myrna.

"Hello Fred, Mother and I are coming home in the morning. It has been a nice visit with my sister. Sister Ann may come to visit us in a few weeks. I hope you have not messed up the house while I was away. Have you seen our old dog? I do miss him. Are you doing the house repairs on my list? I do hope you are not wasting all your time on that dumb novel. Well, see you in the morning. Bye".

Panic flooded every cell of Fred's body as he tried to think of ways to explain the Corvette to Myrna. *Maybe if I return to my writing a mental butterfly will make that beautiful car disappear from our garage,* he reasoned.

*****

Even beginning writers know stories have to be realistic to fan readers of crime novels. P.I. Mike would find it difficult to reach Harlan Casey, especially with all the media heat the trucking boss/governor candidate would receive after the possible death of his wife. No one had seen Mrs. Casey for several days. Casey would be surrounded by layers of protection keeping legal and news reporters from getting too close. Mike had to think of a way to penetrate those barriers. He would know from his Corps days every protection defense system had a flaw, an opening where it can be overcome and penetrated. It was time for Mike to check in with Angel and see if she had uncovered information useful to help him set up a meeting with Harlan the governor candidate.

Mike needs a car of his own. He could not rely on taxis and rental cars. A private investigator needs quick access to transportation to be successful in their work. Fred contemplated. A Monarch butterfly drifted by his cellar window reflecting its orange color on his desk. Looking at the moving colors on his keyboard, Fred could only hope the Vette would disappear like the fading reflections of a passing butterfly. His concerns for Myrna's discovery of the new car in the garage were set aside when his thinking about the novel took over. Writing reduced his stress about her returning home. How can P.I. Mike get a new car after his Classic Charger burned?

Words Can Kill

He should have the Corvette in my garage. My P.I. Mike needs a Vette. TV's Tom Selleck had his borrowed Ferrari. No that would not work. Mike could never afford a sports car in my story. P.I.s barely get by on the fees they charge clients, clients who often did not pay on time, if ever. Fred was not aware of the latest mental butterfly. Like the orange and black Monarch, each drifted by with its own gift. One gave beautiful colors of light. The mental butterfly delivered a solution to his Corvette dilemma. These words appeared on the screen. **Gift Mike your Vette**. Fred's fingers continued to write.

The office light was on as Mike turned the door knob setting off warning in his brain. Angel would not be working this late. She would be in class at the community college. She was, after all, only his part-time secretary. Her part-time salary That was all he could afford to pay. Mike's right hand moved to the grip on the nine-millimeter pistol in his shoulder holster. His other hand reached for the light switch by the door. Stretching his arm around the door jam, he flicked the light switch off. The office went dark with the exception of diffused light from the yellow glow of a street light in front of the bakery across the street from his office.

Mike's cop training kicked into gear as he realized there was no point in giving the prowler a door framed target. Mike kicked the door open. Diving through the opening, he rolled behind his old worn-out stuffed chair. His entrance was orchestrated by an unending scream from a woman's voice choked with fear.

"Who are you? What do you want?" the woman screamed.

This was a voice he had heard many times as a kid. Mike remembered the scream coming from his Mom Terza when a mouse ran out of an opened kitchen drawer, and up her arm.

"Mom? What are you doing here?"

"Mike, is that you?"

Mike picked himself off the floor, hit the light switch, and holstered his pistol. His mother was standing in the corner by the window with a stiletto letter opener in one hand, and his little league ball bat in the other.

Words Can Kill

*"You scared the life out of me, Mike. Angel called me to
ask if I would come to your office and give you the
information you requested. She was afraid to leave it in the
office unattended when she went to her evening classes."*

"What did she leave for me?"

*"Here are some papers listing the owners of some cars.
Don't know why these are important. And here is a DVD of
something. You are not taking porno pictures are you?"*

"No Ma, no porno pictures."

*"You never tell me much about how you make a living in
this business, son. I don't think it is the kind of job I would
be proud to tell your Aunt Sadie about. Are you in trouble
Mike?"*

"Nothing I can't handle."

*"When are you going to make Angel an honest woman?
You know it just isn't right stringing her along. She spends
too much of her time in this dingy office for the little you
pay her. You know she loves you. She waited for you to
return from Iraq; and what did you do? You disappeared*

George W. Clever

for days on your return after she had everyone over for your welcoming home party. Where did you go Mike?"

"Not now, Mom. I have to look at this information she left me."

"We all thought you and Angel would marry after you took the cop job. What a disappointment it was for her, me, and your dead father, when you quit the force."

"Let it go, Ma. You can go home now. I'll call you a cab."

"Can't you take me home? It is very late, and your office is in a very bad part of town."

"No, I have to go out again. Got to see a guy about this case I am working on."

"Don't bother calling a cab. I will call my own cab. Fine son who lets his mother stand out by the curb late in a rainy night, and never even says thanks for her waiting in his dirty dingy office guarding some "important" papers."

"Ok, Momma, your guilt game worked. Give me a minute, and I will take you home."

Words Can Kill

"Mike, are you sure you are not in some kind of trouble?"

"No Mom. Give me a minute please."

A mental scan of the names attached to the recognizable license plates in Kelly's Bar parking lot did not register anything outstanding until the last one nearly jumped off the page. Mrs. Casey's car was in the parking lot that night. Where is her car now? Mike thought

"Ok, we can go now, Mom."

"Mike, aren't you going to watch the DVD I gave you?"

"No mom, I'll watch it later after I drop you off at home."

The DVD fit snuggly in his inside pocket next to the list of license plate matches. There was still time for Mike to make one more stop before calling it a day. He had a curiosity about what cars were still in the parking lot of Kelly's Bar. Then his office phone made a heart stopping ring.

"Hi Angel, all finished with your classes? Thanks for the information you had Mom guard here at the office. Yes, I

know I owe you a dinner. Now? It is very late, and I have to drop Mom at her home. Bring her along?"

He turned toward his mother, eyebrows raised in expectation of Terza's answer, and showed her a free hand, palm turned up, to indicate Angel was waiting for an answer to her dinner invitation to his mom.

Terza shook her head and whispered, "I need to go home. It is very late."

"She wants to go home Angel. Ok, meet me at Kelly's Bar in an hour. The cook is in the kitchen till midnight, and I have a few questions I want to ask Kelly. See you then."

Mike hung up the old office rotary phone, and looked directly at his mom to be sure she had heard his conversation with Angel. Her tired eyes and a slight nod of her head told him she did.

"Ok, Mom, let's go."

*****

Mike reached the street a few moments before his mother. When she closed the building storm door he was

Words Can Kill

standing at the curb where he had left the cheap rental car, a KIA Rio. Mike was never comfortable riding in a car with the initials KIA, Killed In Action. Now, he would not have to do so. His rented Rio was gone. In its place was a white Corvette convertible with a maroon stripe.

"Oh, where did you get this beautiful car?" his mother asked.

"It's not mine. My rental KIA Rio is gone."

"Was it towed?" Terza asked.

"I don't know. There is no meter parking here. Who would tow or steal the damn cheap thing?"

"Where is your old car?"

"It burned up last night."

"Mike, are you in trouble?"

"No, it just burned in Kelly's parking lot. Probably a fuel leak."

"Look Mike, there is a note here on your windshield."

George W. Clever

"What does it say?"

"It says a gift to Mike from an admirer. Keys are under the mat."

"Well, Mom, as pappy always said, 'don't look a gift horse in the mouth', but then again, he also said, 'nothing is ever free'.

Mike found the keys, and put the DVD and plate list in the glove compartment buried beneath the owner's manual. Under the hood of the Chevy Corvette Stingray was the latest performance small-block, a 6.2-liter LT1 V-8 generating 455 horsepower and 460 pound-feet of torque.

"Hop in and buckle up."

Like a kid with a new toy, he fired up the ghostly beast, and peeled away from the curb burning a nice pair of black tire streaks on the asphalt.

*****

12

Photo Shot Glasses

A writer can only sit in front of the unblinking eye so long. It was time for a potty break. On his way to the john, Fred peeked into is garage to see if the Corvette was still there. It was gone. He would regret this mental butterfly inverse, but he could never explain the new vehicle to his wife. Mike now had a set of wheels more in line with his PI profession. Tom Selleck from the Magnum PI TV series would be proud. There are times when a PI has to get out of a tight spot in a hurry, and the Corvette was certainly a better choice than a KIA Rio for those times.

Fred's novel was not going to write itself. He had set a goal of ten thousand words a week. There were a few weird moments in writing where his storyline seemed to be writing itself. Fred knew this was one story he could not bury in the "finish someday" file. He would get this job done with mental concentration, and no interference from those obscene mental butterflies. *Now let me see what Mike and his Angel will uncover when they have a late*

George W. Clever

dinner at Kelly's, Fred considered. *Just a few more moments in the "reading room" and I will get back to writing. My bathroom john is the safest place in the house for me away from Myrna and her mother. In this place I can do some of my very best creative thinking for my novel. He thought beginning to type the first line.*

Mike and his mother had a quiet ride to her home. Both were thinking, "What kind of friend gives away a Corvette, and did it have anything to do with the possible murder of his latest client? Mike saw his mother to her door checking one more time to see if she wanted to go to dinner.

"Are you sure you don't want to have dinner with Angel and me?"

"No Mike, you go ahead. I am very tired. Maybe this will turn out to be a romantic not business dinner," she said with a twinkle.

"You never give up do you?" Mike said. "You will have me in marriage chains before I know it."

Words Can Kill

"Tell Angel, mission accomplished and have her come visit me soon, son."

The Vette rumbled to life before Terza waved goodbye and closed the front door. It was at least a fifteen-minute crosstown drive to Kelly's, and Mike wanted to check the parking lot for Mrs. Casey's car before he met Angel.

*****

Only a few cars were in the Bar parking lot at this late hour. Mike recognized most of the cars owned by regular patrons and the bar gang he knew well. His quick check of the remaining license plates for a match to Mrs. Casey's car was unsuccessful. Her vehicle must have been moved, but by who? Kelly or one of the bartenders might know, and if not, maybe there was a surveillance video to finger the mover. Kelly's old RV was parked by a little garage in the far corner of the lot. Two other cars were parked beside it. The cars probably belonged to the restaurant staff so customers would not have a long walk from their cars. When he entered by the side door to the

George W. Clever

dimly lighted dining room Angel was seated at one of the
tables closest to the bar.

"I had to take Mom home. Have you been waiting long?"
he asked Angel. "She said to tell you 'mission
accomplished', whatever that means, and for you to come
visit her."

"I have only been here a few minutes. Class ran late. How
is Terza?"

"She was a bit shook up when I busted into the office with
my gun drawn thinking we had an intruder."

"You must have really scared her. She offered to stay and
give you the information I found. Was the information I dug
up of any value?"

"Yes, Mrs. Casey's car was in Kelly's parking lot the night
my car burned. I just checked the lot, and it is not there
now. Question is, did Mrs. Casey or someone else move it,
and where is it now?"

Words Can Kill

"Can we eat now, Mike? The kitchen is about to close and I am starved."

"Business before pleasure love. I want to find Kelly or one of the bartenders to ask about Helen's car. Also would like to know if she came in the bar Friday night? Just order me a steak and a beer. I'll be back in a minute."

Well so much for the pleasure part of this dinner, Angel mused. What will it take for me to get his mind off a case for some personal time? His mother Terza was right. It will take more than doing his leg work for case information to help him. It will take a little bit of action from my sexy legs!

Two men and a woman sat at the bar. The men were news reporters from TV4 and the woman was Kelly's wife Stephanie. Kelly was in the kitchen. John a retired truck driver and part-time bartender was holding down the bar.

"Look who's here, the man who lost his classic Dodge Charger rust bucket in last night's fire," John shouted as his greeting.

George W. Clever

"Hey John, Hi Stephanie, is Kelly around? I have a few questions I would like to ask him."

"Hello Mike, my husband is finishing up in the kitchen. He should be out in a few minutes. Sorry about your car burning. Any idea who might have torched it."

"Not yet. I didn't expect to see you here so late."

"Well, Mike, if you can't find your man at home you had better go where he is. Kelly has been working long hours here. I hardly ever see him home. Didn't I see Angel come in a few minutes ago?"

"Yes, she and I are having dinner in the dining room."

"She is a beautiful girl Mike. You had better not let her get away."

"You and my mother working this marriage gig together?"

"No Mike, just saying."

The two news reporters pushed away from the bar and turned toward Mike.

Words Can Kill

"Say Mike, we are looking for an angle to the story last night of your burned car and the woman's body police found in the trunk today. Do you mind if we ask you a few questions?"

"Well, guys, in my business I am the one who asks question. I am truly sorry you both have to make a living in the nasty, slimy media business. First thing I know on the news, you all will be making me look like an eco-polluter for driving a gas guzzling Charger. Keep your ears open and you might learn something from the questions I am asking."

"John, do you know what happened to Mrs. Casey's car last night? It was in the parking lot, but I don't see it there now."

"No Mike, I only work nights, and I didn't see it when I came on this evening. It was there last night when I came to work. I parked beside Kelly's old RV; you know the one back in the corner by the storage garage."

"Do you know her car, John?"

George W. Clever

"Oh yes, she was a bar regular."

"Do you think I could get a look at the surveillance tape from today?"

"I think you had better talk with Kelly about that, Mike."

"Well I had better get back to the steak Angel ordered for me. Nice seeing you Stephanie. Will you tell Kelly to stop by our table when he clears the kitchen? Thanks."

"Hey Mike! Before you go, just one question," the reported asked. "Was the woman in your car trunk Mrs. Helen Casey?"

"Don't know. If you find out, you let me know."

The reporters finished their drinks and headed for the door. They would be back after running down the lead Mike had given them about the identity of the woman in the burned car. By now, the police forensics lab should know.

The bar was quiet again, except for the elevator music noise always played louder than needed for good conversation by the patrons. It did, however, make loud conversations heard by anyone within earshot distance.

Words Can Kill

Maybe someone at the bar the night of the fire had overheard useful information, Mike considered. He slid off the bar stool and returned to Angel in the dining room realizing not much information of value was received from John or Stephanie.

*****

When Mike was out of sight, Stephanie turned on her stool to see if anyone was near who would hear what she was to ask the bartender. When she was sure her question would not be heard, she leaned over the bar, and waved at john pointing to her drink for a refill.

"John, would you be interested in making a quick hundred?" Stephanie asked in a low voice.

"Well sure Stephanie if it ain't illegal. What you got in mind?"

"It is a little joke I want to play on my husband. Give me four of the shot glasses he uses for his 'start of the day lifter'."

George W. Clever

*John reached under the bar and pulled up four shot glasses
with square bottoms. "Will these do?"*

*Stephanie reached into her purse, took out a photo,
a pair of small scissors, and a tube of rubber glue. She cut
the photo into four pieces the size of the bottom of the shot
glass, and glued each piece to the glass bottom so if one
looked into the glass, part of the photo picture could be
seen.*

*"Now you must be sure one and only one of these shot
glasses is placed under the bar each day for four days. The
shot glass has to be right where Kelly will choose it when
he comes to work in the morning. Be sure you do this
without him seeing you. Do it just when the bar closes. All
you have to say when he asks about the piece of photo
pasted to the bottom of the glass is this. You have no idea
how it got there. Act surprised. After the second or third
day he will demand an explanation. Play dumb. On the last
day I want you to put the last glass in the second spot. I will
be here on that morning to have an eye opener with Kelly.
That second photo glass will be for me. Got it?"*

Words Can Kill

"Sure, some kind of mystery photo no?"

"Don't mess with the glasses to figure out what the photo is or there will be no hundred bucks. Be a good soldier now and make this happen."

*****

13

Bar Talk

"Mike, you do know how to keep a hungry girl waiting. Was it worth my wait?" Angel said with a half- smile.

"Not sure. John only works nights. He knew Helen Casey's car was in the lot Friday night, but didn't know when or where her car was taken the next morning. John said I would have to ask Kelly for today's day tapes. His boss was in the kitchen making your steak. Here he comes now bearing your long awaited dinner sweet thing."

The bar owner, Kelly, entered the dining room. Sweat was pouring down his forehead from the heat generated in a busy kitchen. He wiped his face and hands on his apron, and approached Angel and Mike's table.

"Hello Mike. How much did you have to pay this beautiful woman to be your dinner companion?"

"You say such nice things Kelly. I actually had his mother threaten him for this meal," Angel responded.

George W. Clever

"Hey, Kelly if you were any longer in the kitchen, Angel would be eating out of your refrigerator. Got a minute? I have a couple of questions I would like to ask you about last night's car fire," Mike said.

"Sure, sorry you lost your classic ride. I see you picked up an even sweeter Vette already."

"How did you know?"

"Oh I have a security camera TV in the kitchen. Sure looks like a bitchin ride. The gumshoe business must be paying you big overtime bucks. Those 'Vettes are pricey."

    Mike nodded, but did not explain his acquisition of the metallic white Corvette. He was focused on the questions he hoped to ask Kelly.

"I wanted to ask you if Helen Casey was here at the bar anytime yesterday?"

"I don't think so, but I do get so busy running around like a chicken with its head cut off when help calls in sick. Even when they are here I get stuck in the kitchen. Only bad help is available these days. With so many out of work

Words Can Kill

it doesn't figure. Guess the State gives them more money not to work than I can pay them for working here."

"I understand her car was here after the fire. Do you know who moved it, and where it is?"

"No I don't Mike. It must have been moved this morning before I checked in."

"Could I look at today's security tapes? They might show how and when her car was moved."

"Oh sure. That's what I would have said any other day Mike. Odd thing is, no tape was in the recording machine when I went to put one in for the night shift. Sorry. I guess when the cops took the tape last night we forgot to put in a new one. Well enjoy your steak. I'm going to clean up the place a bit, and then take Stephanie home. John can close the place. Why Stephanie sits on her favorite bar stool every night lately is beyond me. This place makes even me bored."

Kelly made his apologies for not being able to answer any more of Mike's questions as the dinner hour was busy, and there was a lot of clean-up to do before calling it a night. He wiped his sweaty hands on his apron again, and returned to the kitchen.

"Not much information there." Angel said in a soft whisper. "Maybe it is just woman's intuition, but I think he knows more that he will share Mike."

"Yes Angel my love, he does. Tomorrow I will hit the neighborhood and see if I can turn up someone who saw Helen Casey's car being moved from the parking lot. Now finish up my hungry one. I still have time to curl your hair with a fast coast highway drive in the Vette before it turns into a pumpkin, and our parting becomes short, and sweet sorrow. Can you imagine the note on the Vette just said, 'a gift to Mike from an admirer'? What kind of person goes around gifting Vettes, and stealing KIA Rios? Don't know how I am going to explain all this to the rental agency. They may want the Corvette in exchange, but I will be damned if I will give this beautiful car away."

*****

14

Silent Return

Being a writer is a little like being God. One gets to create human beings, plus the world they live in. Writers can plan their destiny, and find delightful ways to mess up their lives. Fred was beginning to enjoy his unlikely profession. Any thought he ever had about becoming successful writer would never have come his way if it wasn't for the computer age revolution. His handwriting in elementary school always received a D grade. College courses, requiring hand written papers, were artfully avoided. Only one of his English teachers offered any encouragement for his writing, and that was because Fred became a fan of the authors Thoreau and Emerson. He and his professor was especially drawn to one of Henry David's quotations: Any fool can make a rule, and any fool will mind it.

It was the Dawn of Aquarius in Fred's college days, and it included his protesting of rules. The hippy mantra of rebellion to the status quo and rules was tailored to Fred's life. He endured so many heavy handed controls in his growing up, dished out by an obsessively dominant mother. Fred knew the fleeting freedom he found in college was lost in marriage. Myrna was an equally obsessively and controlling wife. Her rules were re-enforced by his overbearing mother -in law, Bertha. They were a tag team act just like WWF wrestlers. Nagging was their game. Their home was an arena mat. Mother and daughter would test his temperament by a million daily demands, all interrupting his writing.

Fred contemplated the return of Myrna and her mother from their visit to his wife's sister. He would experience verbal abuse when they returned home to find fault with all he had not done. *What would be a way to avoid their verbal abuse? Is there a reasonable solution to ending their torture*? One of those uncontrollable butterfly thoughts floated through his mind on an undetermined flight path. *How wonderful it would be if they could not talk?* The computer screen on his desk rolled, steadied, and printed out **Mother and Daughter cannot talk.**

*****

Words Can Kill

Traffic to an airport and flight delays appear to be the work of the devil. Fred deduced if one leaves to meet a flight just a little bit late there would be six lanes of bumper to bumper traffic traveling three miles per hour. His belief was re-enforced the day he drove to the airport to pick up his wife Myrna and her mother Bertha. The traffic made him late. Fortunately, for him, Myrna's plane was late. He waited by the screen showing the flight and gate change for Myrna and her mother. He had arrived on time to meet them. At least he would not have to hear their complaints about his tardiness.

A sea of passengers passed him on their way to baggage returns. Last in the group was Myrna and her mother holding cardboard signs. How odd, I don't see any of the other passengers carrying signs. Neither of the women could talk. Something in the air circulating throughout the aircraft created throat irritation and the inability of Myrna and her mother to speak. The Friendly Skies of Condor Airlines printed hasty signs for them which read: I am not able to speak. Please see this pad given to me so I can write what you need to know. On the front of each pad was the airline's logo of two Condor birds circling a 747 aircraft. All good things always seemed to have an end for Fred. The airline company assured his pickup passengers their irritated throats and the inability to speak would only last a few days.

Damn! Only a few days. I could do with this kind of mental butterfly for the rest of my married life, Fred brooded. Passing notes of demands and instructions became routine, but labor intensive for Myrna and her mother. It was especially difficult when Fred was down in his inner-sanctum basement pecking away at what Myrna called his trash novel. Eventually, the women gave up writing notes. They each decided to save up all the instructions for the things Fred was to do until they could once again speak. Fred gave up trying not to laugh at his good fortune. His mother-in-law saw his smirk and wrote in her notebook.

"Why are you laughing?"

He simply said, "It's a funny part of my novel."

*****

15

Kidnapped

It was three A.M. by the time Mike gave Angel the promised Corvette thrill ride down the coast highway. He parked in her apartment complex lot away from the resident assigned spaces.

As they walked to her apartment door Angel asked, "Would you like to come in for a while?"

"Not tonight love. I have to get a handle on the possible murder of Helen Casey before our police friend, "Detective Keith Clumsy", makes his move drying up all my sources of information. I also need to try to get some sleep. It hasn't come easy lately. I keep waking up more tired than before I go to bed. Bed covers are thrown all over the floor from dreams I remember.

In my dreams or nightmares, they all involve me driving a hummer that was belching fire and smoking from an IED hit. I was trying not to have it explode before I could bail out, but I couldn't leave because my team in the Hummer were all wounded. They were yelling. 'Mike get us out.' I had to save them."

Angel and Mike stood there for a quiet moment. Their goodbyes usually included a quick non-committal kiss. This time the kiss was illuminated by flashing blue lights and a harsh command.

"Put your hands where we can see them."

Two boys in blue came to the doorway on a run.

"You Mike Dunmore?"

"Yes."

"You are under arrest."

"Arrest? For what?"

Angel chimed in with a demand, "Why are you arresting him?"

"You are under arrest Mike Dunmore for the murder of Helen Casey."

Words Can Kill

The second officer slipped plastic riot handcuffs on Mike while the first cop padded him down.

Finding Mike's 9mm piece, one of the cops asked, "You got a permit for this weapon?"

"Yes, I'm a concealed licensed holding PI."

The officer slipped Mike's handgun into his duty belt and lead him to the squad car leaving Angel standing stunned by her door.

Turning before he was shoved into the back seat, Mike yelled, "Angel, call my attorney and my mother."

*****

Did this piece of writing lead me down a blind alley? Fred considered. *Who will get Mike out of jail? And will he be released on bond? If not, who will find the real killer of Helen Casey if the woman in Mike's car trunk is his former client? Could it be that Mike did kill her in an unexplainable act caused by his PTSD? No that would be too expected at a time when every crazy act in the news blames PTSD. Now they say it comes from all kinds of*

George W. Clever

sources from serving in combat to stressful marriages, car accidents, and even school discipline from an overzealous teacher. I will have to spend some serious time thinking about the problem just created for Mike. What evidence did his old force friend Detective Keith have to initiate Mike's arrest?

It was 'Miller Time' and Fred wanted a good snack to go with his beer. Maybe after a couple of TV shows Fred hoped his creative writing juices would be jump started. If he got motivated to write again, the answers to all those story questions rolling around in his head might magically appear on the computer monitor.

After watching three straight brain numbing TV re-run episodes of Gilligan's Island, Fred returned to the basement computer to do battle with his story's dead end.

Mike knew something was wrong with this arrest besides the fact that he did not murder his client Helen Casey. The boys in blue did not Mirandize him, the squad car was not marked, and there was no light bar on the top. As he settled into the back seat, he noticed there was no

Words Can Kill

protective screen between the cops in the front seat and any perps in the back seat. That was the last thought he had as one of the uniforms reached over from the front seat and hit Mike with 4.5 million volts from a Stun Master. The car stopped, and a cloth was tied tightly around Mike's head over his eyes. By the time his brain was again able to communicate with the rest of his body, Mike was out of the car and dragged into what appeared to be an abandoned gas station. The smell of oil and gasoline filled the hollow sounding room. Mike was pushed down a short set of stairs and tied to a metal chair in an oil change pit.

A strange voice echoed around the oil change pit. It sounded like it came from a telephone voice changer use to make secret calls.

A raspy female vocalization said, "Where is the Harlan Casey file?"

Mike could not be sure it was a woman or a man. Voice changers could make even the gender deceiving.

"I gave it to Helen Casey, he shouted."

George W. Clever

No sense prolonging this, Mike thought. I might as well tell them what I did with the file. They will either kill me now or after I give them what they want, Mike considered. Maybe I can learn who they are if I hold information they want a bit longer. I need some negotiation power if I can hope to avoid a dirt nap.

The 'Phyllis Diller' sounding speaker delivered words in a controlled tone. Even the voice was painful to his ears.

"We know you keep personal files on your cases. Where is your personal file for the Casey case?"

"Never made one," Mike replied. "Now let me ask a question. Who are you and what the hell am I doing here?"

"You are in no position to ask anything Mr. Dunmore. You will answer our questions the first time they are asked or we can help you find the answers."

Mike felt someone unbuckle his belt, and pull his shorts and pants around his knees leaving his "boys" exposed. Excruciating pain jerked him about in the chair as

Words Can Kill

two sharp clamps punctured the skin on either side of a gonad.

"Once more, where is your file on Harlan Casey?"

His answer through grinding teeth was, "Go to hell. There is no other file."

Mike's answer was punctuated by what could be described as electro-shock therapy from a car battery to a man's junk parts the Creator mistakenly left outside the body. Fire shot out of every single one of his pores. The heat was followed by his screaming and moaning. The sound bounced around the empty walls of the oil change pit, and out on to the main bay.

His screams were enhanced by a cry for mommy. A desperate call for Mom comes from all men when their personal pain goes beyond the level men learn to tolerate. It is the pain known before death. Tall grime coated window panes, no longer emitting light to the station, rattled from the force of every scream. The smell of burned flesh, his own flesh, rose to Mike's nose.

George W. Clever

"Once again Mr. Dunmore, where is your Casey file?"

Mike forced his tortured mind to concentrate on his Marine training and what few options he was sure he had left. He could tell them where to find his personal file, and they could then kill him. He could again deny there was another file, and probably receive another shocking treatment. To stay alive, he could tell them he had the file in a place only to be retrieved by himself. Maybe then his persecutors would give him the opportunity to retrieve the file. By choosing the last option he might find an escape opportunity. It sounded like this plan would be his best shot, but what story could he make believable. Perhaps the best story would be the truth.

"The file is in a safety deposit box. Only my eye scan and fingerprint will open it."

Ball in their court. A long quiet pause followed while the strange voice seemed to be in conference with someone else about their next move. The crackling of speaker sound preempted the next instructions coming from the voice as an order to the goon squad.

Words Can Kill

"Take Mr. Dunmore to retrieve the file. This had better be the only copy Mr. Dunmore. We would hate re-enacting this wonderful party for you. Keep him blindfolded if possible until you get to the bank. Do not give us any further trouble or you will be killed after you give us the file Mr. P.I. Then I want him dropped at his Mother's home. You know the one he was screaming for when we applied our persuader. And I mean dropped!"

Someone released his foreskin from the jaws of the jumper cables, and pulled up his shorts and pants not bothering to wipe or stop the flow of blood only partly stemmed by the electro-shock cauterizing. Mike was lifted from the chair by two strong arms, dragged out of the pit to the outside of the gas station, and thrown into the back seat of a waiting car. He guessed it was probably the fake unmarked squad car.

"Where is this file?"

It was a voice Mike remembered from his arrest scene.

"It's in a safety deposit box at the 22nd street Bank of America. That's where I put it."

George W. Clever

"How in the hell are we going to get him in and out of the bank with a blindfold on? One of us will have to go with him after we take off his blindfold. If you have any thoughts of pulling a fast one get them out of your mind. We will kill you, your mother, and your secretary, before the day would even be over. Do you understand?"

"Yes."

The car pulled away from the curb and rapidly gained speed. Mike tried to sense the start location of the parked fake police car by memorizing each turn, and the time it took before the next car turn. He could sense a right or left turn based on the way gravity moved his body. It was a tough memory assignment to do only by body senses without his eye sight. If he survived this ordeal, Mike would return to the scene of his pain to find out who was responsible.

"Pull over in the alley just after the bank. We need to make sure he looks presentable. Be sure he has no blood stains and no cuts that can be seen. Can he walk?"

Words Can Kill

Mike was pulled from the car by the same two bulky biceps that threw him into the back seat. He was held upright until it was possible for him to stand. Mike's blindfold was removed bringing a new pain from the bright, penetrating light to his eyes. He tried to memorize the faces of his captors who discarded their cop clothes, and were now in civilian duds. Only one stood by his side. The other two goons stayed out of sight in the car.

"You have the box key?"

"No, the box is only opened by eye scan and finger prints."

"Ok. Let's go."

The biggest of the thugs led him out to the sidewalk where they walked around the corner to the bank.

"You tell them at the bank I'm your brother, and we both need to look at our mother's papers. Got it!"

"Yes."

The bank teller was most obliging leading them to the security box vault. Mike stared at the door optical receiver and pressed his thumb on the lock pad. When the door opened, Mike and his strong-arm assistant followed the clerk to a table. The file was retrieved in a few moments after Mike pressed his left hand thumb on to the safety deposit scanner. Outside the bank once again, Mike and his guard returned to the waiting car. Pushed into the back seat by a door window, Mike was once again bound with plastic handcuffs and blindfolded. His friendly 'brother' helper pressed a gun into his side. The driver pulled away slowly and drove in a reasonable manner to avoid being noticed.

"What are we going to with this slab of meat?" The driver said. He saw your face you know. We need to eliminate our witness."

"No, the boss said to remind him we can do the final touch to his mother and girlfriend if he runs his mouth to the police. Just drop him as we were told to do."

The car began to pick up speed. Tires squealed as the vehicle made a hard right and left turn. At the third turn, the back seat goon reached over, opened the car door and gave Mike a powerful shove out of the speeding

Words Can Kill

automobile as it roared down a quiet tree lined street. Bouncing along the pavement, Mike's clothes gave way to shredding by the course cement. Layers of skin followed and finally bone as he skidded across the street to the curb. His head rested on a fire department number stenciled in black by the driveway. It was number 234, his Mom's street number. Mike was home. At least what was left of him.

*****

16

Angelina

Those troublesome mental butterflies had not made their presence known to Fred for some time, and he was grateful. It was becoming more difficult to manage the shock value some of the brain farts had made on his life, his family, and neighborhood. Fred was making good progress with his new novel nearing thirteen thousand words. Storm clouds filled the sky with a promise of steady rain and another dreary day. Not much could be accomplished completing Myrna's list of outside chores. He considered his options deciding it would be a good day to concentrate on moving the novel story along.

Thinking out loud Fred said, *"I have a solid list of possible murder suspects developed for the story. Kelly the Bar owner is on my list as well as his wife Stephanie, Governor candidate Harlan, and possibly John the part-time bartender. I think all these suspected people will be just too obvious to a reader. It would be almost like the butler did it. Now I must think, who had the most powerful motive?*

George W. Clever

There was Mike the P.I. himself of course with no motive developed as of yet, and perhaps another character killer I could introduce later. Yes, it was time for me to introduce a new suspect, but first Angel, Mike's mother Terza, and his attorney friend would be looking for Mike. When they find out he didn't show up at his usual places, those who know his habits would expect 'Missing Mike' to be in jail or the morgue. Angel thought he was in jail from the shock she received watching the cops arrest him the night before."

*Boy would I like to have a secretary like Angel to do my editing, and have someone to bounce off my character ideas. Fred mused. The computer flashed a new green light with sounds like an old typewrite carriage sliding across the page. **Editing Secretary like Angel** appeared on the flat screen.*

"Hello Fred. Sorry I am late. I missed the bus from campus to your home, and had to take a taxi. Where do you want me to start? I could be working on character development or perhaps reading your manuscript for first edit?"

Words Can Kill

"Who are you and how did you get into my house?"

"Fred, I am Angelina your part-time secretary of course, silly. You do remember hiring me and giving me a key to your computer room basement door?"

"You can't be here!"

"Why not?"

"My wife and her mother are here. They are upstairs!"

"Well come on Fred, you didn't say anything about those kind of extra job opportunities. I am not here for anything that would concern your wife. I am only here to help you with your book."

"No, you don't understand. My wife is a very jealous person, and you are so... Fred paused looking for the right words, "...beautiful, just like Mike's Angel."

"Angel? Who is Angel?"

"She is a character in my book. Never mind that. You cannot stay!"

George W. Clever

His voice was loud enough to be heard in the kitchen above as the sound traveled up the cellar stairs.

"Fred, who are you talking to down there?" Myrna's voice tumbled down the cellar stairs.

"No one honey. I am just voicing some of my story characters."

"Well who ever she is, she has, or you have a very sweet voice. I want to come down and meet her," she said with a giggle.

"Give me a minute, and I will be right up. Don't we need to go to the market this morning?"

He turned to Angelina, and pleaded for an inverse to his unintended secretary request.

"Look Angelina, I don't know where you came from, but you will have to go back there at once."

"Oh! I can't go back anywhere Fred. Once you have a mental butterfly, you do understand from the website warnings, there is no going back."

Words Can Kill

"Well, I have found inverses before. There must be one for you to go back to wherever."

"Please Fred, let's just get to work. I have evening classes I must attend."

Fred grabbed a handful of pages from the manuscript pile by his printer and pushed them into Angelina's hands.

"Ok, just edit the first twenty pages. Do it quietly, and then leave," Fred told her as he turned and hurried up the stairs.

There would be no more writing that day. He had to keep Myrna out of the basement. Fred needed time to think of a way to reverse his Angelina butterfly thought. Maybe he was just daydreaming, and it would all go away.

*****

17

Hospital Hours

No one was in the computer room when Fred returned the next morning. Myrna and her mother were collecting roadside pop and beer cans carless people had tossed along a section of highway 44. This was their volunteer work for the Naked Clowns Foundation, a charitable organization for homeless clowns. The section of the highway Myrna and her mother were to clean was part of several miles assigned to the Naked Clown Foundation. With his wife and her mother out of the house, Fred was free to continue writing his novel.

A smirk settled in one corner of his mouth as he thought about the foundation receiving donations from cans collected by supporters cleaning the roadside. What a cool way to keep American's highways beautiful and the country free of homeless clowns. Fred knew where he wanted the mystery story to go as he began to type.

George W. Clever

Angel's cell phone rang in her purse. Frustrated as she fumbled with the zipper trying to get it open, Angel hoped the caller would not hang up before she could answer. Maybe it was Mike, or at least some news about where he was after being arrested by the cops.

"Angel?"

"Yes."

"This is Jessi, Mike's attorney. You called me last night. Well I have contacted just about all our jails, prisons, and law enforcement agencies this morning, and Mike Dunmore is not on their arrest lists from last evening to this afternoon. Are you sure he was arrested last night?"

"Yes, I was with him when two uniformed officers showed up at my home arresting him for the murder of Helen Casey."

"Maybe it was a mistake. Do you have anyone on the force you could contact?"

"Well I could call his former patrol partner Detective Keith Farrell. Maybe he would know something."

Words Can Kill

"Yes, do that, and call me if anything further turns up."

"Thank you, I will."

Angel hung up and called Detective Keith. If anyone could find Mike it would be his best friend.

"Precinct 54 Detective Sergeant Keith speaking. How can I help you?"

"Keith this is Angel. Mike was arrested by two of your boys in blue last night at my home. They arrested him for the murder of Helen Casey. Did you send them?"

"No Angel, I did not send them to arrest Mike on any charge let alone the murder of someone we are not sure is dead."

"Well, Keith, I called his attorney this morning, and she could not find any arrest record or a jail where Mike might be held."

"Doesn't surprise me Angel, he is in Streams Memorial Hospital. The EMTs took him there after his mother's paper boy found him by the curb in from of her home early this afternoon.

George W. Clever

"Oh no! Is he alright?"

"He was in very bad shape. Mike is a tough bird, and alive as far as I know."

"Keith do you think this might have something to do with the Casey case and the burning of Mike's car?"

"I don't know Angel. We are still not sure it was Helen Casey in Mike's car trunk. Seems, all day Mike was one step ahead of me in that investigation. Just on my way now to Streams to see what happened to him. Why don't you meet me there? We will know more then."

"Yes, I am on my way. See you at the hospital in fifteen minutes."

The cellar computer room door lock turned and then opened. Angelina entered and stood before Fred's desk. She was wearing a one piece, thigh length, black suit with a white collared blouse open to the waist. Angelina's office attire showed all but a portion of her ample bare breasts. Black bra lace discretely covered the rest.

Words Can Kill

"Good morning boss. I am ready to do some editing work if you have no other plans for me," she said twisting a curl hanging in the middle of her forehead.

Fred could feel his face heating to match its crimson skin color that always appeared when he was embarrassed. It really did not take much to change his pale face a deep red when he looked at a beautiful woman.

Clearing the stress frog in his throat he said, "Accaa. here Angelina, sit at the desk next to mine. I will print out several pages from my book written today. You read them silently. Mark any corrections I need to make. For heaven sake, do not talk, do not ask me questions, and do not make any kind of noise when I go upstairs."

Pushing back from his computer, he shoved a folding chair toward the corner of his desk for Angelina. His heart rate kicked into high gear watching her settle into the seat so near to him. Fred stared at his 'new secretary'. He noticed she made no attempt to adjust her skirt, now creeping up to mid-thigh. Logic prevailed in his thinking. There must be a way to get rid of her. There must be some way and yet, he stopped in mid thought rising to cautiously move around her. Fred looked up toward the cellar stair landing, and back at Angelina. Do I really want her to go? He thought. She is so beautiful with a ten body that rocks. She's not hot! She is smoking.

The door upstairs opened. Myrna's shadow appeared on the cellar wall as she stood in the doorway.

"Fred are you coming up or should I come down?"

"I'll be right up Myrna."

"You know, Fred, you really are convincing when you voice your characters. I could swear there was a real woman with you downstairs."

Whispering to Angelina, Fred said, "Ok do the editing for just the first chapter. Above all do not call for me or make any loud noises while I am upstairs at dinner. When you finish leave quietly for your evening classes."

With those instructions out of the way, he climbed the stairs to wash up before dinner. Fred ran hot water in the kitchen sink scrubbing each hand with a passion. He

Words Can Kill

tried to ignore the penetrating looks he was receiving from his wife.

As he moved to his place at the table Myrna said, "Do you have an interest in any other women Fred?"

"No dear, one woman, you, is more than enough for me. The only other women of interest to me are those in my novel."

"I am so glad to hear that from you. It would be most difficult for you to try and write your novel with broken fingers," Myrna said with a crooked little smile as she wiped her hands on a dish towel.

Fred knew there would be no inverse to the arrival of secretary Angelina by any normal thought process. How will I ever keep Myrna, her mother, and Angelina from meeting? He considered. Maybe a butterfly will just arrive to take Angelina away. Oh it is so conflicting with these damn butterfly thoughts.

Finishing his dinner in silence, Fred was unaware each person at the table also were lost in their own world.

George W. Clever

Myrna was staring at her wedding rings. Her mother, Bertha, was polishing tableware with her napkin.

"Good dinner Myrna. If you both will excuse me I would like to finish a chapter in my novel before bedtime." Fred said.

He carried his dishes into the sink, and quietly walked back down the stairs to the computer room. Angelina was gone. Fred took in a deep breath, and gave out a sigh of relief as he settled into his desk chair. *Ok, let me see what Mike is doing at the hospital when visited by Detective Keith and Angel.* Fred considered the possible hospital conversations and started to type.

*****

"What are you doing, Mike?" Keith said, in a firm voice."

"I am getting dressed so I can leave this damned hospital."

"You can't leave just yet. You were seriously injured, and I am here on official as well as personal business. You could have died. Now get back in bed. Look at you with your two

bandaged arms, torn flesh on your back and legs, and maybe a concussion. Who did this to you?"

"I don't know, but I have a pretty good hunch who ordered it done. Did you send those uniforms to arrest me?"

"No, I did not. You shouldn't have to ask. The trust we had as beat cops hasn't gone away when you quit the force."

"Didn't think so, but I had to ask with all the rogue cop business these days."

"Do you think it was Harlan's goons?"

"That is number one on my "top ten" list as of now."

"What did they want? For sure it was not to hold you for ransom. We all couldn't raise even a sawbuck for your kidnapping ransom."

"They wanted my file on the Casey case."

"You mean the one you told me you did not have? Did they get it?"

"They got a file I kept in my bank safe deposit drawer, only after some major persuasion on their part. I am going to *tell you something I would not admit to anyone else. Electro shock therapy is not fun when battery connected wires with pinchers are clamped on your balls."*

Mike returned his clothes to the room closet and settled back in the hospital bed with its nasty plastic sheets.

"Knowing you as I do, there is another file copy. Am I correct? Do you have another copy? I will need to see it. I want you to know the department has an undercover who is building a case against Casey and his trucking firm. You didn't hear that from me. Got it? I will try to tap into the investigation to see if I can learn who might have been involved in you being snatched. The team is very tight about anyone poking into their child slavery assignment, but I will be more discrete than you ever were."

Sergeant Keith heard the hospital room door open. Automatically, he went on alert. If those goons had tried to kill the P.I. once, they may try again. He turned with relief to see Mike's gorgeous secretary.

"Oh, Hello Angel."

Words Can Kill

Angel walked in the hospital room with determination and concern on her face. Finding Mike alive and safe was an answer to mom Terza's and her prayers. She obviously had a long night of no sleep and crying after witnessing Mike's arrest. Her violet eyes filled with tears as she surveyed the damage done to Mike by his abductors.

"Hello Keith. Ohhhh! Mike! What did they do to you?"

"Nothing permanent I think. I'm all right."

"Angel, will you keep this lug in his hospital bed at least long enough for his wounds to stop bleeding?" Keith ordered. "I'll be back to see you tomorrow Mike. You had better be here. From what I got from your doctor you have some healing to do if you ever expect to be a father in your crazy lifetime."

Keith closed the door as he left the hospital room thinking it was important to give Angel some private time with Mike. He considered the next few hours would be a time for his cop personality to tread lightly as he tried to link the two events of the last few nights together. Homicide is my bailiwick, he thought, so there is some room for me to poke around the Casey lair since the burned body in the car trunk could be Helen Casey. After confirming the dead woman was killed by blunt force trauma before being burned in the fire, it became a homicide case for my department to solve. The coroner still could not identify the body by DNA. We should have more in that soon. He considered.

Fred continued with his writing pausing only to think about the reality of his story. Something was not quite right about the autopsy. Police special investigation department teams can jealously protect their cases. Going undercover was a dangerous business. Perhaps they and the coroner already knew the identity of the corpse. If it was Helen Casey, a condolences call to Harlan Casey would certainly in order by Detective Keith. Casey would be expecting the police anyway. Cop shows on TV have let everyone in on the police expectation all surviving spouses are suspects in murder cases. Fred continued to write.

Keith returned to his unmarked car considering his next move. The trick would be for 'Detective Sergeant

Words Can Kill

Farrell' to learn all I can about the Casey business before I step on the toes of any undercover task force assignment. Hopefully I can do this before Mike is well enough to do a sledge hammer visit to the possible future Governor Harlan Casey. It is time for a 'condolence call' at the Casey residence. Maybe Helen Casey has returned, and is no longer a missing person.

"Officer Burr, take me to the Casey mansion, please."

There was an uneasy quiet in the hospital room after Sergeant Keith left. Angel studied Mike's face to find a place without abrasions, contusions or bandages as she looked for a less tender place for her kiss. Finding no safe place, she pressed her lips softly on his.

"Mikey…Mikey…I am so worried about you. I know you will not walk away from finding out who torched your car, and the identity of the woman in your car trunk. It is so dangerous. If it is Helen Casey, Candidate for Governor Harlan Casey has money, power and political connections.

George W. Clever

He can have you killed and leave no bullet holes in your beautiful body. I don't want to echo your mother, but couldn't you find something safer to do to earn a living? Maybe you could be a lion tamer in the circus?"

Mike smiled, and then winced in pain. He twisted and flexed his shoulders trying to find a more comfortable position on one of those hospital slab beds.

"Any more of your jokes and they will rush me back into surgery. You know after Iraq I became a thrill junky with the unfortunate handicap of night sweats, flashbacks, and violent flare-ups I could not control. That is not the kind of guy you want teaching Sunday school after a week as a bank teller. Either they get me or I will figure this one out, and get them. You've got to help me out of this hospital soon. Do me one more favor Angel. My mother is sure to be freaking out. Please give her some re-assurance I will be ok. Maybe you could take her gift shopping for her poor invalid son in room 245 Streams Hospital? I need to sleep

Words Can Kill

now. They gave me something for pain that is slamming my eyelids shut. See you tomorrow sweetie."

Angel found new places to leave her kisses. She lingered for a while straightening out his sheets, and tucking him in before saying good night.

"Love you Mikey."

With Angel and Keith gone, Mike closed his eyes, and gave his weary brain instructions to run its files. His orders were to map out the best way for him to learn if Helen Casey was murdered. He knew as few as 25% of murder cases are solved after the first forty-eight hours.

*****

Sergeant Keith and his driver followed the GPS to the home of Harlan Casey. It was set back from St. Regis Parkway behind a gated fence monitored by security cameras. A camera was mounted next to a stone lion on the top of each brick gate pillar. Keith's uniformed driver punched the call button at the gate, and waited for a response. The security cameras moved in a ballet of

George W. Clever

information seeking, and focused on the detective, his driver, and their car.

Officer Burr spoke into the communications box, "Officer Burr and Detective Farrell to see Harlan Casey."

"One moment." After a few minutes a voice in the box responded. "Mr. Casey is expecting you. Follow the circular drive to the front of the house. He will meet you at the door."

An ornate, iron latch clicked as it opened the massive black iron gate. Two sections of the gate slid away on tracks like a snake in a hurry. Officer Katie Burr drove along a gravel drive lined by Eucalyptus trees. The trees with their shaggy bark and faded olive green leaves seemed to blot out the sky above the police car. In a few minutes, the house of Harlan appeared high on its own observation knoll, looking more like a stone fortress than a home. Heavy drapes covered all the windows. Several suits stood by the front door. One turned to open the door as Officer Katie parked the squad car to an echo of its one squeaky brake. A massive carved, oak door opened. A tall man

Words Can Kill

appeared standing in the home foyer entry above any of the guards standing on the stone landing in front of the door. It could not have been a more orchestrated introduction of Harlan Casey to Sergeant Keith Farrell and his driver officer Katie.

First out of the car, Keith said, "Mr. Harlan Casey?"

"Yes, I am Harlan Casey."

"Good afternoon, I am Detective Sergeant Keith Farrell. I want to express my condolences for the disappearance of your wife. The department is doing everything it can to determine if the body found in the burned car was your wife. If our coroner determines it is Helen Casey we will find out how she died. At this point, I think I can say whoever we found in the trunk of the burned car was a murder victim. I assume Mrs. Casey is still missing?"

"Yes, she has been gone for several days now."

"Any help you can give us in this matter would be appreciated Mr. Casey. Could we come inside you home? I

George W. Clever

have a few questions I would like to ask you. The information you provide may help us solve this case."

"Yes you may come in. I want you to know first, I do realize as in all TV cop shows, the husband is always one of your main suspects in any foul play involving his wife. If your questions begin to take that direction, I will ask you to leave. Any further questioning will be done in the presence of my attorney. Is that understood?"

"Yes, of course. This is just routine police procedure. We only ask questions to learn where we must look for the perpetrator of such a horrible crime or the disappearance of a loved one. I am sure you will agree, if your wife was burned to death in the trunk of a car it was a terrible way for her to die"

"Yes, it is unthinkable. Come in to my study. I will send for something cool to drink. It is very warm today."

Sergeant Keith and Officer Katie followed Casey and two of his muscles into the study while a third man disappeared down the hall. He returned promptly with a tray of cold drinks.

Words Can Kill

"Your library is quite impressive," Sergeant Keith said. "Are you an avid reader?"

"There has not been much time for my reading of late. Mrs. Casey thought the library was a necessary refinement to a substantial home for any candidate for Governor. Please have a seat."

"Did Mrs. Casey have any enemies?"

Harlan hand motioned toward a chair in front of his massive desk. Officer Katie stood by the detective's side as the trucking executive seated himself behind the desk. He opened a cigar box on his desk offering one to Keith who shook his head as he was a non-smoker. Then with enough time for him to organize a well-planned reply, Governor candidate Casey responded to the question about his wife's possible enemies.

"Helen had no enemies as far as I know. She did have her own life independent of our married life. My trucking business is not a 9 to 5 work deal. I was away at work long into the evening on many days. The demands of running for Governor have taken me away from our home quite often."

George W. Clever

"On the night she disappeared, or was perhaps killed, was it one of those long work days, Mr. Casey?"

"As a matter of fact it was a late work session for me. My accountant and I were preparing State tax reports."

"What time did you arrive home?"

"This is beginning to sound a bit like you are looking for my alibi."

"Oh no, Mr. Casey, I am more interested in knowing when you learned Mrs. Casey was not home."

"Yes, I see. Well, she and I have not been sleeping in the same bed for some time. This is a big house with many bedrooms. It wasn't until the next morning when two of your uniforms arrived with the news of her disappearance or possible death that I discovered she had not come home the previous evening."

"Can you tell me if Mrs. Casey ever was missing previously for unaccounted amounts of time?"

"No. She loved being in her home, but Helen had her own philanthropic interests that involved some travel."

Words Can Kill

"Did Mrs. Casey ever ask you for a divorce?"

"No, Helen was content with our arrangement. She did not have to work outside the home, and there was plenty of money available to keep her happy here."

"Did you have a pre-nuptial agreement?"

"Yes, but it never was an issue. I gave her everything she wanted."

"Why then did you have separate beds? Did she have an outside lover?"

"Again Detective Sergeant you are getting very close to those questions where my lawyer should be present. Do you have any other questions? I really must leave now for my office."

"Yes, what is your accountants name and where can he be reached?"

"His name is Noah Carver. He can be reached at the Casey Trucking office. I think it is now time to say Goodbye Sergeant."

George W. Clever

"Oh....one more thing Mr. Casey, I may need to speak with you again. I would advise you not to leave town until Helen Casey is found, or heaven forbid, we have determined she was murdered.... and one more question, did you have your wife killed?"

"Now you will be talking with my attorney should we meet at any time in the future. Good bye."

Two of Harlan's suits moved between the Governor candidate and Sergeant Farrell. Using their body motions, they created an unseen force directing Officer Burr and Detective Farrell out the front door. The door closed with a thud and a bang.

"That is what I would call a hostile witness," Officer Katie remarked.

"Yes he was not very co-operative in helping us find his missing wife, but his actions are not necessarily incriminating. I do think he is hiding a great deal from the police. I would like to make our next stop a short conversation with accountant Noah Carver before Mr.

Words Can Kill

Casey reaches his office. Call in one of our motorcycles and have the officer make a car stop of Harlan Casey limo before he reaches his place of business. I am sure the officer can find some minor traffic violation to delay him long enough for us to speak with his accountant, Noah Carver."

"Yes sir. What shall I tell the motor about your need to have Casey's car stopped?"

"Tell him there is suspicion the driver has felony warrants."

"10…Officer Burr with Detective Farrell. 10-20 Fairway Drive. Signal 13 We have a 10-8 black Lincoln limo, license YB 485 leaving a residence on St. Regis Parkway. Possible driver with felony warrants."

"10-13 Dispatcher. Do you need assistance?"

Affirmative. Black and white, or Motor stop needed. Detain at the scene to verify identity. Signal 0 May be armed and dangerous."

"All units in sector seven respond to signal 13 St. Regis Parkway. 10-8 black Lincoln limo, license YB 485. Driver with possible felony warrants. Signal 0 advised. Detain at scene and verify identity."

George W. Clever

"Ok Katie, step on it. I need all the time we can get to talk with Noah Carver."

*****

18

An Introduction

Alone at the computer again, Fred thought about the problem of his part-time secretary editor Ms. Angelina. How was he going to explain her to his wife Myrna? Surely they would meet the next day when Angelina returned from her university studies to do his editing work. There would be no way to hide her. Myra would know there was certainly no money in their tight family budget to pay a secretary. His brain did a little fart and blurted out She is an intern working free for college class credit. *The computer eye spelled out **Free editing as a college intern**.*

That just might work, Fred concluded. He would give it a try in the morning and introduce Myrna to Angelina. The next morning Fred made his usual breakfast of cranberry juice for his pills, Special K, coffee, and a chocolate donut he knew would not be approved by Myrna or his doctor. He fed their dog "killer" the expected dog treats while Myrna tidied up the kitchen.

George W. Clever

"Is this another writing day for you Fred?" Myrna asked.

"Yes, I have a dead line of 20,000 words this week."

"Mother and I will be at the beauty parlor having our haircuts and perms this afternoon."

"There is something I would like to share with you, Myra, before you go. I received a call from the University English Department Dean. He has an intern editing program going on and would like to place one of the students with me part-time for class credit. What do you think about that?"

"Well, Fred, do you think some undergrad would be qualified to edit your book?"

"I think the intern would be a graduate student with some competency in editing."

"Will it be a she and pretty?"

"I don't know or care as long as the intern is a good editor. The intern could be a 'he' you know. If you are here for another hour you can meet this person."

Words Can Kill

Fred tried to mask his lie answering Myrna's question with a bored look. He knew it would be a she and very pretty indeed. Angelina had all of those model college girl attributes. She was a very healthy woman, and easy on his eyes like PI Mike's girlfriend/secretary/college student Angel. He finished his breakfast and returned to his writing place just as Angelina opened the basement door.

"Hi Fred, I'm ready for another day editing the wonderful and exciting book you are writing. Made any progress since yesterday?"

"Yes, I am at 15500 words now. Before we get started I would like to introduce you to my wife Myrna before she and her mother go to the beauty parlor. Give me a minute. I will call her to come and meet you."

Fred stood at the foot of the stairs and called Myrna. "Myrna…will you come down here for a second. My editing intern is here."

Myrna appeared at the top of the stairs and said, "Be down in a minute. I have to find mother's coat."

George W. Clever

A few seconds later she descended the stairs, surveyed the room with a puzzled look, and stood by Fred.

"Myrna, I would like you to meet my editing intern Angelina. Angelina, this is my wife Myrna."

Myrna's lips parted with a startled look soon forming into a Mona Lisa smile.

"I'm very glad to meet you Angelina. I know you will be of great assistance to my husband. Mother and I must be off now or we will forfeit our place at the beauty parlor. Good luck with your bookwork today Fred."

She turned abruptly and ascended the stairs. Myrna said something to her mother Fred could not hear as she closed the kitchen door.

"Mother I am very concerned about Fred. He introduced me to his university student editing intern just now."

"Why would that be upsetting to you dear?"

"Because, no intern was there!"

*****

Words Can Kill

"Angelina, I would like you to do a read of the first three chapters to see if I have left any dangling story directions. If so, please make notes in the margin of the printed manuscript. I am sorry I have only one computer here. I will try to have another one available for you on your next work day. A good proof read and copy edit would be appreciated."

Fred handed a pile of recently printed papers to Angelina, and returned to his desk. Myrna surely took my introduction to Angelina well. He mused. No more worries about being alone down here with a very attractive secretary. Funny though, Myrna did not shoot me one of her intensely jealous looks. It will be a relief to sit here appreciating Angelina's beauty without any guilt. Perhaps something more exciting will develop between us later.

Now, what will Sergeant Farrell expect to find out when he meets the Casey accountant Noah Carver? And how long will it be before Mike Dunmore checks himself out of the hospital disregarding the advice of his doctors, mother, and secretary Angel? What web is he connecting with this case as he rests in his hospital bed? The computer chattered with letters between each clunk for spaces as Fred's fingers flew over the keys. He was aiming at 16000 words before the day was over.

Corticosteroids and Antidepressants dripped from Mike's I-V bringing some relief to his pain and world of black despair. Every once in a while, the pain between his legs would send a jab north causing him to lift the sheets to see if indeed his male junk was still there. It was, but not without some bandages covering the burns, and a growing blue black bruise on each thigh. In between those moments, he built a mental marker board to link the events of the last few days, the people involved, and perhaps find the murderer of the body in his car trunk. He tried to find a link to his work for Helen Casey and the car fire.

His mind fought the drugs the former Army nurse had administered. She must have been an Army nurse because he could bounce off the sheets she had fitted to his hospital bed. Mike's PTSD flared again as his mental

Words Can Kill

questions roared through his brain like the zip and zing of AK-47 rounds he ducked in Iraq.

What had he missed? Who was the missing person able to shed light on the events of his night of abduction? At the Seneca Downs race track, he had given Helen Casey the file of damning information about the sinister and illegal child smuggling operation involving future governor Harlan Casey. It had been a quick slip of the file into her huge purse as they walked together through a crowd of people headed to the betting booths before the third race. Could it be she was followed?

How did the thugs who snatched him know the file delivered to Mrs. Casey by him had a second copy? Yes, he knew he had bragged at Kelly's Bar about finishing a job with a good payoff, but never gave any details about his employer or the type of job he did for the client. Why was Kelly O'Conner out in the parking lot on a busy Friday night? Oh yes, to dump bar trash. Surely he could have ordered a waitress or bartender to do the trash dump. Did he see anything besides the burning Charger? Was Mrs.

George W. Clever

Stephanie Kelly in the bar that night? What could she have seen?

Mike pushed his brain to remember his own abduction as he heard the sound of RPGs hitting the hospital room door making brain numbing explosions real again. They were real enough for him dig deeper into the thin hospital pillows on his way to possible dive under the bed. He probed his drug fuzzy brain to remember if he had seen Helen Casey in the bar that night. His damaged legs began to build the sheets and covers into a foxhole as the pain killers opened up night sweats again.

The effects of the stun gun slam and the battery shocks had barely worn off. He was remembering being blindfolded during his torture, but able to see when one of the goons took him to the bank for the Casey file in the deposit box. That was a big and costly mistake for the thug who dragged him through the bank vault, and tossed him on the street. Mike could recognize that goon. The bank employees could I.D. him also. Why didn't the muscles just kill him? The hoods knew I could be a witness if and when

Words Can Kill

they were caught. Obviously, their instructions were to avoid any killing, killing that would bring more heat to the Casey file problem. One thought kept slamming Mike's review and reasoning. I know a lot about Harlan Casey, but what did I really know about Helen Casey? It was a good place to start when released from the hospital.

The Helen Casey starting line was to be his last thought until morning. The shadows of the hospital room merged with the pain killers working their way through Mike's veins closing his conscious curtain for the night. Lights out. Sleep came when his brain was turned off. Maybe he could ask better questions the next time he was able to down a cool brew at Kelly's Bar.

Morning sunlight sneaking through the hospital room blinds announced the arrival of the day nurse with Mike's breakfast tray. She brought the news his hospital stay was over. He would be released by noon. It was time to find his clothes, and ditch the too small bed rag they call a hospital gown. Tie it in the front and your junk is naked. Tie it in the rear at the nurse's request so your junk is not *exposed, and…how in the hell do you tie it in the back? He had to see if Angel would work the computer and his other connections to learn more about Helen Casey.*

*****

"Come on Katie. You can drive faster than this. Put the pedal to the metal. Don't know how long those rollers will be able to delay Harlan Casey. I want to have enough time with Mr. Carver before his boss arrives at the office. We need to nail down Casey's alibi for the night of his wife's disappearance"

Officer Burr spent her weekends at a dirt track in a modern stock car she had built herself. Storming the streets at speed as directed by Sergeant Keith was an order she was thrilled to obey. It took only seven minutes for her to pull into a parking space at the front of the Casey Trucking Company office. She did it without flashing lights and a siren.

"Wait by the car with the motor running. I prefer not to be confronted by Mr. Casey or his lawyers yet."

Words Can Kill

Keith entered the front door and was met by a suit who introduced himself as Harlan Casey's secretary. It didn't take a metal detector to determine the bulge under the secretary's expensive suit was not an I Pod.

"Hello, I am detective Farrell. I would like to speak with Mr. Carver and you. I have a few questions to ask regarding Mrs. Casey's disappearance."

The 'secretary' led Keith down a short hall to a door with gold lettering stating Mr. Noah Carver-Accountant. As the secretary opened the office door Ferrell heard someone say.

"Sergeant Farrell I presume. I have been expecting you."

"Ah! The wonders of cell phones, I believe Mr. Casey must have just called you as I left his home a few minutes ago. You must be Noah Carver."

"Why yes he did. I was told he was detained on his way in to the office. Some misunderstanding with a motorcycle officer about the identity of his driver, and a burned out

George W. Clever

license plate light I think. How can Noah Carver be of assistance to you?"

"I would like to ask you a few questions regarding the disappearance of Mrs. Casey."

"Oh yes, a tragic affair and very devastating to Mr. Casey. She was the rainbow light in his eyes you know. Has the coroner been able to identify the burned body as Mrs. Casey?"

"No, not at this time, body was badly burned. I understand you and Mr. Casey were working late in the office on State taxes the night she disappeared."

"He was here helping me with the excessive State tax forms that are the bane of small business everywhere."

"I am not sure I would exactly call Casey Trucking small business. The company grossed over fifty million last year I believe."

Words Can Kill

"Sergeant, you have been doing some research on our company. Perhaps we should have called you for consulting on the tax problems that Friday."

"What time did Mr. Casey leave the office that night?"

"I believe it was, no I am sure it was 2 A.M. My wife called at that time to see if I was really working in the office. She is a very jealous woman."

"Do you know of anyone who would benefit from Mrs. Casey's disappearance or death?"

"Certainly not anyone I can think of. Mr. Casey and his wife had a prenuptial agreement you know."

"Yes I do know of the prenuptial agreement document. How do you know, Mr. Carver?"

"I met with Mr. Casey's lawyer providing financial information as the prenuptial document was being written."

The office door slammed opened. Harlan Casey stormed in with two other extra- large size suits standing on either side of him.

George W. Clever

Between gritted teeth Casey said. "We meet again, Detective. This time it is an unpleasant meeting. It would seem one of your misguided motor cops had nothing better to do than harass my driver on our way here. I am sure you had nothing to do with that. You had better leave before I bring this unwanted harassment to the attention of my lawyers."

"Just on my way out, Mr. Casey. Your accountant has been most helpful providing information I can use to find your missing wife. I'll be in touch as soon as I have found her."

"You do that. Goodbye."

*****

Fred's writing was interrupted by the clomp-clomp of Myrna's sensible shoes walking down the cellar stairs.

"You know Fred I work all day at the candy factory to pay the bills now that you are out of a job. When are you going to get serious about finding a new place of employment? All you do is sit in front of that computer day and night. Are you on one of those social or sex websites? Mother and

Words Can Kill

I never see you upstairs night after night. I am really getting sick of your novel writing excuses. You still have not found my dog Killer. This yappy thing you brought into our home is driving me crazy. You must get rid of it. And another thing, you never take me anywhere. We never have a date night anymore. Your excuses are always dependent on my mother being here. We could take her along you know."

Myra's rant went on for some time, but after the first few minutes Fred was already in his mental 'Happy Place.' His selective hearing was turned off. He was lost in a place where his comfort zone was thinking about writing what Mike Dunmore, Private Eye, was planning to do after he left the hospital. Fred rose once more feeling guilty for taking a mental escape as Myrna was saying the same think in repetition.

"You never want to be with mother. You never want to be with mother, Fred."

"Your mother smells." He mumbled under his breath. "She has a terrible skin condition, wears Icy Hot, with Arthritis Cream for deodorant and perfume."

George W. Clever

His mumble was covered over by a blanket of loud television white noise made when mother Bertha accidentally punched the TV clicker for a channel not on their cable list.

"I'm leaving for work now, Fred. I expect you to feed mother and do the laundry load I have left in the washer."

Myrna completed his marching orders for the day, and slammed her way through two doors into the garage.

When Myrna and Fred had disagreements, it was Fred who looked for a hole to crawl into and release his stress. Myrna never felt any resolution to their arguments nor to her concerns. The place Fred created in his writing was one he could always control. Yes, he could always control the plot, characters, and events. This was true, at least up to the one time he used his clicker to end his writer's block. Now he was not so sure he was in control of anything, especially the results of one of his mental butterflies. Those brain farts seemed to show up on their own, and were in no hurry to leave.

Words Can Kill

These "mental butterflies" could make real and potentially dangerous events come into my life he reasoned. Myrna's latest unpleasantness clouded Fred's creative writing brain. He knew it was time to hit the computer 'Save As'. *Maybe after feeding Myrna's mother there would be time to do more writing. What would Mike be planning to do after his hospital stay? There must be a way to control these brain farts. Maybe just pinching myself every time I feel a loss of focus from the writing. Perhaps some sort of shock or pain would keep those weird thoughts from slipping into my mind. He considered.*

*****

Mother Bertha was in rare form when Fred returned to the kitchen to prepare lunch for her. She waddled into the kitchen with her walker, pulled a pot from under the cupboard and began to heat some water.

"Well, are you just going to stand there and make me do all the work making my lunch?" She barked. "Don't you remember I am an invalid? Do you want your wife to come home and find me scalded because you were too lazy to make me soup?"

"I'll make you soup. What are you going to do with the boiling water?"

George W. Clever

"I'm making soup!" she shouted.

"What kind of soup is hot water?"

"See that catsup on the table? It makes tomato soup if you pour it in hot water. Dumb ass."

"That is just red hot water. We had plenty of soup cans. What kind do you want?" He asked.

"You got no canned soup. I looked under my bed. There is no canned soup there!"

"Bertha, we don't keep cans under your bed." Fred replied in an exasperated tone, shaking his head. "Sit here at the table and I will make you some tomato soup."

He found the crackers, and poured Bertha a beer she requested. *Myrna hates it when I give her mother beer. I do it so the old bag will nod off leaving me some peace and quiet time.* While the soup he found in the cupboard was heating, Fred gathered up the dirty laundry in their bedroom hamper, and started a load of dark clothes. Bertha finished her lunch, and clumped her walker into the den to watch her favorite Jerry Springer TV program. *That should keep her quiet for hours. She usually falls asleep in the rocker after watching Springer and one episode of her favorite soap story. Don't think she will even know if I go back to my writing for the rest of the afternoon. Fred considered.*

*****

19

Round-Two

The morning nurse had just taken Mike's vitals, and dressed his wounds with cleaned bandages when he heard a quick knock on the hospital room door.

"Hello Mike."

"Angel, what a nice surprise. Why do I rate a hospital visit from you so early in the morning?"

"I wanted to see how you were doing before I headed to the university. This is one of my long days full of classes. How are you feeling, and why are you dressed and out of bed?"

"I'm fine. Just need to get back on my feet, and get answers to a few questions I have mulled over in my sleep last night. I need a favor on your busiest day. Will you do your computer magic and dig for information about Helen Casey. I just realized how little I really know about her."

"You probably never thought about anything more than little Mrs. Hotness and her body."

George W. Clever

"Ok, her attributes did occupy and divert my inquisitive mind at times. I need her background information by this evening. Can you do this for me?"

"I am sorry Mike any other day would be fine. But today I have a paper to finish, and a final test to take."

"I really need this one, Angel."

She looked at his wounded face where his eyes told of damages that may never heal. How could she refuse his request?

"No guarantees, I will try. Where will I find you this evening?"

"I'll be at Kelly's Bar, and later at Mom's place. I need to show Mom I am quite alive with just a little body mending to do."

"I would say you need a lot of body mending. You may be doing more if you don't take it easy for a while. Ok, I will find you if those goons don't come back for second helpings. One more thing, Sergeant Keith was parking his

Words Can Kill

car as I entered the hospital. I am sure he wants to see you before you check yourself out."

"Ok, I'll wait for him. Good luck on the exam, and better luck with Helen Casey's bio."

Angel found the only undamaged, resting place for her lips on Mike's face again. It was a much longer kiss than one of those quick social goodbyes.

"See you this evening tough guy."

Flexing his fingers to ease his carpel tunnel hand pains, Fred thought about the warning posted on the writer's prompt website. 'Once you click this icon you will never stop writing.' It sounded like a wonderful promise to any writer looking for a never ending source of things to write about. He welcomed the motivational energy to crank out book after book in an all too short lifetime. But was this promise really a gift? Nothing was said on the website about those pesky mental butterflies showing up, and turning a writer's life upside down. At first he envisioned smoke bringing a genie out of a jar to grant whatever wishes Fred's brain butterflies would produce. The result of his pinching experiments to control his brain fart thoughts were very disturbing. It didn't work. How does one explain major changes in life to those around him who know there is no logical way these changes could be a result of a mental wish? Even the wishes he mentally initiated never materialized. The thoughts over which he had no control were the ones intruding on his reality.

Fred did realize his commitment to writing, "Puking out a novel" as Stephen King would say, was running on warp speed. That was a good thing. Fred wondered, *how many more crossroads will be reached with these brain farts before the novel is finished? Where will these computer prompts lead me? Hopefully they will lead to a best seller novel.*

He knew it was a good thing his doctor gave him anxiety pills after losing the job at the call center. Anxiety over mental butterflies was so much more intense than getting fired from a job he hated. It was almost as stressful as living with Myrna and her mother. Getting fired for

Words Can Kill

telling some caller an expired warranty was only good for wiping their ass was probably the best thing he did that day.

Fred hated that job. It was a job he only took because his wife's Aunt was the call center's personnel director who owed Myrna a favor. Myrna whined and cried to her Aunt how she married a good for nothing husband who could not find a job. Her Aunt soon tired of the conversation and gave Fred an interview. Working in a cube was the worst way to spend a day in his otherwise dull life. Being on the phone all day, and listening to the whining of callers as a 'Tele-communications Service Representative' was personally demeaning.

Losing the job may have been good for him, but it was very bad for Myrna and her mother thanks to Aunt Mildred's gossip spreading. Fred was now a family joke among all of Myrna's relatives. Writing was a life saver for Fred. It provided power to control all things around him, at least in the basement in front of his Dell computer. Once again his fingers found their way without an eyesight guide as he wrote.

George W. Clever

"Good morning Mike. How's the ole body doing this morning?"

"Hey Sergeant Keith, you bring any donuts with you?"

"No, but Krispy Kreme stock took a dive since you left the force. What are you doing up in your clothes?"

"Time for me to go. I have to see some people about the torching my car."

"Mike, I need to have your copy of the Casey file. I know you well enough to be sure you have one."

"Keith, I thought I told you in my groggy state of mind last night those thugs dragged me to the bank and emptied my safe deposit box of the file copy."

"I think you planted one there as a decoy. I want you to get your file copy, and meet with Lieutenant Meagan Glade and me when you are feeling better. She is working undercover on a child prostitution and smuggling case. Understand me clearly Mike, we need her assistance to solve Mrs. Casey's disappearance and possible murder."

Words Can Kill

Sergeant Keith looked at Mike's bandages covering visible body parts and considered body damage not visible. Keith gave a shiver thinking how close his friend came to being killed in his street slide for life. There had to be away to keep him in the hospital where he would be safe until police detectives could crack the case.

"Yes, it is now a murder case. Our crime lab has examined the DNA they recovered from the body in your car trunk. It was a match with Helen Casey's DNA. We took hair samples from her brush Harlan Casey begrudgingly brought into the precinct. Harlan is a hard nut to crack. He may be the killer, but more likely, he had someone do it for him. He has money, power, and political connections to cover his tracks. Still working on his motive. I already fenced with him yesterday. You know we have our own interdepartmental rivalries on the force. I have to tread lightly in my homicide investigation because another investigating team is focusing on Casey Trucking. Glade is a good cop. If we can provide some information for her, she can be persuaded to work with us."

George W. Clever

Mike was not thrilled with the idea of some undercover woman getting in the way of his search for the person or persons who torched his car, and left a body in the trunk. Placing Harlan Casey off limits in the case was like wearing handcuffs to a swim meet for P.I. Mike.

"Ok Keith, set it up. I will bring the file goods to the meet. For the time being, I will avoid a 'discussion' with Harlan Casey, and use what energy I have left to squeeze what I need from those who were at Kelly's Bar that night. All I got last time was some tight lipped answers to my questions. Now I have some questions that will open their tight lips. Call me when you are ready to meet."

"Ok you had better take it easy giving your body time to mend."

"One more thing, Keith. Is that Glade woman a real cop who can stop traffic with a stare or is she a looker?"

"She is gorgeous enough to keep Harlan's attention while she digs into his trucking business. Why do you want to know?"

Words Can Kill

"Well, it makes meetings with you easier when there is eye candy in the room. Your office coffee is nasty. It reminds me too much of the Corps."

Mike followed Sergeant Farrell out of the hospital room and placed a "Do Not Disturb" sign on the outside of the hospital room door.

"Where did you get that sign?" Farrell asked.

"Don't ask. It should keep the nurses out long enough for me to grab a cab without having to run the hospital administrative gauntlet."

"Stay out of trouble, Mike. I will be calling you with the meeting time and place in one hour."

*****

Scanning Myrna's list of marching orders taped to his computer; Fred read a familiar item. #1.) Feed my mother. A strange thought buzzed through his brain. *Why don't I just make her a trough, and shovel the contents of the kitchen refrigerator into it*. **Make her a trough and**

George W. Clever

shovel refrigerator contents into it appeared on the flat computer screen.

"Oh no! What made me think of that? How do I control those damn thoughts?" He shouted.

It was too late. He rushed upstairs, and found the kitchen refrigerator door open. A large wooden v shaped box was on the floor before it. Closing the frig door he reached to pick up the trough at the very moment Bertha wheeled her walker around the hall corner into the kitchen.

"What are you doing Fred?"

Writing his novel seemed to help his ability to think and lie quickly. He had to say something believable or he would hear it from Myrna when she got home.

"Just getting ready to deliver this trough to the kid next door, he is raising a Four H Club pot belly pig."

"Well, that certainly seems odd. You know I am really hungry, and it is way past lunch time." Bertha replied.

Fred's hands shook. A wrinkled brow formed on his face as he lifted the trough. Hurrying to the back door he reflected

Words Can Kill

on what had just happened. *Wheew! That was a close one. I don't know how many more of these mental butterflies I can take. Now what am I going to do with this wooden dinner plate for Bertha? It won't disappear by itself.*

Fred pushed the wooden box out the back door grabbing a sledge hammer leaning against the cordwood pile. It only took a few seconds and a couple of hefty swings of the sledge to break the trough into pieces. *Myrna will never know all this kindling wood was once a pig trough, and now is just some more kindling wood in the scrap pile.*

Returning quickly to the kitchen, he made a melted cheese sandwich with chicken noodle soup lunch for Bertha and himself. Finishing the last spoonful of soup, Fred read the next item on Myrna's list of demands. #2.) Do the whites laundry. Two piles of clothes were separated on the laundry room floor, one of colored items and the other of whites. *I don't have time to hang here until two loads of clothes are washed and dried. These two piles are small. Might as well just put the two together and be done with it,*

Fred reasoned. He opened the washer lid, and stuffed all the clothes in the gaping washer cavern with plenty of room to spare. Pouring a cup of washing soap over the clothes, he added the softener in its indicated place. As an afterthought, Fred remembered the bleach for the white clothes.

The machine made its electronic voice known as he pressed the start button. *That should take care of her list for this day. I know what she will say. 'You didn't do any of the things on my list', he speculated. I never can please her. Drying that wash load will have to wait. Got to get back to my story if I am to reach my word count goal today*. He closed the laundry room door and returned to his computer.

*****

A P.I. was no good without his wheels, and his weapon. The cab ride took Mike to Angel's apartment complex where he remembered the Corvette was parked. With luck it would still be there. It was, and the keys were under the mat where Angel had placed them. Good thinking

Words Can Kill

girl. *You knew I would not stay in that hospital bed for long. Now it is time to see Carmichael, and pick up a locker key. It felt good for Mike to be mobile again with some control over his day. Pauper's Pawn Shop was busy for a Tuesday with Carmichael and his sales staff all attending customers who were buying and pawning anything of value.*

Mike moved to the display of Elvis stuff pretending to have an interest in buying one of the pieces. Carmichael, free of his last customer, came over to stand behind the Elvis display case in front of Mike.

"Hey guy, good to see you are interested in my Elvis memorabilia. All of these Elvis things are hot items right now. You can double your money buying here, and selling on eBay. What can I sell you today? Maybe I should find a personal nurse who worked for the Pelvis? You look like the shit truck ran over you."

"Had a tough night with a couple of guys from Arena Cage Fighting. I need the key Angel gave you, and one more favor. The two pretend cops took my Beretta, the one I have

registered. Can you find me one without numbers to replace it?"

"The key is easy. The replacement may take a while. Can you give me an hour?"

"Sure, I need a shower, a shave, and some clean clothes. See you in an hour."

Carmichael was alone in his office when Mike returned. He looked up from his examination of a Rolex watch on the counter, and smiled.

"Hey Mike, you do look a hell of a lot better since I saw you last. Those medics are doing wonderful things with super glue."

"Oh funny Carm. Did you find my replacement?"

"Yes, and here is the key Angel left."

"What do I owe you?"

"The same money I owed you when you took care of that scum bag my daughter dragged home. She dumped him

Words Can Kill

after crying for three days when he never showed or called her. You must have scared the bejesus out of him."

"Oh, I just reminded him it is difficult to dance with broken knees. Thanks Carm for the piece and the key delivery. I do appreciate the help."

Carmichael slipped a brown paper bag to Mike. He knew better than to pry on a 'Private' detective for information about case. He did have a serious concern for his friend as he studied the visible damage Mike's face had received.

"Are you in some heavy trouble? Is there anything I can do?"

"Just keep the home fires burning, and your shop open. You still on for Thursday night bowling?"

"Do you think you will be able to lift your ball?"

"I'm not too worried about that ball. See you at Ten Pins around nineteen hundred, and thanks."

*****

George W. Clever

The Browning nine-millimeter pistol felt comforting tucked in his belt pressing against Mike's right hip. Another Corvette passed him going in the other direction. The driver gave a salute to Mike as an exchange of understanding about the pleasure of driving a Vette. The purpose of Mike's next scheduled stop at his Mom's was to try and reassure her he was in better shape now than the day she saw him at Walter Reed Hospital after his second Iraq tour.

Then it would be time for a short snort at Kelly's Bar. This time he expected to fit together a few pieces of the Casey puzzle. He pulled in the driveway and exited the Vette like he was in top shape and ready to run a marathon. His mother might be watching from the window. Mike rang the doorbell, and waited on the porch swing for someone to come to the door. His mother cautiously opened the screen door.

"Well, look who the cat has drug in. I was so worried when Angel told me you were going to be away for a short time. I knew what

Words Can Kill

she meant. You were in the hospital again, and didn't want your mother hovering over you. Are you ok?"

"Yes. I'm ok. Just a little skirmish, and I am ready for round two."

"Please Mike, get some another kind of less dangerous job. Maybe you could use your GI Bill and go to college to be a lawyer or even to a trade school where you could learn motorcycle mechanics. I saw that ad on TV."

"I like what I do Mom. P.I. work is mostly just boring stuff like watching someone's errant spouse."

"Oh no Mike. I know PI work is all dangerous. I've watched the Rockford Files on TV you know. Will you come in and stay for some supper?"

"Can't tonight. How about tomorrow night? Today, I have to do some work on the Casey case before I call it a night. If Angel stops by will you say I'm at Kelly's Bar, and for her to meet me there?"

"Yes, I will tell her. Be careful. Your beat up face tells me there is more damage hidden under your clothes."

George W. Clever

"I'm ok Mom. See you tomorrow night. Do you think you could make pigs in the blanket for me?"

"Of course I can. I know it is one of your favorites. Can't remember when we sat down for one of those dinners together. Guess it was before your Dad died."

"See you tomorrow."

Mike gave his Mom a long hug before jumping into the Corvette driver seat in a manner he saw on TVs Dukes of Hazzard. He wanted to do a bit of 'show boating' for his mom so she would see he was physically ok. All the slide over the Corvette hood did was to re-enforce Terza's memory list of all the dangerous things Mike had done since he was able to walk as a kid.

*****

20

Puzzle Pieces

As the Vette powered up the interstate on ramp the cell phone in his pocket on vibrate began to buzz. Mike chose to always keep it on vibrate so the phone would not give him away at the wrong time with some kind of cute ring.

"Mike, Gunny here. I think we should have a powwow. Can you stop by my home this evening? Got some intel for you."

"How urgent? I am meeting Angel at Kelly's this evening."

"Bring her along. I haven't seen that lovely woman in many moons."

"Ok, but it will be late."

"No problem. I'll be up. See you then. Bye."

On the way to Kelly's Restaurant, Mike made a mental check list of people he wanted to see in the bar. He wondered how many would be there in the middle of the week. Friday nights were the busiest at Kelly's Restaurant with their exceptional fish fry. His questions would not wait until another Friday rolled around. He had questions for Kelly, his wife Stephanie, the bartender John, and anyone else he could identify as a person who was there last Friday.

Mike knew from his past police work the clock was ticking on any chance to solve this case. He needed to clear himself as a police suspect involved in the disappearance of Helen Casey. Fumbling through the glove compartment, he searched for the DVD and license plate list Angel gave him. His driving was a bit erratically weaving down the express lane as he considered whether the list and DVD would be reachable in the glove box. Maybe the fax cops tossed his car, and took the DVD with the list. His hand closed on the plastic cover, and then the paper around it held by a rubber band.

If he made a quick stop at Pauper's Pawn, he could use Carmichael's electronics to examine the DVD security video. It would be important to run the names and license

Words Can Kill

plate connections through his brain one more time to see if there were any names he could connect to the Casey Trucking. Carmichael runs a twenty-four-hour pawn shop, but would he be there now? He was. The three balls of the neon store open light were on.

"Hey, what up dude, back so soon?" he shouted from the back of the shop. "Car, I need to find a TV and box that plays DVDs. You got one?"

"Yeah, I got a half dozen. They're all plugged in. Help yourself. Anymore customers like you tonight and I will apply for membership of the unemployed and out of business club."

Firing up one of the sale computers, Mike popped in the DVD to a connected player and leaned over the counter. Carmichael was at his side, curious to see what was on the recording.

"What you looking for Mikey?'

"Oh, just some face in the security video DVD from Kelly's Bar who might know more information than I do about who torched my car."

They watched the video recorded on the DVD scroll through various security camera footages until Car said, "Hey isn't that Helen Casey?"

"You know Mrs. Casey?"

"Oh sure, she used to be one of my pawn shop regulars leaving expensive stuff when she was short of cash. That was all before she met and married that Trucking boss."

"You do have such an honorable clientele list. Recognize anyone else in this video?"

"Yes that woman over by the bar, Mrs. Stephanie Kelly. She came in here one time trying to get me to buy her husband's old classic 1940s Buick. That was before her husband bought the bar. You see anybody you recognize Mike?"

Mike pressed stop button on the DVD player, then hit the reverse, stop and play button again. Two faces were

Words Can Kill

barely visible in shadows as the people sat in a booth near the bar. Placing a finger on the TV screen, He pointed at people in the booth and asked Carmichael again.

"You know those two guys at the corner table?"

"Yes, I think I do. Kind of hard to see them. I think the one on the right has been in with a roll of cash to buy one of my Super Bowl rings. Word is he hires out to 'fix' things."

Mike recognized him as the thug who escorted him to the bank. Helen Casey was seen coming in the front door of the bar, and Stephanie, Kelly's wife, was on a bar stool at the right. She looked at Helen and moved off the stool to intercept her just as Helen was about to enter the dining room.

"Look at their faces do they seem happy to see each other?"

"No, they are anything but happy. Looks like they're in an argument."

George W. Clever

Helen entered the dining room and left through the side door. Another camera change showed a shot of the bar and the corner table.

"Car, the fixers are gone."

"Maybe they slipped out the front door?"

"I don't see Stephanie Kelly either."

A different security camera switched on showing the parking lot. The picture was grainy and fuzzy, but the people were still recognizable.

"Look there in the far corner of the parking lot by the little garage where Kelly parks his car alongside his old RV. Is that Helen getting into her car or Stephanie?"

"Where did Stephanie go? I guess we know where Helen went or do we?"

"Here is the shot I have been trying to find. Kelly is coming out of the side door with the bar trash."

In the video, Kelly looks toward the RV first and then turns to Mike's Charger which is now in a fire ball.

Words Can Kill

He drops his trash and runs back inside by way of the side door of the bar. The Charger burns on the other side of the trash dumpster.

"Mike, do you always park behind the Dumpster?"

"Yeah, sure, don't like to advertise when I am at Kelly's watering hole."

"I think it is in a dead spot on the parking lot security camera sweep."

"You're right. I wonder who else knows about the dead spot. Give me a re-play of Mrs. Casey where she meets Stephanie in the bar, please. Do you notice anything unusual about these two women?"

"Well, they are about the same height. One dresses like a Baptist preacher's wife, and the other like the woman the preacher is trying to save from hell and damnation."

"What else?"

*****

George W. Clever

It was going to be one of those days when all Fred could do was sit and stare at the computer screen. He had no motivation to write and not much interest in completing his novel. Still, he found the only comfort available to him was just sitting in the basement. Somehow it was his safe place away from the crazy world above. *"If I could find some kind of work it would get me out of this house, and away from the chores Myrna expects me to do as a care giver for her mother. But what kind of job could I do, and why would I abandon Mike Dunmore in his time of need to find the killer of Helen Casey, and who torched his car?* He thought.

Maybe I could find a job where there is a lot of down time with little to do, a place where I could write with a laptop computer. If I only had a laptop instead of a PC, I could work and keep on writing. That would shut up Myrna for a while, He said out loud to himself. The flat screen went dark for a few seconds. *When it appeared to re-boot, he saw these words.* ***If I only had a laptop instead of a PC bought of the back of a truck at the flea market.*** He heard the front door open and Myrna's voice.

Words Can Kill

"I'm home Fred. Where are you?"

It was only a moment before he saw her piano legs on the stairs. She was coming down to his cave with a determined tromp-tromp as her heals echoed off the oak stairs. Fred knew by her determined steps it would be the prelude to some argument about his short comings.

"Mother said you told her something about building a wooding trough in the kitchen for some kid. Why? Don't you have more important things to tend to than building something for some kid in the neighborhood?"

She stopped in midsentence, and looked from her towering stair pulpit directly at his desk. Something was not right in the picture of his desk she had filed in her mind.

"Where did you get that laptop? You know we have no money for this kind of thing. I work all day just to keep the roof over our head now that you have decided to swell the ranks of the unemployed. And what is that plugged into your PC?"

George W. Clever

Fred turned from his obedient focus on Myrna's rant to look at his desk. A new, out of the box, HP laptop was beginning its upload of Fred's novel.

"I need a fast laptop if I am to keep up with all the social media like LinkedIn as I search for work."

"You take that machine back to the store where you bought it now! How did you manage a shopping tour when I left you in charge of mother's care?"

"Your mother was sleeping and I was only gone for a few minutes."

"Fred, take back that laptop!"

"Yes dear, I'll take the laptop back."

"That will never happen," he said to himself. Guys that sell off a truck at the flea market don't take returns.

Myrna turned and stomped back up the stairs almost shouting, "Could you just try a bit harder to disappoint me?" Slamming the door to emphasis her frustration with his laptop buy, the noise echoed around the cellar room. Fred shrugged off her anger and settled into his office

Words Can Kill

chair. He was ready to escape Myrna's condemnation with a mental drift into his novel.

*****

Kelly's Bar parking lot was surprisingly full for a weeknight when Mike pulled the Vette into his old space by the dumpster. Angel's yellow, VW bug convertible was not in the lot. Her absence gave Mike a few minutes to see if any of the key players in the Casey case were in the bar. He had plenty of questions to ask now. He would take no dodging and dancing from anyone during this question session if they tried to offer canned answers. Kelly was wiping off the bar when Mike walked through the side dining room door.

"Mike, what brings you to your favorite bar stool this early in the afternoon?"

"Just thirsty Kelly. I'll have a Black Label draft when you get the chance."

George W. Clever

Kelly put his bar rag into the sink below the bar, and pulled the BL beer tap leaving just enough room for a proper head in the glass.

"There you go sparky. Learn who torched your car yet?"

"No, I haven't heard anything from Sergeant Keith either. Would like to ask you a few questions about that night, if you have a minute."

"Sure, at your service."

"Was you wife here last Friday night?"

"Yeah, she came in about seven and left shortly after you came in. Why?"

"Did she know Mrs. Casey? I saw them together in the security video."

"I don't think so. Maybe she was just doing a little bar PR with female customers, you know promoting our dinner menu."

Words Can Kill

"Does she usually park her car out in far corner of the lot by your RV?"

"I guess so. All the staff was told at the last meeting to leave the close spaces for the customers, but I think she took a cab home that night. Her car needs some brake work. I have just been too busy to get it into the shop."

"Will she be in tonight? I would like to talk with her. Maybe she saw something in the lot when she left."

"She probably will be in sometime around closing. That's the time we like to have a nightcap, and chat about events of the day. Sometimes we do the same thing for our morning opener if she is going shopping."

Kelly continued to clear glasses from the bar and rinse them in the sink. He was thinking of a way to ease out of Mike's interrogation while wiping the bar with a clean cloth.

"Did you see anyone in the lot when you went out to dump the trash, anything besides my car blazing? You know like someone getting into their car?"

George W. Clever

"I don't remember seeing anyone."

"Not even Mrs. Casey or the cab that picked up your wife Stephanie?"

"No Mike, scouts honor! All I saw was that blazing car. I didn't want to lose this bar so I ran in and called 911. Guess I haven't been of much help. I got to tend to bar business Mike. Let me know if there is any way I can be of help in finding who torched your car."

Kelly left Mike as he cleared a few glasses from the side tables near the bar, wiping the dark red checkered oil table cloths and straightening the empty chairs.

"Hey Sparky, here is someone to take your mind off unpleasant things." Kelly hollered as he returned to the far end of the bar.

Angel walked into the front door and took a stool beside Mike at the bar.

"Hello boss. You are a tough one to track down. Almost didn't get away from my stop at your mom's place. I'm starved. Let's eat."

Words Can Kill

Mike and Angel found a quiet table in the dining room where room noise would not interfere with their conversation.

"Did you find the Helen Casey information I needed?"

"Oh yes, and something very juicy about her twin sister."

*****

Closing his laptop lid with a snap, Fred pushed away from the computer desk on a mission of anger needing a release. He climbed the stairs to the kitchen where Myrna was making dinner.

"I WILL surely try harder to disappoint you tomorrow. I have an interview with the Geico Insurance Company. You know the one on TV with the talking gecko lizard They are looking for phone insurance adjusters."

"What makes you think they would ever hire you? Do remember you were fired from your last job as a service rep. You really have no personality nor people skills."

"I can do this job. The ad says, the service representative we hire will receive customer requests for an accident adjustor. The ad reads 'We at Geico need someone to relay appropriate claims information to the appropriate satellite agent adjuster.' Now how hard could that be?"

"For most people it would be not very hard, but for you, impossible."

"Thanks for the vote of confidence, Myrna. I thought you would be thrilled if I found a new job."

"Who will watch my Mother?"

"She can watch herself. Been doing it now for more than eighty years I think."

"I think you would not say that if it was your mother."

"My mother is dead. She was smart enough to pull the grass rug over herself before she had to live here with you."

Fred returned to the basement, reopened his laptop, and dialed his selective hearing to off. Myrna threw the spatula she was using into the sink, and followed him down the stairs.

Words Can Kill

"This conversation is not over Fred. You resent my mother being here with us even for a short time. Before you take any job, should the company be so desperate, you had better check with me. Mother will be back at her home in a few months so your precious job can wait."

Funny how Myrna uses good news about the possibility of her mother returning to her own home to win our arguments. I know Bertha will not be going back to her second floor slumlord apartment. She fell twice, being unable to get her bulk up the stairs to the dingy place filled to the ceiling with her crap. Fred reasoned.

"Well, Myrna, I thought you would be thrilled with the possibility of me working again. As usual, I was wrong according to you and your mother."

"You always are a disappointment to me Fred," Myrna said, as she stomped back up the stairs.

A whisper of a though blew through his mind. If only Myrna and her mother Bertha were gone this would be such a better world. This thought, unfortunately, was not the type of mental butterfly bringing him a desired result.

George W. Clever

Fred understood deliberate thoughts he could control would not bear fruit. He was thinking, *where was I in the Mike and Angel story? It is becoming more and more difficult for me to keep all the players in the story connected, and moving toward a story ending. It is just the same with people and things showing up in my own life. How will each story end, the one I'm writing, and the one I live every day? How soon will they both end?* Fred needed time to work out the novel story line. He felt compelled to keep his fingers pounding the keyboard to hammer out some phase of the story every day. *Could that damn icon be cursing me? I am supposed to be writing forever. Oh yes, now I remember. Angel was saying….*

*****

Words seem to fly on the computer screen as Fred hammered out the dialogue between Angel and Mike. He was in a writer's groove, an unstoppable rhythm, as the story unfolded in his mind.

"Helen Casey had a twin sister, not an identical twin, but one so close in looks it was difficult for most people to

Words Can Kill

distinguish them apart, at least when they were young. That changed in high school for the sisters when one of them stole the boyfriend of the other. After that incident, one of the girls altered her looks, dress, and style."

"What else did you find out?" Mike asked.

Angel flipped through her note pad looking for the page containing the information she had collected on the sister's parents.

"Well, their parents were both killed in an automobile accident when they were in their teens. No one stepped forward to provide foster care. There was no estate of substance, and they were kicked out of their parents rented home. Out on the street they joined a street gang. One of the girls began a prostitution career. Her work favored truck stops. At age 14, she become what truckers call 'a lot lizard'. The other sister found pole dancing to her liking and tried to talk the other sister into joining her at that job. Helen Casey met Harlan when he was just beginning his trucking business as a regular driver. Rumor has it, Helen's sister met a young bartender and married him. I *got most of this from on-line documents. Helen had a rap sheet for solicitation and a shop lifting misdemeanor. Couldn't find anything on the other sister, but I have a friend Shawn, from one of my classes, who has a sideline as a street gambler. He says he wants to have a "legit" job in medical services like me. He wanted a real job as a place to hide away if his gambling street gig got too hot. Shawn filled in the rest of the information about Helen Casey you needed. He is pretty connected to those who walk on the dark side in this town."*

Mike reached into his leather jacket pocket, and removed a small notebook and pen. The serious look on his face faded to a smile as he processed the information Angel provided about Helen Casey. Scribbling a few sentences in the notebook, he folded it quickly placing it back in his pocket with the pen.

"Good work love. Now my pie has some tasty filling."

"You just mentioned food. Can we eat now? Please?" Angel smiled.

Words Can Kill

"Ok, but I can't stay long, and you can't either. We have a late night date with Gunny Jackson. Seems he has more filling to add to this pie. He asked specifically for you to come along with me. Gunny misses you."

"Yes, I miss the old fart too. Let's eat."

*****

21

Don't Mess with Gunny

There must be more to this writer prompt website than its devilish motive to make my life even crazier than it is now. The few good mental butterflies are far outnumbered by the bad. And yet there is this implied promise of positive brain farts coming through to the computer screen, making my life better. If only I could control those butterfly thoughts somehow, Fred considered. *Oh well, at least I am writing more, and will finish this novel soon. Perhaps Myrna will never know I made up the interview story about the job at Geico.*

What kind of job could I find that would give me time to keep writing my novel, and as a bonus, get me out of the house away from Myrna and her mother? Just like tapping brain keys, an answer came through from his troubled concerns. Be a night clerk in a hotel. Slowly the words began to form on the screen. **Be a night clerk in a hotel.**

George W. Clever

Fred's cell phone buzzed as it vibrated. He hated the ring choices, but liked the vibration. He only wished the phone vibration could be like a massage.

"Hello. Yes, this is Fred Fonsworth. Who are you? Oh, yes Morgan Cleb. Now I remember. You sat in the cube by the window at the call center. I haven't seen you since I left the telemarketing service company. How you been?"

"Oh Morgan, I am fine working on writing a novel. Wife Myrna is a bit unhappy with me out of work, but I really must finish my novel by September. This call center layoff gives me that time. Yes, I was a bit out of line to tell a customer what to do with an expired warranty. You always wanted to do the same thing? No kidding?

It had been a long time since Fred had the opportunity to talk with someone other than Myrna and her mother. He felt like prisoners must feel when they are finally paroled. Talking on the phone is generally not a 'guy thing', but he wanted this call to go on for a long time.

"What am I doing next Friday? Well, I should be home. You want me to sub for you on a bowling team?"

Words Can Kill

"Well, Ok, I will have to check with Myrna. She is really pushing me to find another job. Oh, you could help me with that? Your brother-in-law is a hotel manager looking for a night clerk. Sure I will be interested. An interview Friday morning? Yes, I could be there at eight o'clock. Ok, an interview, and bowling all in the same day. Sounds swell. Thanks."

When he ended the call his thought took a positive turn for a change. *Maybe something good is coming to me from this website after all. I need to finish at least another five hundred words for this story by tomorrow. Not much time for writing on that day I think. Now where was Mike going? Oh yes I am sending him and Angel to visit with Gunny.*

Angel and Mike finished their dinner at Kelly's and drove in Angel's VW convertible to Gunny Jackson's home at River Walk. Gunny's home was in a small enclave of retired military homes along Lake Belton close to Olin Teague Veterans Hospital. As they neared the house, Mike could see no lights in any of the house windows. The house

George W. Clever

was darker than pitch. It was not like Gunny to say he would be up late in his home, and then go to bed early. A car was parked by the curb with its motor running. Someone was hunched over in the driver seat. Two dark shapes could be seen on the porch, one on each side of the front door.

"Keep driving Angel and fast! When you get to the next corner turn right. Stop behind the first house. Wait for me there. Something I don't like is going on at Gunny's. Don't leave your car."

Angel parked around the corner in the shadow of the first house. Mike quietly opened the car door, and ran in a crouch toward the front of Tom Jackson's house. Following the cover provided by scrubs, he sprinted from one house to the next until he was able to see Gunny's front door. The breaking of a glass was followed by the sound of a door being kicked in. Two gun shots rang out as the shadow men entered the home. Mike vaulted over the porch rail at the side of the house and plastered himself against the wall by the door. One of the dark shapes exited the

Words Can Kill

door, but not before falling spread eagle on his face when his legs changed direction from one of Mike's kicks. "Don't move dirt bag, Mike growled. He expected the second shadow man to emerge from the house. When he didn't Mike yelled inside.

"Gunny, are you all right?"

"That you Mike?"

"Yes sir. Two guys went in. I got one here. Where is the other one?"

"On the floor here Marine. I nailed him when he crashed my front door," Tom Jackson yelled back.

Mike grabbed the man on the porch floor, threw him up against the broken door, and patted him down for weapons. Holding the Browning 9 he had acquired from Carmichael to the man's head, Mike relieved the perp of a short barrel 38 pistol.

"Ok, scumbag on your feet. Let's go find your partner," Mike commanded.

George W. Clever

He pushed the home invader toward the smashed door and into Gunny's Living room. The two Marines in the living room gave each other the same long stare they often shared after a mission completed in Iraq.

"Ok Gunny?"

"Yeah and you? Looks like the only collateral damage was to my front door, and a few serious holes in one of the perps lying behind the couch. I caught him with 00 buck. Leave the other one with me and I will interrogate him before the cops arrive. He will tell me who sent these two thugs to break into my home. Can't rely on the 'feel good' police force to get the answers I need. Meet me at your office tomorrow morning. I will have more to tell you then. I think it is better you are not here when they arrive."

"There is another one in the car out front," Mike cautioned."

Tom Jackson looked toward the street, pumped another shell into his twelve gage shotgun, and held it on the ready. Tires screamed as the get-away car roared down the street.

Words Can Kill

"Looks like that one was too nervous to stick around," Tom said. "You had better get going."

Mike gave Gunny Jackson a quick quasi salute, and bolted over the porch rail back to where Angel was waiting in the car. As he opened the car passenger door he saw fear dancing around in Angel's eyes.

"Oh Mike I heard shots!"

"It's ok sweetheart. Just get us out of here quickly. I will tell you all about it on our way to your crib. Be sure we are not being followed. The car we saw parked in front of Gunny's house disappeared after the shooting. It may still be lurking around here somewhere. Did you by any chance get a look at the car when it passed the corner?"

"Silver Chevy Impala with a New Jersey license plate. I could only get the letters CVM." Angel replied.

"Well call your friend in the DMV tomorrow. I know it is a long shot, but maybe that info will turn up something."

Angel threaded the side streets with her eye on the rearview mirror before taking the ramp to the interstate.

George W. Clever

"What happened back at the house Mike? Is Gunny Jackson ok?"

"Yes, he had a home invasion and took care of one of the perps with his short twelve gauge. I slowed up in time to dropkick the second invader. Gunny is having a serious talk with my field goal punk about bad life choices, and who sent him to the Jackson house party. I am sure the neighbors have called the police by now after hearing gun shots. Gunny sent me on my way, and said he would meet us in my office tomorrow morning."

"Why would anyone want to break in to his home?"

"My guess is it had to do with whatever Gunny was going to tell us this evening. Pull into this fast food place and through the take out. I want to check for any tail we might have picked up."

Mike watched the street for a moment as Angel pulled by the drive through window and ordered two coffees. When she handed Mike is usual black coffee he looked at her with a nod of thanks.

Words Can Kill

"Ok love, I changed my mind. You had better drop me at my apartment. No car followed us," Mike said.

"No Marine, I think you should not be alone tonight. We have to meet Gunny together in the morning. My place might be safer."

*****

Door locks were no guarantee unwelcome visitors might be waiting for a single woman's return. Angel checked the scotch tape she always placed in the lower corner of her front door when leaving. It was not broken. No one had entered while she was gone. She removed it and unlocked the door. Mike closed the door as they entered, snapped the dead bolt, and slid the door chain into its slot.

"Are you thirsty Mr. Tough Marine?"

"No, sweetie, just tired. All I need now is a pillow and blanket so I can crash on your couch."

"You don't have to sleep on the couch," Angel replied.

George W. Clever

Mike pulled off his torn jacket, looked at her for intently for a brief moment. She would mistake for his serious stare for a considering her offer. He turned reaching for both of her hands.

"We tried that before if you remember. It didn't work out."

"Yes Mike, I remember. When my cell phone sleep alarm rang you almost killed me jumping out of bed, rolling to the wall, yelling something about "Get out of the street! Snipers! You must have dreamed you were back in Fallujah. Don't you think it might be time to check into the VA for some help with those dreams?"

"Oh yeah, sure, and have them make an entry in my file "Potential Terrorist" or add me to the ATF list of those who cannot own firearms. You heard the news on how screwed up VA is with a death list for those needing care."

"All right, here you go." She handed him a blanket and pillow. "See you in the morning. You can dream tonight about what you are missing found only in my bed."

*****

22

Employed Again

Time for a writer break before I head to the bowling alley. Wonder what snacks are available upstairs? Not much to add to the story word count today after my hotel interview. Sure was surprised when they hired me on the spot, and told me to start work the same day. Fred mused. He entered the kitchen to find Myrna emptying the dishwasher returning the silverware to the cupboard drawer.

"How did your interview at Geico go today?" Myrna asked.

"I didn't go."

"Why not?" Myrna said with and biting edge to her voice.

"I received a better offer from Best Eastern Hotels. It pays better, and I like the work."

"When do you start?"

"Well, tonight."

George W. Clever

"What do you mean tonight, Fred?"

"They hired me today, and I will be working the night shift right after bowling. Maybe that will be good for us."

"I just don't understand you anymore Fred. You seem too occupied with your writing. We never do anything together anymore. Now we won't even be sleeping together. Is that what you want Fred? Do you want me out of your life?"

"Myrna, I want a job. You wanted me to get a job. Now I have one. Are you satisfied?"

Fred put on his coat, and looked in the closet for his bowling bag. His satin yellow bowling shirt hung in its usual place. The shirt had his name embroidered on the pocket with the 'Ten Pin Split' team logo and sponsor, Martin's Garage, on the back. Wearing the bowling shirt always gave him a sense of belonging to something special.

"Where are you going now?"

"I'm a substitute on Morgan Cleb's team."

"Who in the world is Morgan Cleb?"

Words Can Kill

"He's a guy I used to work with at the old call center job."

"What am I supposed to do here alone tonight Fred?"

"Play some cards with your mother. I'll be back in a few hours."

Myrna was left standing in the hall with her mouth half open, and her brain working overtime to find an answer to Fred's newly exerted independence. *We always bowled on the same team Monday nights. How can he be bowling without me?* She wondered.

After bowling, Fred began his new job early in the evening before the shift began. He was assigned a hotel teammate instructor. The instructor's first lecture was on the fine art of customer satisfaction demanded by Best Eastern Hotels. None of the tasks in his job description seemed too difficult or too demanding. His instructor had worked the desk for many years, and gave him a list of useful 'front desk lies', especially useful on the night shift. They were printed on a card under the front desk for his reference. 1.) All rooms are basically the same size. 2.) Of course I remember you! Welcome back! 3.) There is nothing I can do. 4.) I appreciate your feedback. 5.) I'm sorry the bellman made you uncomfortable. I will certainly alert management. 6.) I didn't mean to sound insulting. 7.) I will mail this immediately. 8.) It is my pleasure to serve you. 9.) I would like to offer my deepest apologies, and the instructors favorite, the star of the list, 10.) We do hope you have a safe trip and return again soon.

It was very late in the evening before Fred could take his laptop out of the black zippered bag, and plug it in to the nine slot surge suppression strip under the front desk. He was ready to write again after the usual evening rush of those travelers seeking the comfort of a quality room for the night. There were only a few late night stragglers. These were couples seeking the use of a bed for a few hours. Their interruption his writing on the laptop was painful.

*****

"How did you get in here Gunny," Mike said as he opened the door to his office early the next morning.

"The door was open Mike. Look around, you had visitors."

Words Can Kill

The office file cabinets were open. Files were thrown around the room. The locked center desk drawer had been jimmied and its contents thrown on the floor.

"There's coffee and donuts on the side table for you Angel. Don't know how you can look so beautiful this early in the day, or for that matter, why you are hanging around this grunt? You may want to heat the coffee in your microwave a couple of minutes. I have been here since the cops finished their interrogation of me early this morning. They collected my shotgun like good government brown shirts, and hauled away the living and the dead bodies. I don't think they believed me when I said the perps broke in to steal my shooting trophies.

Gunny waved his hand with a sweep around the room. He stopped speaking to pick up two of Mike's Corps shooting trophies, returning them to a shelf.

"It looks like the bad guys hit this office first before paying me a visit. This place was a mess when I arrived. I think the cops had thoughts about keeping me longer at my house,

that is, until Detective Sergeant Keith showed up. He told me to say you are expected to be in his office for a meet and discuss this afternoon at two. Now it is time for you to tell me what I got myself into when you paid a visit to my work place?"

Angel took the coffees to the microwave while Mike gave Gunny Jackson an update on his search for the torch perp, the goons who worked him over, and the disappearance of Mrs. Casey.

"What was so important you asked us to visit your humble abode last night? I am sure it was not in anticipation of the fireworks you provided," Mike said.

"No Jarhead, that gun play was a bonus. Sure do miss the old days busting down doors and blowing things up in Iraq. Don't you? Here's the deal. Some of my drivers have been approached by suits from Casey Trucking Company to make a few runs into Mexico, and bring back a special cargo. They weren't told what the cargo was, but figured what it something to do with the high traffic of child prostitutes roaming the truck stops. That kind of cargo pays

Words Can Kill

so much better than a load of weed, and is least likely to put the driver in the slammer."

"This much I know Gunny. I spent a month on the border shadowing trucks from the Casey dock. I had enough pictures of loading and unloading suspicious cargo to satisfy Mrs. Casey. She would be well armed with the file I gave her to squeeze a big time settlement from husband Harlan in court, regardless of their prenup. What else have you got?"

"Well, Mike, you may not know Helen Casey was a player in this smuggling game. Some of the old time truckers remembered her when she was a teen lot lizard before she married Harlan. All her marriage did was change one unknown pimp for her husband pimp. He got her to sign the prenup, and then set her up as a madam with a string of pimps specializing with the offering of child sex to truckers. It was an environment she knew too well. My guess is trouble came to Harlan when he kept all the money and would not share. He may have threatened her with cement

block shoes, and a dip in the river if she didn't deliver the goods from her end of the enterprise."

"Why were those goons busting your door, Tom?"

"I guess I may have gotten too close to their boss's money pipeline with some of the questions I was asking truckers on the loading dock. Oh, and one more thing Mike. Helen had a twin sister."

"Yes, I know. Angel dug that out in her on-line web search."

"Did you know her sister was a pole dancer in the past. Now she is married to a bartender named Kelly?"

"Stephanie Kelly is Helen's sister?"

"That's the way I hear it from one of our drivers who knew her from the old days when she was billed as Candy Sparkles. The driver said she had a candy cane tat on her right shoulder. He saw her shopping at the mall recently. Almost didn't recognize her dollied out in that 'Baptist Lady' dress. She was not alone. There was a "hottie" in a short, too tight, leather skirt with her. Looked almost like

Words Can Kill

Candy Sparkles twin, at least from the neck up. That's all I got Mike. You be careful. These creeps are playing for big money. You could get permanently dead after a one-way ride."

Angel returned to Mike's side hearing the last part of Tom's warning. She placed her arm on his shoulder in a manner often used to get his attention.

"Oh, he already had that ride Gunny. Even electro shock didn't wake him up to the land mines in this Casey case." Angel said. "Coffee's hot". She passed out the steaming cups, reached for her purse and headed to the door. "Well, dudes, it is time for me to hit the university library before class. You lazy Jarheads, with no work schedule, can clean up the office for me when I am gone. See yah."

The office phone rang just as Angel closed the door. Mike was picking file papers from the floor. Tom was putting drawers back in the desk.

"Answer your phone Mike, Angel is gone." Gunny said.

George W. Clever

"Hello, Dunmore Detective Agency. Hey Sergeant Keith, what's up? You want to meet where? How soon? Yes, I will bring the file copy. See you then."

Mike hung up the phone, shook his head, and turned toward Tom with an apology on the ready.

"Time for me to go Gunny. By the way, did you learn anything from the B&E perp I left you?"

"No, he clammed up, but he went to the jail with extensive bruises in unseen places."

"Ok Tom, finish your coffee and lock up the store on your way out. I'm off for a meet and discuss with Sergeant Keith after I do a pick up at Pauper's Pawn. Keep in touch."

*****

23

Undercover Meeting

Mike had two stops to make before his meet with the local police establishment. First stop was to pick up a key for the bus locker from Carmichael, and then a quick retrieve of the Casey file. Things had changed at the old Alhambra Police Station #4 since Mike left the force. Entrances were blocked, and routed with cement barricades. Metal detectors and sniffer scanners checked out all who entered. Security cameras monitored every room. Even those in blue had to clear their weapons on entry to avoid any incidence of cop on cop.

For all that upscale security it was still no place for the kind of secret meeting Sergeant Keith had in mind with P.I. Mike and Lieutenant Meagan Glade. They were to meet in the local public library, out of uniform. Each person was to enter the library individually, find a book, and go to the sound proof listening room B. As an extra precaution, Keith would bring along a "bug catcher". The MCD-22H all in one bug, phone tap, GPS and spy-cam detector was a *device to prevent the hearing of private conversations. Keith wanted to be certain no one was recording the conversation held during their meeting. The device in his briefcase would scan the room for listening recorders before anyone spoke.*

Lieutenant Meagan took every precaution to be sure no one followed her. If she was seen with someone as well-known as Sergeant Keith or his friend Mike, her undercover work would be compromised; and her life at even greater risk. Sergeant Keith was first to enter listening room B followed by Mike. After a few minutes, Lieutenant Meagan opened the listening room door. Yes, she was easy on the eyes, but even more exciting was her voice. She had a way of turning cop conversation into ear worm music. Any man listening to her speak wanted to play it over and over again. It was no wonder Harlan had taken her into his confidence. She was dressed in a modest business skirt and jacket that strained hard trying to contain her D bra.

Words Can Kill

"Ok, what is in that file folder you are squeezing?" Keith said.

Mike spread the contents on the table along with the photos he had taken at the border, papers dugout of the Casey dumpster, and a video of hidden truck compartments where the illegal children were hidden as they were unloaded at the Casey Trucking dock. It was a dark and grainy video taken in the shadows at night. If one looked closely, it was possible to see the little people being loaded into short buses. A few of the DVD videos were of Harlan and a variety of his mistresses in rather X rated activities.

"You have been a busy boy Mr. Mike," Meagan said. "These items will be very welcome by the D.E.A. and our undercover task force. How did you get the pictures of the children hidden somewhere in an eighteen wheeler?"

"Well, first I had the video of the special tanker truck hauling the kids. So I called around local tanker truck firms as an accountant for Casey Trucking complaining about a drunk driver who delivered fuel and made a major spill. Most told me flat out they didn't deliver gas or diesel to

George W. Clever

Casey Trucking, but the manager at South Coastal Transport Company was most apologetic telling me he would check into the driver problem immediately. My friend Carmichael, owner of Paupers Pawn, knew a driver who worked for South Coastal. The driver had a kid with serious health problems. He had pawned just about all the valuables he possessed, and still had to raise cash for the treatments his kid needed. For a few Cs he was willing to take me into the Casey Trucking compound on his deliveries, hiding me in his sleeper. Day deliveries were a bust until he was called in for a run to Mexico, and a special two in the morning delivery. That's when I was witness to the "special kid cargo" delivery.

"Keith, I thought this was a meeting of mutual interests. What do I get out of this gathering that will help me find the person who torched my car?" Mike replied.

"Well, you get off the hook for the murder of the woman found burned in your car trunk" Keith remarked.

"I need a little more than that if you please Detective Sergeant. I need something to help me find the firebug, and

*the location of the thugs who gave me a new understanding
of electricity. What did your lab find out about the woman
who was a crispy critter in my car?"*

*"Nothing much. Her body was almost incinerated. They
worked overtime trying to collect useable DNA from the
body. They tell me now it is almost certain the woman in
your trunk was Helen Casey. The two guys you and Gunny
dealt with were not connected to Casey Trucking as far as
we can tell. The lug who survived Gunny's double o buck is
not talking about who sent him to do a number on the ole
Marine either. Looks like these guys were independent
muscle hired by an unknown, so far as we can tell."
Sergeant Keith said.*

*Lieutenant Meagan leaned closer to speak to Mike.
Her perfume sent his private thoughts in another direction.
She spoke almost in a musical whisper.*

*"I really am not able to help you with information from my
undercover work at Casey Trucking. We do know Casey's
income far exceeds his OTR cargo, and he is running up
big bills with his Governor campaign. I will tell you one of*

George W. Clever

the household servants said she saw Mrs. Casey at home, briefly on the night of the car fire. Mike, I need you, and Keith, to stay away from Harlan Casey, his home, and his business until I can wrap up an indictment against him and the child smuggling ring I believe he heads. One more thing Mike, your revenge for the burning of your car and later kidnapping does not play higher than what those poor smuggled kids endure. Some are sold into sweat shop slavery and others kids into prostitution. Please help me nail this Harlan operation. If you have any other information I can use, please give it to Sergeant Keith. I got to go now."

She moved quietly to the listening room B door. Her departure had the effect on Mike like she was leaving her voice behind. Carefully she opened the door only wide enough to slip out never looking back. As the door closed, Mike and Keith were left to their own confusion about whether they were ass men, leg men, or Tata aficionados. They watched her sensual walk through the library stacks.

Words Can Kill

Her body motions seem to leave a trail of irrefutable promises which Harlan Casey would surely try to collect. Seems it really didn't matter if a guy was a leg, or ass, or Tata man. Lieutenant Meagan had the Miss America prize in all categories.

*****

Another boring night at the hotel desk, and Fred was still being observed as a trainee. All the booked reservations had been filled as travelers arrived at the start of his shift. He shuffled the hotel chain brochures looking for something to do. Looking up from his orderly accomplishment, he had an unwelcome surprise in front of the desk.

"Angelina, what are you doing here?"

Angelina stood in front of the hotel desk clutching a stack of papers. "I couldn't find you at home and wanted to give you my first edits of your book."

"How did you know I would be at the Best Eastern Hotel? This is my first night on the job."

George W. Clever

"I overheard your wife telling a neighbor about your new job in the Best Eastern Hotel on 5th street. You do remember I work here part-time cleaning rooms, don't you? A girl has to make ends meet. Your editing job is an unpaid internship. It is just a part of my college class assignment."

"Oh yes, I guess I forgot you mentioned the cleaning work. What do you want?"

"What do I want? Why I want what you want of course. I am with you to assist in any way possible with your novel writing or anything else than might drift into your mind. Do you have more of the manuscript for me to edit?"

"No, I was hoping to get some writing time here when work is slow. Not much to do at the front desk late in the evening.

"Is there anything else I can do for you, anything, anything at all?"

Angelina almost whispered those last words as she leaned over very close to Fred's ear. Anything, anything at all, what did she mean by that? He wondered.

Words Can Kill

"No, just go now. I will have something for you later."

The day shift manager and Fred's trainer stepped out of the office directly behind the desk. He spoke with an overly assertive tone that played like a xylophone on Fred's spine. It was not pleasant music to be sure.

"Fred, who were you talking with a few moments ago?"

"Oh boss, it was just the woman editing of my novel. She had some of the work completed and wanted to give it to me here. I told her not to bring any personal editing issues here when I am at work. She won't do it again."

"Funny, I never saw anyone in the lobby."

"Sir, she is very short. Probably could not see her over the desk," Fred replied.

"Well, Fred, be sure you don't register any 'stealth' folks' tonight with invisible money."

The manager's sense of humor was lost on Fred, but not to his staff. It became all too common to have some day shift desk clerk or maintenance person toss a burn line at Fred. They would say, 'Did you check in the Invisible

Woman last night?' or, 'Looks like you had a very busy night filling all our empty rooms with spirit people.' As irritating as these comments were, Fred tolerated the barbs, not responding to their comments. He hoped the day shift people would leave as soon as their shift was over if he just ignored them. He wanted as much time to work on his novel as possible.

Once Fred's laptop was powered up, he had no difficulty finding new motives to write again as the promo for the website promised. *Now where did I leave off last night? Oh yes, the undercover cop just left the library, and now I must write the conversation Sergeant Keith and P.I. Mike would have as she was leaving.* Fred considered. His next thought was not one he planned to write.

'Someone should take an icepick to the tires of the day manager every time he or one of his staff burns me with a comment about my unseen secretary Angelina.' That peculiar mental butterfly drifted through his mind as he began to type the next line Sergeant Keith was to say. No words appeared on the laptop for several seconds. Then the

screen blinked twice and these words appeared. ***Four of the manager's car tires are holed by an icepick.*** "Oh no, not again. I could lose my job if this happens." Fred mumbled under his breath. His first reaction to the computer announcement was followed by a more logical decision. *"If I don't spike the manager's tires, certainly I would not be blamed. No matter what happens now the manager will probably have his own list of people who would do such a nasty act. Why should I be the one the boss accuses?"* he said to himself. Fred pressed on with his story writing before the late evening 'short timers' crowd showed up to rent a room for quick sex, nasty love making, and romance.

*****

24

Gunny's Recon

"Mike stay away from Harlan. We don't want to blow Meagan's cover." Detective Keith ordered.

"Sure Keith, you know me well enough. I would never do anything to put the lovely officer Meagan in danger. I will keep my search spotlight out for the person who torched my car, and not shine it on the Lieutenant. But I will need some help from you in trade. I need the DNA information from your corner as soon as he or she is able to recover it from the body left in the trunk of my car. I also want a look at the police record for Helen Casey and her sister. The sister went by a stage name of Candy Sparkles."

"Ok. I will do what I can, but it will risk my pension. I am too old to start a new career with ITT Tech. fixing computers."

Mike was the last to leave the listening room. He picked up the three books left on the study table, and returned them to the distribution cart. Looking at one of the book titles, he thought it was funny Lieutenant Meagan had chosen a book of story poems. The title was Dancing with Grandfather, by some guy named Clever. Odd choice for an undercover detective. I'm at a dead end with the Case of the Flaming Charger. He thought. I might as well admit it. I feel like I am now chained down by Keith and Meagan after this meeting. Harlan Casey was on my list of possible suspects, and now I can't in good faith squeeze him a little for some of the puzzle pieces in this case. Well, if I can't knock on his door maybe I can knock on the door of Casey Trucking to find a few answers.

Perhaps Gunny can give me a crash course in OTR. Not much money coming into my P.I. business. A few extra bucks as a truck driver might be a start in finding another classic Charger to replace the burned out hulk I used to own. I need to call Tom now, Mike decided.

"Gunny, Mike, I need some help. Will you do me another favor? Meet me at my mother's home about seven and I will explain. Thanks, see you then."

Words Can Kill

It was a short ride to Mother Terza's home, but it gave Mike time to give some thought to the logistics of his next move. His Mom hated it when he called her 'Mother Teresa'. Sometimes the name fit. It was exactly the way he saw her as she found so many ways to help those down on their luck. Even after Mike warned her about 250,000 street people being mentally ill, she still made her daily deliveries to her 'people of the cardboard boxes'. Terza passed out her cookies, free burger coupons, and at times, some money.

Mike knew he had to be cautious about getting closer to Harlan Casey without blowing Lieutenant Meagan's cover, or even creating some suspicion that the law was interested in the Casey Trucking Company. He had a special goal of finding the torch who used his car for a crematorium. But it was no longer the prime motivation for his investigative digging. If children were being smuggled into the country, abused, and used, it was time to see if he could put a stop to that outrage. He had seen enough of that as a Marine in the sands of Arab countries. Maybe he could do his small part in stopping it here in the ole USA.

George W. Clever

His NA elders taught him to at least paint one room, and not try to paint the whole world. Gunny's mean, green jeep was parked on the street in front Mom Terza's house when Mike pulled the Vette into the driveway.

The old weathered, wooden screen side door with its long tension spring slammed shut as Mike entered the kitchen. He was sure Gunny would be there at the table with Mom. Tom would be eating her latest batch of peanut butter cookies, and slugging down a tall glass of cold milk. Yes, he was.

"Hey Mom, Gunny, glad you both are here. I wasn't sure you would be home Mom. No food bank duties today?"

"No, that's on Tuesday. Sit down, and I will get you some hot cookies from the oven. Tell me what's new? It isn't often I get to revel in the wonderful company of my son and my favorite Marine Corps Gunny."

"Cookies first, and then I will bring you up to speed on my wild and exciting, mostly boring P.I. life."

Words Can Kill

"Ok, from your phone call I understand you need a favor. What kind of favor?" Tom asked.

"For reasons I can't share just now, I am at a dead end with three mysteries. The first is the question of who torched my car? The second mystery is the name of the person who was behind my abduction? And last mystery is the identity of the woman found burned in the trunk of my car. Some of the pieces are beginning to fall in place, but the big piece about the Casey Trucking connection is not within my reach just yet. Gunny, I want a truck driving job with the Casey Trucking Company. Can you fix me up with the tickets and background I need as an OTR driver? I have driven a Duce and a Half in Iraq. I should be able to do the eighteen wheelers with some quick instruction and practice."

"You would need a CDL, commercial driver's license, and pass the FMCSR, Federal Motor Carrier Safety Regulations exam. My question is, why do you want to do this Mike?"

"If Harlan Casey's trucking company is smuggling children into this country I want to get into the middle of it to see if I can stop even one load of children from receiving pain, neglect, and abuse. Will you help me?"

"What else do you need?"

"In addition to the OTR driver's license, I'll need a quick driving lesson or two, and a resume showing where and when I worked with some truck company. Mom, I need a few of Dad's old truck driving clothes to make me look like a trucker, and a list of your church contacts who work with illegal aliens and smuggled children. I know you have a relative working to help young prostitutes escape from the mean streets of Las Vegas. If I can talk Sergeant Keith into giving me a minor rap sheet, not one that would keep me from a truck driving license, but one that will help make me be more interesting as a driver to those in the smuggling business."

"What's your plan Mike?"

"If I can talk myself into a job driving for Harlan Casey's trucking company I probably will be happy just drawing a

Words Can Kill

much needed check for local or OTR loads since my P.I. income has dried up. Could drop a few hints to the grapevine about my need for fast money. I might find more about how Harlan's system works, and perhaps return a load of the kids to their families in Central America as my last act before slamming the lid on the child smuggling ring."

His mother's face showed a seriousness that would not be denied. She interrupted the Marines conversation with a mother's concern for her son.

"Mikee that plan sounds so dangerous. Isn't there any other way? Couldn't you just forget about losing your car, and get a nice safe job in an office somewhere, maybe in the medical field repairing laser equipment? There are a lot of those jobs advertised on TV now."

"No Mom I can't. Most of my day this old bean head feels like all the daily routines are crushing me with boredom. I get numb to everything and everyone around me. On those nights, I wake up from a dream watching myself in a firefight. I am trying to load my M249 Saw with one hand *while stopping the blood flowing all over my arms and weapon from the big hole blown in my squad leader's shoulder by a sniper bullet. When I am doing dangerous jobs now, things get more normal."*

"I know a grunt that runs a truck driving school for CR England. He owes me a favor. He will give you a crash driving course in two days where it normally is twenty-one. Another Devil Dog is working for a truck company that keeps lousy driver records. We will get you that driver history," Tom offered.

"Why don't you do the twenty-one-day course, and make driving your regular employment? You would make me, your loving mother, so much happier if you were safer doing the trucking job. When your Dad passed, I kept all his clothes in a green trunk in the attic. Go find what you need. I can't do this for you. Touching his clothes makes me cry."

"Ok. Mom. Thanks for your help also Gunny. After a stop in the attic for clothes, I'm off to see Carmichael at

Words Can Kill

Pauper's Pawn. He does business with a printing guy who can crank out better looking driver documents than the DMV. I'll see you in two days, Gunny, for all the working paper tools."

As the attic door closed, Terza Dunmore turned with pleading eyes toward Gunny Jackson.

"Can't you talk some sense into him, Tom? He needs to find a safe job, and settle down."

"It's more complicated than that Mrs. Dunmore. I have seen so many Jarheads wrestle with their demons after combat, just as Mike is doing now. Given time, if they survive, this PTSD will all pass. Well most of it anyway. A good woman can help. I have even seen amazing changes when other Marines gets war dog gifts for pets."

"You mean a woman like Angel might help Mike? I don't know where to find a war dog, Gunny."

"Maybe Angel can help, but Mike seems to want to keep her out of his own crazies until he can work it out. Got to

George W. Clever

go Mrs. Dunmore to make those calls for Mike. Who knows, I might even find a good war dog needing a home."

*****

There were few normal night shifts at the Best Eastern Hotel for Fred. The front revolving door began to spin like a tornado as the day manager burst into the foyer.

"Call the police, then call my wife. Ask her to pick me up." He shouted at the front desk. "Call AAA to have them tow my car to the tire shop. Someone has made holes in all my tires."

Two other day clerks rushed through the revolving door and shouted, "Boss, somebody cut all the tires on our cars. They are all flat!"

The day manager gave a piercing look at Fred who was standing at the front desk with a phone in his hand. It was a look of accusation with no room for denial.

"You wouldn't know anything about this would you Fred?"

Words Can Kill

"No sir, I just got here a few minutes ago. You know I do remember one guy who was complaining about his room at the front desk yesterday when I arrived. He was very mad about being given a noisy room next to the hotel utility room. Do you think it could have been him?"

The day manager reduced his accusing manner as he approached the desk. He remembered the unexpected and disturbing glimpses of life all desk clerks receive from guests who are the dregs of society.

"Don't know Fred. We do get some loony tunes here every day, especially that late night crowd. Remember the couple who left their room filled with quacking ducks? And then there was the wife who carved up her husband in the shower, and filled the snack refrigerator with his junk. We even had a shootout in the hall on the third floor. Playing the shootout surveillance video is a highlight of our Christmas staff parties. The cops will find out who spiked all our tires if they can pull themselves away from the donut shops. I hope they don't see this vandalism as just another minor pain in the ass for them."

George W. Clever

All the excitement cut into Fred's writing time as his shift was almost over by the time the police had cleared the 'flat tire' crime scene. With cop cars in the parking lot, there were few of his regular night visitors checking in to interrupt his writing time. He began to think about his story ending, and of course, his trouble at home. *My wife might be more understanding of my need to write this novel if we didn't have her mother to contend with all the time.* He thought.

His thinking returned to the novel story as he planned P.I. Mike's next step in securing a job driving for the Casey Trucking Company. Fred considered the fact Harlan Casey had never seen Mike. No trucking employees knew P.I. Mike Dunmore. These facts would make easy to write about Mike's search for a job with Casey Trucking. Fred lost his writing concentration with thoughts about his problems at home.

What would it take to be free of my wife Myrna's mother? If she had a fall we could put her in an assisted care home, but what kind of fall? Fred was still thinking

Words Can Kill

about Mike Dunmore's next move when one of those brain farts skidded through his mind. *Maybe it could be something like Bertha fell down the cellar stairs.* He considered. The words, ***Bertha fell down the cellar stairs,*** *appeared on his laptop.*

*****

25

Bertha Problem Solved

Fred's cell phone rang. It was Myrna. She was screaming, repeating her words, and sobbing.

"Fred, I found my mother at the bottom of the cellar stairs near your computer desk. I don't know how long she has been laying here. She must have fallen and is not moving. The EMT's are here giving mother CPR. Oh, come home, Fred. I need you now!"

"I'll be there shortly, Myrna. Try to calm yourself," he said, closing his geezer style, out of date, flip cell phone.

His phone had none of the hip features found on an I-Phone or Galaxy. It just provided for making phone calls and an occasional picture. Myrna said he was not smart enough to have one of those more complicated devices. He was in no hurry to go home. After all what could he do? The EMTs were there and probably the police. Fred informed his night manager of the problem at home, gathered up his laptop, cleared his desk money drawer, and walked out of the hotel into the employee's parking lot.

Maybe there was something he could do to erase the troublesome writer prompt. Why would he really want to do so? Fred considered. *He could always change his mind later or maybe not. He would stop at Tim Hortons for coffee, and use their Wi-Fi to write a little more on his novel before facing the 'Myrna's mother's fall' brain fart results at home. A new page for his novel began to form in his head as he slowly drank his café mocha.*

When Mike walked into Pauper's Pawn, Carmichael was with a customer who seemed interest in an eighteen century jade Buda. The kind of conversation Mike wanted to hold with Carm was not one open to listening customers. He would wait and shop for his surprise going away present for Angel before he hit the trucking road. There were so many fascinating possibilities in unclaimed pawns filling the showcases, glass displays and book shelves. Shrunken heads, motorcycle jackets, and military hardware didn't seem good choices as a gift for Angel.

Words Can Kill

He would need something sparkly if she was going to be happy about his absence. Carm finished with his Buda customer and joined Mike at one of the displays.

"Can I help you?"

"Yes sir, I need to purchase something for Angel that will soothe her tribal temperature when I tell her I will be out of the office for a month or more. What you got, Carmichael, that doesn't spell engagement, and is in the budget for an out of work P.I.?"

"You might like this, Mike."

Carmichael walked over to a glass case, opened the lock, and lifted out a dazzling white, Samsung Galaxy Tablet, 8.4 inch, with Wi-Fi. He re-locked the case and place the tablet in front of Mike.

"Does she have one of these?"

"I don't think so. Can I afford it?

"Well normally they sell for a shade under four Cs, but for you only two Bennies. This one is new in the box. I just bought it yesterday."

George W. Clever

"Is it hot?"

"I don't think so. It came from a guy I know in the neighborhood who needed to cover his bookie bill in a hurry."

"Ok, I might as well be dead broke as nearly so."

Carmichael placed the Samsung tablet in a more attractive plastic gift bag. He sealed it with a strip of box tape before handing it to his friend.

"No clients Mike?"

"That's the second reason I came to see you Carmichael. I need some working papers."

"What kind of 'working papers'?"

"I need to be an OTR driver in a hurry with a CDL, and the proof I passed the medical exam and the FMCSR. Do you still have Mr. Inky on your connection rolodex?"

"Sure Mike, but a quick job like this would bought by big K cotton. How soon do you need it?"

"In three days."

Words Can Kill

Three rows of wrinkles lined up in front of Carmichael's receding hair before he asked the next question.

"Do I ask you why? I know jobs are hard to find these days, but you could get cheaper service finding work at the State Employment Office."

"I can tell you a lot of innocent kids will be safer if I make this trucking job work. The documents should be for a guy named Mike Torcher. Do this for me and I owe you a big one. Get'er done. See you on Friday."

Just outside Paupers Pawn shop Mike placed his gift for Angela in the pocket behind the driver seat, and retrieved his flip phone from his inside jacket pocket. He dialed a familiar number.

"Sergeant Keith please. Keith, this is Mike. I need to see you this afternoon. Can you meet me at Vincent Park near the fountain about three o'clock? Thanks, see you then."

The park was quiet for the afternoon. Kids were still in school. A few dog walkers were trying to keep leashes untangled. Others were scooping dog poo with one hand inside a Wally World blue plastic bag. Mike watched the activity as he waited by the fountain for Sergeant Keith. He wondered why someone would own a dog in a place that required poop-scooping with one's hands.

Sergeant Keith was dressed in one of the colorful spandex jogger's outfits runners often wear. As he approached Mike, Keith kept his pace by running in place.

"Might as well get my run in here as long as you have dragged me away from the precinct desk. What's up, Mike?" He said gasping for breath.

"What are you, some kind of health nut? Stop for a minute before you have a heart attack. I need to ask a big favor. That favor in itself may stop your heart."

"Ok, Mike, what is it?"

"I need a rap sheet. Not one that will keep me from being employed by a trucking company, but one to make me a person of interest to those who step outside the law. Can you do it?"

Words Can Kill

"Didn't you get the message from Lieutenant Meagan? No contact with Harlan Casey."

"She didn't say I could not get a job as a driver for Casey Trucking did she?"

"Well, no, but I know you. Driving will not be all you are doing. What's your plan? I need to know if I am to mess with CJIS Criminal Justice Information System. That is a big risk for my pension unless I care to spend retirement years in the slammer with all those fine people I put there."

"Here it is in bare bones. I get a job with Casey Trucking. Raise some attention by my rap sheet, and maybe get to drive a smuggling run. I would have international information about the child smuggling ring by driving. Lieutenant Meagan would not have to get honeying up by Harlan."

"Not so interested in who torched your Charger anymore?"

George W. Clever

"I leave that small challenge to you and your blues. Stopping child slavery and prostitution is a much bigger fish, and more important in my book."

"What you really mean is it is more dangerous. You know getting killed will not bring back the grunts on your team you left behind in Fallujah. You didn't know what was in the building your squad went too clear. Yes, it was filled with propane tanks and diesel fuel that blew the moment they were inside, but it was not your fault."

"I need to do this Keith. Will you help me?"

"On one condition, you call your mom every other day, and give her code messages on your progress. I will get you the code phrases before you go."

"I may be around this town for a while if Casey Trucking puts me on local freight hauls. You will know if that changes when I get some international work. The name on the sheet should read Mike Torcher."

"Ok, give me a day or two before you apply for a job. If you get picked up by our boys in blue before that time, I

Words Can Kill

will have my work cut out for me trying to keep you from standing before a judge with a rap sheet. Off to do my heart healthy mile jog. Be careful. Don't mess with those Mexican Police. They find great pleasure in jailing our Marines for any reason of their own choosing. And they keep them."

Three days later Mike received a call from Sergeant Keith. It was in a generic pleasantry code necessary when personal calls at the station were being monitored, and recorded.

"Have a safe and pleasant drive Mike. Your mom has the travel guide you requested."

Any call from detective Farrell was typically short. Moments after ending the call, Mike's cell phone buzzed again. It was a call from Carmichael.

"Your 'get out of town' gifts are ready. I am sure Angel will like the sentiment of a new Galaxy phone. It is not the most romantic gift Michael."

George W. Clever

Things were beginning to fall in place for Mike. He selected the saltiest of his dad's old truck driving clothes from the trunk in his mom's attic, and stopped by Paupers Pawn to collect his travel documents and the gift for Angel. He was ready for his interview at the Casey Trucking. The receptionist for the trucking company was not.

A familiar woman greeted him at the receptionist desk. She did not look up from the papers on her desk.

"Good morning, may I help you?"

The smile on the receptionist's face faded as her eyes met those of the man before her desk. She recognized Mike.

Lieutenant Meagan made a quick recovery swallowing her impulse to ask under her breath, "What the hell are you doing here Mike!"

"Yes madam I would like to apply for a truck driving job." Mike said with a steady coy reply and smirk.

Meagan stumbled through the usual screening questions the receptionist was to ask job seekers. All of Meagan's questions about his qualifications for

Words Can Kill

employment was answered by the documents secured from Carmichael's friend Mr. Inky. His truck driving documents included a phony Social Security number, and a new name, Mike Torcher. It seemed an appropriate new moniker, but Mike knew it was always better to use your real first name rather than a phony one. Using one's first name would prevent slipups if someone were to call him by name.

"Our personnel director is down the hall, second door on the left. Fill out this application, and give him your documents," Meagan said, pointing in the direction he was to go.

As Mike Torcher walked down the hall Meagan turned to one of the accounting clerks near her desk and whispering a request.

"Helen, I need an early lunch. Time of the month and nothing in my purse. Also need to pay a late bill. Will you please take all the calls until I return?"

Once outside the office in her car, she called Sergeant Farrell's private cell phone as she drove toward

George W. Clever

Rite Aid at the mall. Meagan always checked to see if she was being followed.

"Keith here."

"Keith, what the hell is Mike doing in the Casey Trucking office? I thought we had an agreement he was to stay away from Harlan Casey until I wrapped up this investigation. Do you two want to get me killed?"

"Easy Meagan, all he wants to do is drive truck for the company, and maybe get the smuggling system figured out first hand. He promised not to meet or confront Harlan."

"And you think he will keep that promise? Well I do not."

"He's a friend of mine, and Mike will keep his promise unless his hand is forced. Meagan we all need the info Mike can get from his truck driving recon. Trust his judgment and stay cool. We all need each other."

"If this blows up Keith I will go to the Commissioner for your badge."

"Well I think you will have to take a number. Got to go now."

Words Can Kill

Sergeant Farrell hung up before Meagan was through with her rant. Two cups of expresso with the vegan lunch special at the Turtle Pit Café filled Meagan's hunger, but did not end her anger. Those thoughts boiled, like hot coffee, with what she would say to Sergeant Farrell the next time they met. She was only a bit more composed returning to the office. Meagan wondered if the Casey Trucking personnel director hired 'Mr. Torcher'. He did.

*****

Bertha was dead. Her neck was broken by her fall down the cellar stairs. Fred gave a statement to the investigating police detective as to his knowledge of the accident, and his activities that day.

"Mr. Fonsworth, do you have a moment. I would like to ask you a few questions about your mother-in-law's accident."

"Yes, of course Sergeant. Haskell," Fred replied.

"The coroner places the time of death about 9 A.M. Were you home at that time?"

George W. Clever

"Normally I would have been at home working on my book, officer, and of course, keeping an eye on Bertha. I am usually home at that time writing my novel. Today after my wife went to work, I left a few minutes later to do a little car shopping. After visiting a few car lots, I had a drive through lunch at the Golden Arches. Oh, I remember spending some time by the lake feeding the ducks before clocking in for my job at the Best Eastern hotel. I had the three to eleven shift as a night desk clerk."

"Did anyone see you during your tire kicking shopping, Mr. Fonsworth?"

"No, I don't remember seeing anyone I know while car shopping. You know, I like to wander the car lots without drawing any attention from some overzealous salesman. Sometimes, I just drive through the lots and look at the cars from my vehicle."

"When you were feeding the ducks at the lake do you remember speaking to anyone who might remember you?"

Words Can Kill

"Oh no, Sergeant. I always try to find a quiet place at the lake to have no interruptions to my thinking about my writing. I need a quiet place to do my story planning."

"Were you ever concerned about leaving Bertha home alone when you left the house?"

"No sir, Bertha was a very independent woman. We never thought she needed our constant supervision. She was quite capable of taking care of herself. Is there a reason why you are asking me these questions?" Fred asked defensively.

"No sir, just routine," answered Sergeant Haskell.

Bertha's death was ruled accidental by the county coroner the next day. Her funeral was held in St. Agnes's RC Church the next Friday. Myrna attached some of the blame for her mother's death to Fred although she never told him so. She did tell everyone else who would listen.

Myrna would say, "If only Fred had been at home working on his book, he might have prevented her from making the trip to the basement where she fell."

George W. Clever

Still, Myrna believed there was something not right about her mother's fall. Bertha seldom went into the basement. She had no reason to do so. It was odd that Fred chose this day to do his car shopping before work. He didn't have any money to do much shopping. He got paid by the hotel management on the same Friday her mother's funeral was held. Myrna could not accept the thought that Fred was somehow responsible for her mother's fall…and yet he was acting so odd lately.

It was more than a week of his bereavement leave from the hotel before Fred could return to writing his novel. There was so much to do settling Bertha's estate. He helped Myrna empty her mother's bedroom and closet, packed all the unwanted items off to the attic, and delivered some boxes to the Salvation Army store. He finally returned to his writing routine and hotel desk clerk job feeling somewhat relieved to be free of caring for his wife's elderly mother.

Fred remembered thinking about his relationship with Myrna after the funeral. He was hoping their marriage might take a turn for the better with her mother dead. Sadly, it was not to be so. Myrna was back to her demanding self by the end of the month. She would call him at home regularly while she was at work, and give him the 'to do' list for the day. She even called him at work with some lame reason he understood to be only a check on where he really was at that moment.

The only real free time he had to write was still in the early morning at home or the late evening hours on a break from working at the hotel front desk. The clerk job gave him time to use the hotel's Wi-Fi to gather research about the business of international trucking.

When challenged by his night manager as to his interest in trucking, Fred explained how it would make him more responsive to the needs of truckers who often sought the luxury of a hotel room for a night as a break from their 24-7 confines in the truck cab. He researched what P.I. Mike would have to know about driving truck on US interstates, and out of the country to Mexico or Central America. It was dangerous undercover work, and he probably would choose to take a gun with him in the truck for protection. Where could he hide it to keep him from ending up in a Mexican prison if his truck was inspected at the border?

Fred studied Freight trucks and trucking videos on the internet looking for an answer. Hammering the keys to tell the tale, he thought of one place to hide a gun that seemed almost too easy.

*****

26

Trial Haul

Mike's first trucking assignments were routine and expected. He would ride as a co-driver or alone on local short hauls. After one of his trips to deliver food bank goods to the Helping Hands soup kitchen, he was told by the Casey dispatcher to report to the load master pic, the dock boss. This could be the break in assignments he needed to begin the Mexico route hauling.

"Where can I find the PIC," Mike asked the nearest dock associate.

"He's over there by the fork lift."

Mike saw a short stocky man in his early thirties who looked a bit like one of the pictures he had seen on a Mayan temple if the artist had put coveralls on the carving.

"I understand you are looking for me"

"I am if you are Mike Torcher," the dock boss replied.

"That's my handle. Why did you want to see me?"

George W. Clever

"We're taking you off locals. You got a run to Mexico next Tuesday."

"Where to in Mexico?"

"You ask a lot of questions. Just follow the dispatcher's instructions, and load your GPS. Don't do anything dumb or your golden goose gets it in the neck. I read your rap sheet. You are, as I read, skating from your probation officer. Guys who don't work out find the cops become real interested in their location. I'm Jesus Amador your boss now. Be here on time, six in the morning."

On Tuesday, Mike took a cab into Casey Trucking's yard, picked up his manifest. He found the assigned Peterbilt tractor with an empty flatbed trailer for his destination Port of Altamira, Mexico. Jesus Amador found him just as he was climbing into the cab.

"You are dead hauling to Altamira. At dock 55 you will be met by another driver, Franco, who works for us. You are to be his co-driver bringing the new load back to the US. No stops outbound or inbound. You will gas at the dock. Franco is to show you where to find the fuel."

Words Can Kill

So much for Mike's plan to stash the Browning nine and two clips into the Peterbilt's air-filter canister. He would gamble on a short stop somewhere along the route to stash the gun. If questioned about the stop, he would claim it was a traffic tie-up. There was no way he was going into a setup like this in Mexico without an equalizer piece he could reach nearby. Chances were the Mexicans didn't do much of a search of the truck's mechanics, maybe only a scan of the empty trailer.

The trip to Altamira was another nine-hour routine travel after Mike's truck cleared inspections at the World Trade Bridge in Laredo, Texas. The World Trade Bridge was located at the northern side of Laredo-Nuevo Metropolitan Area. The bridge was constructed to relieve traffic congestion along Interstate 35 south through Laredo, Texas. Most of the commercial traffic crossed the border through the Juarez-Lincoln International Bridge at downtown Laredo, or the Laredo-Colombia Solidarity International Bridge located farther north of the metro area. The bridge connects to Interstate 35 through the northern part of Loop 20 connecting with Mexico's *highway 2 and 85D. The addition of the new lanes seemed to be working quite well. Traffic south moved through the border check point quickly with moderate flow. Mike could see northbound traffic would be another story. His computer told him over a million and a half trucks moved out of Mexico at this check point every year. He could expect a long delay on his return.*

The guard at the Altamira docks checked his manifest marking the truck's entry time before he lifted the gate barrier. It took the guard several tries in Spanglish before his directional commands were understood by Mike.

"Turn right dos warehouses to Cinco container rows. Park with trucks."

As Mike headed the eighteen wheeler toward the ocean, he drove past two imposing warehouses, turned right, and drove past five container rows stacked four units high. Finding a long row of empty container trailers, he found an open space and pulled in between a red Volvo flat bed and a Freightliner box truck. Ok, what is next? Where is Mr. Franco? He thought. Mike looked through the

Words Can Kill

windshield not quite ready to shut down the truck. Mike jumped when a loud pounding beat began to rattle his passenger side door.

"Oup...Oup!" the voice at the door shouted.

Mike powered down the passenger side window a crack and returned the shout.

"What do you want?"

"Franco, Oup!"

"Come around the other side so I can see you," Mike replied.

A tall man in an orange jumpsuit and hard hat moved around the front of the cab to the driver side. "You Mike?" he shouted over the engine noise.

"Yes."

"Sleep in the cab this night and enter in your log. Food is in this box." He shoved the cardboard carton toward the partially opened driver side window. Mike hit the window switch just enough for the box to slip in.

George W. Clever

"Do not leave your truck. I will be here in the morning with your instructions."

With that terse information delivered, Franco disappeared. Don't leave my truck? Hmmmm. Why not? Mike thought to himself. It was time to open the air filter and retrieve la pistola treasure he had stashed there at a roadside rest stop. Leaving the diesel engine running with the air conditioning on full, he opened the truck driver door and stepped on the top stair. It was going to be a hot night in the sleeper. Any good trucker should do a walk around his rig after a long haul to spot any problems for the next run.

Of course the air filter needed attention. It could be dirty and clogged. It was until he removed the problem. He kept the Browning automatic and clips between his body and the canister sliding them into his hoody pocket. Mike checked the tires on his pre-flight round, and climbed back into the cab to see what culinary delight Mr. Franco had shoved through the window. Sure enough, it was a chicken burrito from Church's Chicken South of the Border. He

Words Can Kill

retrieved a cold bottle of water from the refrig, settled into the sleeper for dinner, and turned on the TV. Three's Company with John Ritter, Joyce Dewitt and Suzanne Somers loses something in Spanish with English subtitles. His eyelids felt heavy reading quick script. Soon Mike was asleep about as deep a sleep as Marine's can afford. His eyes slammed open when he felt the presence of someone or something outside the truck driver door just before daylight.

"Oup! Oup! Open up! We go pronto! Turn right to end of containers. Diesel pumps on the left."

With no other greetings or instructions, Franco slid into the passenger seat and closed the door. Mike rubbed the sleep from his eyes, and dropped the idling Peterbilt in gear, Attendants at the pumps filled the truck tanks full without Mike leaving the cab.

"Follow road to the crane."

A tall straddle carried gantry crane was waiting with a container as Mike's Peterbilt rolled its trailer under the box. The container box was secured with come-along straps and chains before Mike was given the order to move.

"Drive left four lanes now. Pull into el numero tres warehouse."

Mike drove away from the straddle gantry crane as instructed, and pulled into the third warehouse.

"Stay in cab." Franco commanded.

He left the passenger door open climbed out and walked to the rear of the container. Mike could hear the container doors open. He could sense the cargo was being unloaded. A few minutes later, he could hear forklifts moving new cargo into the container. From the truck's rear view mirror, he could see similar boxes with large printing which read in English, Medical Equipment: Caution Do Not Expose to Radiation. The container doors closed, and Franco returned to his perch on the truck's passenger seat.

"Out Gate now. Same roads you came."

Words Can Kill

It was time for Mike to learn where his cargo was going. He didn't like surprises. Recon information was needed for any survival plan to be made.

"Where to Franco?"

"Just drive. I will tell you."

Franco placed the clipboard manifest on the center console, and adjusted the GPS. The dock guard opened the gate without checking the manifest, and waved the Peterbilt out.

"Follow the GPS."

"You're not much on conversation are you? Do we get a pee or lunch break on this trip?'

"No."

"How about we listen to a little rock and roll music?" Mike offered.

"No music."

George W. Clever

Another nine hours of silent driving brought him again to the World Trade Bridge only this time the cue for trucks was longer.

"Pull over to the building on the right after US Customs waves you through."

"What no inspection from Customs or Border Patrol? Don't I have to get out?" Mike was sweating the piece he had in the middle of his back and the clips in his hoodie pocket. Franco's answer came as a relief.

"NO! Do as I say."

Mike pulled alongside the gray cement building at the end of the inspection line. His heart gave a jump when a Homeland Security agent, wearing a gray jumpsuit, black boots, loaded web belt with sidearm, eagle DHS shoulder patch, and lettered cap, rapped on the driver door.

"Open for him," Franco said.

"Ok driver out. I will take it from here," the agent said.

The agent indicated he wanted Mike to leave the driver seat, and join Franco in front of the truck. Climbing

Words Can Kill

down from the cab, he wondered what was going on with this driver change. Franco did not seem disturbed as he met Mike in front of the truck.

"You ride shotgun now. Just do as you are told by the driver."

Without even saying 'hasta luego, or adios" Franco disappeared into the shadows of the fortress like building.

The new driver in his crisp Homeland Security uniform ground a pound of truck gears before he was able to move the semi on to the highway. After fifteen minutes of silence Mike decided to break the ice with a casual talk.

"Hey, I'm Mike Torcher. What do I call you?"

"You call me Jim."

"Jim what?"

"Just Jim."

"Ok, 'Just Jim', where are we going?"

"You don't need to know."

George W. Clever

It was a brief and icy hostile exchange 'Just Jim' carried with him. A black mood filled the tractor cab's spaces. Mike watched the speedo gage and tried to memorize each turn of the truck from the interstate four lane highway to a two lane road. Their last turn was on to a dirt track trail winding through miles of Texas sagebrush. The odometer read fifty miles since the truck left the World Trade Bridge.

Clouds of tan dust filled the road between its boundaries of sagebrush and cactus. The dust blew into the cab from the air conditioner. Trucks in convoys roared past the Peterbilt in the opposite direction as driver Jim negotiated the potholes along some road maze known only to him. Mike would have been lost remembering the travel path if it wasn't for his experiences driving the Al-Dibdibah desert in Iraq. No road markers there either. An hour driving time off the paved road, Mike was able to peer through layers of road dust on the windshield to see a collection of low buildings in the distance.

Words Can Kill

At 3 P.M., driver Jim pulled the Peterbilt in front of a large concrete bunker building with no windows. He left the truck running. A large array of antenna sprouted from the top of the single story industrial building painted sand tan. Camo netting covered the roofs of all the buildings Mike could see.

"You will leave the truck now and go to this building," Jim ordered.

"Any chance I can get a shave and a shower there. Been on the road for two straight days?"

"All of your needs will be met there," Just Jim said as he climbed from the cab and walked around the front of the truck.

Mike could see another uniforms standing in the bunker doorway with a metal detector wand. He climbed into the sleeper, found his ditty bag, and slipped the Browning pistol and clips from the back of his shirt into the bag.

George W. Clever

"Couldn't find my ditty bag," he said to his driver partner Jim as Mike exited the cab.

"Just go. I will find it and bring it to you," Jim replied in an impatient and frustrated tone.

The wheels were turning in Mike's head as he approached the security guard holding the scanner. How could he get his bag holding the gun past the scanner? What if ole Jim What decided to open the ditty bag. The guard scanned Mike, and waved him through the door. Mike looked back at the truck to see driver Jim walking toward the security guard with the bag. From the look on his face, Mike could see he had not opened the bag, but Jim was irritated having to bring it to him. The security guard did not scan Jim. They were after all wearing the same uniform and greeted each other by name.

"Here take the bag. Showers down the hall third door on the left. You left the bag behind your seat in the truck." Jim said passing it around the side of the scanner.

"Thanks, guess I need new glasses," Mike said.

Words Can Kill

No smile came from the uniformed men. Driver Jim returned to the Peterbilt, climbed into the cab, and slammed the door.

"Hey there buddy. I'm really hungry. After scrubbing off this road grime where I can get something to eat?" Mike asked the security guard.

"Cafeteria and lounge are on the right. Bunks are down the hall to the left of the lounge. You will be called when you are to leave."

Just before Mike turned to the shower hall he could see his truck cueing up behind three other trucks near a small warehouse. An off-loader crew followed a forklift toward the truck tailgate.

"Move along bud. Nothing to see out there," the guard at the metal detector ordered.

*****

27

Hear More See More

Fred began to understand the obsession writers have with each novel they write. It is an obsession of control not available to them in any real time life. Unsolvable problems in their stories are solved in a word or sentence unlike his own struggles at home and work. His harassment at work from co-workers about imaginary customers, or a novel editing secretary had been all but eliminated after the flat tires episode. Only on rare occasions did one of the night staff ring the front desk bell for a prank when Fred was in the office away from the desk. They would disappear before Fred reached the registration station. Later they would return to ask with a smile if he had answered the bell and assigned someone a room, alluding to his invisible secretary.

Life at home was more bearable now with Myrna's mother out of the picture. With different work schedules, he and Myrna were each living separate lives. By the time

George W. Clever

he returned from the three to eleven hotel shift Myrna was already asleep. When he awoke in the morning, Myrna was on her way to work and would not return until five in the afternoon. Only on the weekends were Myrna and Fred in the house together, and then not for long.

It was not unusual for Fred to be called into the hotel as a replacement for someone on sick leave. His novel was progressing nicely. The biggest writing challenge was the middle section of the novel. It had been conquered. Middle sections of novels are often the place where creative juices just do not seem to flow. He had a good mental map of where his novel was going now. Better yet, he knew how the story would end. It was time for him to check all the details, making sure locations, time periods, characters, and events were accurate. He relied on the web for the story details he felt necessary to make his novel convincing to his readers.

This was going to be one of those weekends when he and Myrna were alone together in the house. No calls

Words Can Kill

from the hotel to sweep him away from the problems at home. He was stuck with Myrna and her demands. Fred was not prepared for the 'voice' problem when it reared its ugly head.

"Fred did you hear that?" Myrna said as they were sitting at the kitchen table.

"No, I did not hear anything."

"You're so deaf. Why do I even expect you to hear anything in the normal human sound range? It's coming from the cellar stairs. Don't you hear it?'

"What am I to hear?"

"It is a voice. Someone is calling my name."

"What do they want?"

"I don't know. And I do not appreciate it when you patronize me, Fred. If you don't hear anything just say so."

"I don't hear anything."

"How can you not hear someone calling my name from the cellar? Go see if someone is there."

George W. Clever

"No you go if the voice is calling you. It is not calling me."

"Fred, after finding Mother at the bottom of the cellar stairs, I am never going down there again. You go there all the time. Please go and listen for me."

Fred put his paper down on the kitchen table, opened the cellar door, and posed there as if listening for the voice Myrna heard. He was irritated by her unwillingness to check on the voice she heard herself. Why should he have to fake interest in checking out a voice when he believed there was no voice?

"I don't hear any voice," he said closing the door.

Daytime demands from his wife were one thing, but the voice Myrna said she heard did not stop. After the first weekend, Fred could count on hearing her demands in an unending whine for him to check the cellar for the voice. It did not matter where he was in the house, Myrna would insist he check out the voice she heard.

"Fred, someone is calling me from the cellar stairs. I'm frightened. Please go and find out who is there."

Words Can Kill

Every weekend it was like living a NFL football game instant replay. Almost at the same time each Saturday and Sunday Myrna would begin to hear the voice. Her requests turned to unbearable demands when the voice awoke them when they were asleep in bed at night. She began to hear someone calling her every two hours. Myrna would shake Fred awake from his deeply needed rest. When the weekend was over both Fred and Myrna were relieved to return to their work schedules bringing an end to the voice coming from the cellar stairs. Myrna told him she heard the voice calling her whenever she was alone in the house. The voice always came from the cellar stairs. Without the support of Fred in the house, she was filled with fear, and unable to complete even the simplest household chore like laundry. When the voice would start calling, Myrna would grab her car keys, and drive to the mall hoping the voice was not able to follow.

The lack of sleep, constant interruptions of normal activities in the home, and Myrna's confusion was beginning to create excessive stress for Fred. Something had to be done. The answer came to him on the car radio as he headed home late in the evening. He listened to Doctor Bill, a local talk show host psychologist. Doctor Bill was discussing depression and its effects on family members. The voices a caller heard seemed to be similar to the voice Myrna was hearing from the cellar.

Many of the depressed callers relating to this issue had recently lost a loved one. During the program, Doctor Bill offered several suggestions to concerned family members and those hearing voices. He suggested they seek help for depression from a support group called Voice Hearers. Several chapters of the VH organization were available locally. Their meetings were funded by State Social Services or church groups. *Maybe Myrna should join a Voice Hearers group to get the help she needs, and I could receive a good night's uninterrupted sleep*, Fred considered.

He knew she would not seek the help of a psychologist or psychiatrist herself. Shortly after arriving home, Fred searched the local shopping paper, newspaper, and church ads for a Voice Hearers group. On the senior

Words Can Kill

center section of the local shopping paper he found a listing for a VH meeting. Fred left a note on the kitchen table for Myrna with the meeting times and building address. He was sure she would not respond well if he initiated a conversation with the suggestion she could benefit from attending a Voice Hearing seminar. If he made any off the cuff statement like, 'Myrna, you need to seek help for your voice hearing problem.' His well-meaning statement would set her off screaming at him like a demon possessed.

Yes, the note was cowardly. But Fred was not going to ask for more trouble from Myrna. The next evening when he returned from work at the hotel there was a note from Myrna on the dining room table. It read, 'I have attended a meeting of the Voice Hearers Support Group at St. Drogo's Church. I am not crazy. Other people in the group told me so. There is a voice coming from the cellar stairs. You need to go with me to the next meeting on Friday during the noon lunch hour.' Her offer for him to attend the next meeting was not a suggestion. It was a demand from Myrna. It was a demand that surely would never go away unless he agreed to meet the group at St.

George W. Clever

Drogo's Church. He could see no way out of attending a meeting with her.

St. Drogo is the patron Saint of Unattractive People. Fred wondered if being unattractive was one of the criterions for attending mass in that church. Well, what could he lose by attending a session with Myrna? Maybe he would be able to get a few more hours of sleep at night. Those self-help groups always had drinks and snacks at their gatherings. The lunch time smacks provided by the VH organization helped him decide to attend the Friday afternoon gathering. Fred also considered the possibility there could be a self-help group for his dreadful 'butterfly thoughts' plaguing his writing of late. It was time to finish his novel.

*****

A shower and shave sounded just fine for Mike after almost two days in the truck. He was hungry, but that would have to wait. Under a rather cold shower, Mike was mentally cooking a way to get outside and check on the activities going on at the little warehouse. He dressed

Words Can Kill

quickly, and filled the sink with water as he shaved. Mike noticed the facility was first class with a hair dryer in its holder by the sink. What if the hair dryer was accidently bumped into the sink full of water while it was turned on? If it blew out an electrical circuit someone would have to come and reset the breaker. A facility like this certainly had a maintenance person somewhere in its halls. Dressing quickly, he turned on the dryer, and dropped it into the sink. Sparks flew and smoke drifted out of the sink just before all the lights in the room went out.

Mike reached for the door, opened it a crack, and looked out into the hall. All the lights were out as far as he could see in the hall. Beyond the hall, he could tell cafeteria lights were still working. A shadowy form was walking toward the shower room. Mike quickly closed the door, lifted the hair dryer from the sink, emptied the sink, and placed the dryer back in its holder. He returned to the door waiting to see if the person in the hall would enter. The footsteps continued past the shower room door. Mike could hear keys jingling as the maintenance man fumbled in the dark to find the right key for the storage room.

George W. Clever

As the lock snapped open Mike slipped out of the shower room and stood behind the maintenance man unseen. When the man pushed the storage door open Mike lifted his Browning pistol from his belt and hit the unsuspecting workman from behind. The blow to the back of the worker's head knocked him down, but not out. Mike shoved him into the storage room. One such whack was never enough to render a victim unconscious. It was only a stunning blow until Mike hit him a second time to be sure he would not cry out.

The utility room contained the electrical breaker box. Mike used the maintenance man's flashlight to flip the breaker returning light to the hall and shower room. There was a roll of Duct tape on an open shelf in the closet. It came in handy for Mike to make the maintenance man's leg and arm ties. A couple of strips placed over the man's mouth would keep him quiet. Mike stripped off the utility uniform and cap from the worker. Fortunately, the man was a big enough size for his coverall to fit over Mike's street clothes. He checked the ID pin on the uniform. He would be Jose for part of this evening.

Words Can Kill

A trash container on wheels was tucked away in the corner of the storage room. It was just the right size to hold the man on the floor. Mike covered him with trash papers and paper toweling pulled from the closet shelving. Now it was time to empty the trash in a dumpster near the small warehouse.

Pulling his cap down tight, Mike headed to the front entrance and its security guard station. Bent over the cart pushing with both hands, he kept his face low so he would not be recognized.

"Hey Jose, how's it going?" The guard at the entrance said as Mike pushed the cart to the door.

"Estoy muy bien, gracias!" Jose Mike grumbled in reply, passing through the opening quickly and on to the parking lot. He pulled the cart behind the dumpster unloading the trash and the maintenance worker into the bin.

Mike bought a little more time needed for his recon of the trucks in line and the activities at the warehouse by picking up trash blowing around the dumpster. The Peterbilt tractor and trailer he had driven was still in line behind two other trucks. Several trucks were being unloaded with forklifts driving large box loads into the warehouse. A line of children, led by a few adults, emerged from the warehouse and boarded busses behind the staging complex. Another group of children could be seen standing on the truck loading platform at the side of the building.

Two trucks, pulling empty trailers, moved into a separate line close to the building. Another string of full trailers trucks, with their seals intact, keyed up on the exit road alongside of the warehouse. All of the vans were reefers trucks with climate control interiors. Mike used his belt buckle camera with the night scope lens to record the scene he was witnessing before heading back to the bunker with his empty trash container.

No security guard was at the opening as he pushed the trash holder down the hall to the storage room. Stripping from the utility jumpsuit, he stuffed it behind boxes of cleaning solution. Checking the hall to be sure it was empty, Mike picked up his sports bag, close the storage

Words Can Kill

room door, and headed back to the cafeteria just in time to hear his name being called.

The speaker voice squawked and barked. 'Mike Torcher report to your truck now.' So much for meal time and a nap, he thought. Walking briskly across the tarmac to his Peterbilt, he could see 'Just Jim' waiting by the tractor driver door.

"Here is your manifest. The GPS has been set for your trip. Just follow it. You are to take this load to the Casey Trucking Company. No side trips, no fuel stops, no meals, and no layovers. You are being tested this haul. Screw up and you are dead. Do your job and you will be well paid in full. Move out."

'Just Jim' wasn't much on small talk or smiles. Mike climbed into the cab with the tractor already running. He did a quick check of the sleeper for unexpected passengers. Finding none, he stowed his ditty bag. Another fifty miles of dust and dirt filled the cab air as Mike drove many twists and turns of the dirt road following the instruction received from a voice on the GPS. He decided *to call the GPS woman's voice Maryann after the cutie on TVs Gilligan's Island. It sure sounded like her. As a teen fan of the show, he always had the fantasy of being on the island with Maryann and Ginger. It was a relief to be free of dust filled air as he reached the comfort of paved I-35 north highway lanes.*

This would be a long trip to Casey Trucking. His brain was already forcing his eye lids shut not to shut. He needed sleep. Mike still did not know what was in the haul they packed into his trailer. He did know every box loaded in the trailer at Altamira, Mexico was stamped with Medical Equipment labels. There was much to be learned after he pulled into the Casey loading dock where he might get a look at what was packed into his truck container.

*****

28

Voice Whisperer

Many days had passed since Fred was challenged by one of his brain farts while working on his novel. His intensity of writing had not diminished on days when he was not able to write at home or at the hotel. Writing had become his addiction. It was an addiction almost as strong as the pull alcoholics have to the next drink.

This was going to be one of those days when stress could kill him. Fred was to spend lunchtime with Myrna at St. Drogo's Church meeting with the support group for Voice Hearers. He arrived a few minutes early and met Myrna in the parking lot.

"Now Fred I want you to keep an open mind and a closed mouth at this meeting. You may not be a believer in those voices others hear, but they are real to them as mine are certainly real to me."

"All right Myrna, open mind and closed mouth it will be."

George W. Clever

St. Drogo's church was an old building erected at a time when skilled carvers and stone masons could be afforded. The entry was through double carved doors re-enforced with iron fittings. Once in the narthex, Fred could smell the aging and death of a once active congregation of believers. Its youth and employed adults had fled the inner city leaving a mausoleum of a building to find new purposes. Yes, a purpose like a place where the Voice Hearer's organization could hold its meetings before the church was abandoned to the wrecking ball. Self- help groups seem to settle in church basements like a spoonful of instant coffee, some floating on the top to direct the others to settle in the bottom. All these groups needed to be shaken well into some kind of purposeful mission.

As Fred and Myrna descended the stairs to the basement room, they could see a circle of chairs partially filled with unemotionally blank faces of voice healers. Each person attending was prepared to do battle with anyone who challenged their reality of the voices speaking to them. All participants were hoping they would find an

Words Can Kill

authority, a champion, who will say they are not crazy, and those gathered would agree with this pronouncement.

Myrna made the decision to sit in the circle opposite the seat where the moderator always held court. A teenage girl with multiple tattoos and piercings entered with her mother who was wearing a Baptist Bible dress. They chose two seats next to Fred. There was a silence shared by those who are waiting for the center ringmaster. Each individual seemed to be observing the others sitting around circle and people descending the staircase into the room.

Fred studied the scene as an artist selecting characters to possible add to his next book chapter. There was a very tall man who had decided not to remove his hat while sitting with crossed arms and a scowl to match his turned down hat brim. A woman wearing high black leather boots pushed her bleached hair from her face. It was a futile effort as it fell again covering her excessive face make-up. Her elaborate cosmetics were unable to complete the purpose of hiding years of rocky road living evidenced by sagging jowls, a wrinkled brow, and dark circled eyes. Two very chatty professional women, office workers, in their tailor trim business suits with silk neck scarves carefully pinned to the suit lapels, were engaged in a conversation with the ringmaster as they came down the stairs together.

The VH leader followed them into the meeting room taking her rightfully claimed chair in the focal point of the circle. Three participants at the coffee table, coffee and donuts in hand, ended their conversation joining the circle as the meeting commenced. Fred began to pray for a very short meeting. He was impatient to see where his story would go when Mike returned to the Casey Trucking dock.

*****

It was almost midnight by the time Mike pulled his freight hauler to the guard house at the gate of the Casey Trucking Company. The guard focused a spotlight on the cab and asked for the manifest. He read it under his flashlight.

"Ok, pull it up to dock #4 and unload."

Words Can Kill

It would be good to stand on ground that did not move. Mike mused. *He was beat from two days of driving with little sleep or food. There was still work to do before he could rest or eat. What was in the boxes marked Medical Instruments? Were they still in his trailer? Would it be the same load he had moved from Port Altamira, Mexico? It was a good thing the #4 dock had a bumper as his weary judgment was a bit off backing into it with a crunch. The grinding stop was followed by loud shouting from the loading boss as he jumped from the dock and pounded on the driver door of Mike's Peterbilt.*

"Where in the hell did you get your CDL at a pawn shop?"

Mike rolled down the window and said, "Sorry, I've been without sleep or food for two days."

"Let me see your manifest," the dock boss demanded.

Mike handed him the clipboard, opened the truck door, and climbed down from the cab.

George W. Clever

"Take this to the dispatcher." The PIC said. "Don't hit the dock again or you will be working for some other company. Now get out of here."

Following the dock boss up to the loading platform, Mike was trying to think of a reason he should be hanging around during the unloading.

"Hey boss, I left my ditty bag in the truck along with my change of clothes. Only take a second to get it."

Before he could get a no from the boss, Mike slipped down the stairs to the cab and opened the passenger door. He climbed into the sleeper initiating a search for the ditty bag knowing it was tucked behind the driver seat. The stall worked as he heard the dock boss yell,

"Get that dry freight container emptied!"

From the cab window Mike could see a short yellow bus pull up to the side of the loading dock. Large boxes marked Medical Instruments were being fork lifted off the truck and into the warehouse. On closer inspection, he noticed all the boxes had air vent holes. Moments later

Words Can Kill

children in groups of two or three were ushered off the dock into the waiting bus. Mike used his belt camera to photograph the line of children walking from the dock to the bus just before he heard loud pounding on the cab door.

"Hey, what the hell are you doing in there? Get your stuff quick and drag your ass up to the dispatcher," the dock boss yelled.

Shirts and jeans in hand with his ditty bag, Mike hurried out of the truck, up the dock stairs, and into the hall leading to the Casey Trucking offices. He could not leave the dock without looking one more time at the loadmaster and workers moving cargo. Standing with the PIC was a woman partially hidden by the building shadow. At least Mike thought she was a woman, and one he perhaps knew. They were involved in an intense discussion which ended as they both turned in the direction where Mike was pressed into the building shadows. It was time to go.

"Where is your manifest? The dispatcher said. "Come on give it to me. I don't have all day."

George W. Clever

Mike handed the clipboard to him and looked around the office. It appeared to be empty with the exception of the dispatcher. He thumbed through the clipboard papers before placing them in a pile on a side table.

"Ok, you're done. We'll call when you are needed for another run."

"Alright, just tell me when I can get paid?"

"Drivers are paid twice a month depending on their hauls. Next pay is Saturday."

"I need to call a cab. Can I wait here until it comes?"

"Hell No! There's a bus stop out the front door."

P.I. Dunmore, A.K.A. the trucker 'Torcher', left the building and walked to the street where he found the bus stop. Rain began to fall as he huddled in a corner of the bus stop shelter. No one was waiting there in the late hours of the cold wet rainy night, not even the usual muggers and homeless box people. A river of puddle water surrounded his shoes as he placed a call on his cell.

Words Can Kill

"Mike here"

"Mike! Where in the world have you been? What happened to checking in with me with fake calls to your mother?"

"Couldn't chance it, I have much to tell you. Can you pick me up on Fulton Street at the Casey Trucking business office side entrance? I'll be standing at the bus stop. Please drive something less conspicuous than a black and white with flashing blue, and red lights on top."

There are those who can sleep with their eyes open. It is a useful ability for anyone who is required to attend boring meetings. Fred had that ability. His head rolled to one side as he sat on a cold metal folding chair. He began to snore. At first it was only heavy breathing, but then it started to resemble a stick in the wires of a bicycle wheel.

"Wake up Fred." Myrna gave him a not so gentle jab in the ribs with her elbow. "The VH program director is here, and about to start the meeting."

*****

29

Church of the Ugly

"Good afternoon friends, I am Sister Joseph Mary. Yes, for those who are new, it is an odd name taken in reverence to the Saints. Many of us use Mary in our name. My father wanted a son, and my mother a daughter, so the name Joseph Mary seemed to fit me. I received my B.S, M.A. and PhD in psychology from St. Monica University. Some of you may know St. Monica is the patron Saint of Addiction. My studies at this university, and God, led me to lead a group of those who hear voices. Shall we go around an introduce ourselves? Perhaps you can say a few words about why you are here. Let's start with the lady directly across from me."

Sister Joseph Mary pointed directly to Myrna who immediately became flushed as her rosy face looking down at the tiled floor. After a pregnant moment she spoke.

George W. Clever

"I know it is important to introduce ourselves, and say openly, I hear voices. But it really is embarrassing for me to do this. I am Myrna. My mother recently passed away. She fell down the cellar stairs and died. Now I am hearing a voice calling for me from the cellar stairs."

Then it was Fred's turn. He was most uncomfortable, and a bit angry when he said, "I'm Fred, Myrna's husband. I am here because Myrna asked me to attend, no demanded I come with her. She told me to just listen and keep my mouth shut. I don't hear voices in the cellar. I don't believe any of you do either."

There was a look of shock on each of the regulars in the circle, and a hint of a smiles from people they brought to the meeting.

"Well, Fred, we are glad you are here. I do hope you will be open to a change of thinking about those who hear voices by the end of our meeting. All in our group are members of the Hearing Voices Movement. We advocate support groups for people who are hearing voices. Our group is an alternative way to help individuals find a path

Words Can Kill

in life to follow successfully as they deal with the voices they hear that others do not. It is our hope they find their comfort without chemical, electro-shock therapy or psychiatric treatment. We encourage them to bring family and or friends to our meetings. It is my hope supporting people will assist them in their efforts to cope with this living challenge. This may be a good time to have our guests hear the basic positions of the Hearing Voices Movement. I would like to introduce Faith. She is one of our members who offered to be our recorder at each meeting. Faith will you introduce yourself, and read the position statement from our last meeting?"

"Hello, I'm Faith, and I hear voices. At our last meeting Sister gave us the basic positions of the Hearing Voices Movement. They are as follows:

1.) Hearing voices is not in itself a sign of mental illness.

2.) Hearing voices is experienced by many people who do not have symptoms that would lead to a diagnosis of mental illness.

3.) Hearing voices is often related to problems in one's life history.

If hearing voices causes distress, the person who hears the voices can learn strategies to cope with the experience."

"Thank you, Faith, now let us continue with our introductions."

Members in the circle obeyed giving their first name followed by the expected phrase 'I hear voices.' When the circle of introductions was complete Sister gave her next direction.

"This is the moment in our program where we all tell briefly when we hear voices, and what we think the voice or voices are saying."

The young woman with the tattoos and piercing began by telling the group she heard voices when she attends Metallica concerts. The voice she hears seems to be John Lennon who is saying, 'Go home. This is evil music.'

"Do you hear his voice in your left or right ear dear?" Sister Joseph Mary asked.

Words Can Kill

After a few moments of thought she said, "I think it is in my left ear."

"You and your mother are excused from the group now. All those who do hear voices will tell you they hear them in both ears. I'm afraid you are making up your voice hearing. Perhaps you should have a talk with your mother. Explain to her why you are saying you hear a voice."

The mother stood up, and with one hand grabbing her daughter's Living Dead tee shirt. Her other hand slipped its fingers under the daughters belt by her hip.

In an angry voice she said, "We are out of here, missy. I told you this was a phony organization."

She dragged her daughter from the chair, pulled her up the stairs, and slammed the narthex door as they left.

All eyes in the circle began to resemble fine china saucers. Each of the participants were waiting for Sister to launch into some explanation of her treatment of the young girl and her mother. Perhaps Sister Joseph Mary would rise to a defense of the VH organization from the aspersions cast by the irate mother. She did not do either.

"Oh, that was unpleasant." Sister remarked. "Shall we continue with Myrna? I know you have told me you hear one voice with both ears."

Myrna responded with details of the voice she was hearing. At first, her hands trembled. When she saw the smile on Sister Joseph Mary's face the trembling stopped.

"Yes, it comes from the cellar stairway."

"Who is it speaking? Do you know what is being said?"

"Yes, I think it is my mother's voice, and she is saying 'I must tell you…I must tell you.' I hear her even at night when I am in the bedroom. My husband and I are never getting a good night sleep now."

"Have you tried the five techniques we learned at the last meeting? Perhaps after our break it would be helpful if Faith read those five techniques for the new members. Will you do that, Faith?"

"Yes Sister I will."

Words Can Kill

"Ok, let's take a 10-minute break for coffee" the director said, "Please join me at the refreshment table."

Fred did not have a butt built for sitting on folding metal chairs. He was grateful for the opportunity to stretch, and find a cup of coffee. Myrna was still sitting in the circle talking with a woman who hears Marilyn Monroe telling her about John Kennedy. The table of snacks did not show much promise with only two plates of donut holes.

As he poured a cup of coffee from the stainless steel urn, a voice behind him said, "I have looked all over for you today. It has been a while since you gave me any chapters of your book to edit. I need to show my instructor at the college I am working for you. Do you have writer's block?"

"Angelina! What are you doing here? I thought I made it clear you were only to meet with me when I am working in my study."

"I went there for several days and you were not there."

"Yes, I know. Myrna's mother died, and I had no time to write."

"Ok, I will be back tomorrow. Please try to have a chapter for me to edit. My grade is riding on it," Angelina said.

"Who were you talking to, Fred?"

Myrna took a Styrofoam cup from the stack and a tea bag off the table. She poured hot water in the cup and looked quizzically at Fred. He knew she was lining up her list of questions like a priest at the Inquisitions.

"No one."

"I saw your lips moving as you were standing here in front of the snacks when I walked from the circle."

"It was just my intern Angelina. She came to remind me her grade in class would be lowered if I did not give her more editing to do."

"I did not see her by the table."

"She was…."

Words Can Kill

At that moment, Fred was interrupted by Sister Joseph Mary's voice echoing around the reverberating church hall like a ricocheted bullet.

"Will you please take your seats so we can continue? You may bring your drinks and snacks with you. Faith, please read the coping techniques we learned at our last meeting?"

"Yes Sister. There are five techniques we should practice. They are:

1.) Place a rubber band around your wrist. Snap it when the voice is heard.

2.) If the voice says you are worthless, lazy, and worse, just say, 'Yes, right now I am feeling worthless, lazy'…. and whatever other cruel thing the voice offers.

3.) Keep a record noting when the voice is heard, and what you were doing at the time. Perhaps it was after a meeting with your boss or a dinner with relatives.

4.) Play music you really like. Play it loud.

5.) Check your physical condition. Are you sick with fever, a cold or flu? Do you hear voices after you have been drinking alcohol? Make a note of how you feel physically."

Faith offered a slight smile, folded her notepad, stroked her pearl neckless, and returned to her seat. She expected some kind of recognition for her diligence in record keeping. She would not be denied.

"Thank you, Faith. Please continue your excellent recording of this meeting. We have not finished our introductions. All participants need to be sure you give any information you are willing to share about the voice, or voices you hear at this time. Remember by sharing you are coping," Sister said.

Another man in a wrinkled brown suit began his self- introduction by saying, "My name is Tom and I am being told to kill all of you."

"Who is telling you that, Tom?"

"God is telling me that right now!"

Words Can Kill

"And what did we say you should tell God?" Sister Joseph Mary asked.

"If you are really God you would not ask me to do that. I am not going to do it!" he shouted.

"Good thinking. We know our God is kind and loving."

Sister Joseph Mary sorted through her papers in a brief case choosing one to present as a re-enforcement of the normalcy of hearing voices.

"Now it is time to give you your homework for the week. I hope our visitors have gained helpful insight into the problems hearers of voices face, and their struggles in life. Remember we all hear voices. There is one important difference between people here who do hear voices and those who do not. VH will live with a disturbing disability if they let it be so. Gandhi, Anthony Hopkins the actor, Sigmund Freud, and Dr. John Forbes Nash the famous Mathematician, all admit to having heard voices. They learned to cope and live productive lives. Your assignment is to tell the voice they belong to you. Say it more than once. 'You belong to me.' Then ask the voice questions.

George W. Clever

Record the results for our next meeting. Ask this question. What do you want to tell me today?"

Sister closed her brief case and said, "Ok folks that is it for today. See you next week."

Some of the voice hearers stayed to press their case for more personal help from Sister Joseph Mary. Others filed up the stairs with Fred and Myrna on their way to their cars in the church parking lot.

"Now, Fred, do you still doubt me when I tell you there is a voice coming from the cellar stairs?"

"No Myrna, I am sure you think there is a voice speaking to you. I have to go now or I will be late for my three to eleven shift at the hotel. Go home and tell your voice it belongs to you. I'll see you in bed."

"You expect me to walk home in this seedy neighborhood? It is not safe. Not that you care, I am sure."

"I am late Myrna. You will be fine, and it is only three blocks to our house."

Words Can Kill

The drive to the hotel was short, but Fred's mind had its own voices shouting loud enough to drown out the traffic noise. *Angelina must not follow me anymore. I need to finish writing a few chapters to keep her away. Maybe it will be a slow night at the front desk. Thank God I have not experienced any of those mental butterflies while writing lately. Maybe it is because I do most of the writing on a laptop at the hotel, and not at home on the PC where all that nonsense started. Those people at the Voice Hearers meeting should all be locked up. What a crazy Loony Tune group. Myrna must be certifiable hearing voices from the cellar stairs. What am I going to do about her?*

The answer to that question would have to wait as he pulled into the hotel parking lot. He had a more important question in his mind at that moment. *What would the conversation between Detective Keith and Mike Dunmore be all about when they meet after the truck haul from Mexico?*

*****

30

Count the Calendars

Fred was pleased to see the parking lot was full of cars with early check-ins to the hotel. The few rooms left would not be filled until the couples who rent rooms by the hour would show up late in the evening. That would give him plenty of time to work on his novel. He thought about his unexpected visit by Angelina at the church.

I know Angelina's college semester is almost at the end. She will return soon expecting more of the book to be finished so she can do my editing for her class grade. Angelina is very beautiful, young, thin, with long dark hair, golden hoops in her ears, and a special way of wearing shear print dresses draping her wasp waist and ample hips. Myrna once looked the same in her high school years when I first saw her in the cafeteria. Now she is what all middle aged women become with her skunked short hair and Wal-Mart clothes.

George W. Clever

He knew not to stare too long at the bathroom mirror in the morning while shaving. Fred would see his father's tired, sagging face, and thinning hair.

"Ahh! He exclaimed out loud sitting in his car on his way to work. It is true that youth is wasted on the young. I offer in evidence the same young college people who fill in at the hotel part time. They are totally absorbed in their cell phone texting and I-Pad game playing. Every one of them is unable to converse with guests who are asking the simplest questions. Oh well, who cares".

He concluded his self-absorbed remarks while pinning on his hotel badge at the entrance of the hotel. Fred went to his work station standing at the desk pretending to do hotel business. Fred would squeeze as many new lines in the story as possible between answering the desk phone, and registering new arrivals. The day shift staff was eager to leave the building on a Friday. It was party night for them. Unfolding his laptop on the front desk, he thought about the last lines written.

Words Can Kill

As the saved manuscript document filled the screen, his focus changed from the life of a front desk hotel clerk to Creator in a brand new world of crime and intrigue. This was his preferred life, a life of solving crimes with the excitement of fighting bad guys and gals. *What will I do when this book is finished?* He considered. *I will certainly miss my novel characters in their computer world every day. Oh, well, Mike is waiting for his marching orders to call his mother, and make an office stop. Let the click, click of my fingers on the key board begin.*

*****

Sergeant Keith pulled alongside the bus stop canopy where Mike was waiting. He reached over to the passenger door and grabbed the handle to open it.

"Get in quick out of the rain. Don't want the new upholstery rain stained. I just had it re-done to the tune of five hundred bucks."

"Nice car. Where did you get a cool turquois blue Ford Edsel, Keith?"

George W. Clever

"It's been in the family since my father decided to be the first man on his block with a car looking like a vagina."

"Sure will be unnoticed in this neighborhood," Mike said sarcastically. "Step on it!"

Keith stomped the pedal to the metal hoping to surprise Mike. The old Edsel laid rubber for half a block.

"Where to, Mike?"

"Any place where I can get something to eat. I am starved. No food in two days, and not much sleep."

Sergeant Farrell made a quick left turn before backing down an alley and killing the lights. No cars passed the alley and none turned into it.

"No sense of being careless. We are all playing for high stakes with some extremely dangerous dudes."

The Edsel car lights came on again. Keith made two more turns before pulling to a stop in front of a greasy spoon café. The sign read 'Mom's Felony Stop Café'. Mike was going to break one of his prime directives if he ate in this place. Never eat in a place called MOM's. Maybe the

Words Can Kill

*café would have a dozen calendars on the wall. Calendars
in great number were a measure of the food and service
quality in any greasy spoon. These quirky measures of café
quality came from his reading of William Least Heat
Moon's book, Blue Highways.*

*"You will get well fed here. It's a twenty-four-hour cafe
patronized by all sorts of despicable citizens."*

*They entered the café, found a booth at the far end
of a string of tables covered with red checkered, vinyl
tablecloths. Even the menus were trimmed in red. Mike
counted the calendars on the wall. There were three. Not
bad for a dive in this part of town, he considered. There
was no waitress in the café.*

*Mike and Keith were not seated long before a guy
needing a shave, wearing a white paper hat, and a greasy
apron, came to their table with a pot of coffee.*

*"Coffee?" he asked, turning over two cups without
expecting an answer. "Menus are behind the napkin
holder. You want food holler. Give you a minute."*

George W. Clever

The maître / waiter/ cook /busboy headed back toward the swinging doors leading to a kitchen in clear view. It looked like a hobo soup kitchen run by transients. Pots were stacked up on the stove like a modern art ugly sculpture. Near the door an alley cat was enjoying leftovers spilled on the floor.

"Ok Mike let's get to it. Where you been? What did you learn? I have Lieutenant Meagan stomping on my throat every day since you walked in on her at Casey Trucking."

"I took a haul to Altamira, Mexico and back, Keith."

Mike reached for his belt removing a 2GB SanDisk from the back of his buckle camera. He checked it for possible rain water damage, and handed it to Keith.

"These pictures may be of interest to Lieutenant Meagan. One of every three container trucks in the convoys moving from Altamira docks in Mexico to Texas were headed to Casey Trucking. They reached the loading dock after a stop at a distribution center in the desert. Cartons are unloaded at the distribution complex. The flatbed trailers receive

Words Can Kill

shipping cargo boxes containing illegal immigrants, mostly children. Some of the kids hidden in other reefer trailers are loaded into yellow short busses there. All the boxes in the shipping containers are forklift unloaded into a bunker terminal. Not sure what goes on in there. Maybe they are inspected for dead kids, re-distributed, and moved out to the waiting tractors. A few of the cartons might be filled with dangerous illegals, unloaded, and distributed to their paid travel destinations. I don't know where they go from there."

Mike polished off his first cup of coffee and began looking for a refill and scanned the menu as he continued briefing Sergeant Keith.

"Homeland Security is involved in smuggling children and other illegals into America using this system of distribution. After the cargo is sent from the docks at Altamira, Mexico and driven to the border crossings, the civilian drivers are replaced with uniforms wearing D.H.S. shoulder patches. The uniform drivers deliver the trucks to a remote distribution center about fifty miles into the Texas desert.

George W. Clever

Two of the three trucks are emptied at the transfer station and sent back to the port."

"Was there anyone you recognized on the route?"

"No. The only people I vaguely know were on the Casey loading dock when I returned. It was late, and the light was bad, but I saw a woman on the dock in tense conversation with the PIC. At least four of the Casey employees I could recognize are tapped into this gig, the PICs, the dispatcher, two heavies on the dock bay unloading, and perhaps the woman I saw briefly before they hustled me off to the dispatcher."

Keith lifted his coffee cup a second time, and motioned for the waiter for his re-fill. Watching a very hungry Mike eat was going to be tough enough without ordering one of their famous donuts. Trying to get vital information about Mike's travel between his mouthfuls would take some time.

"Why didn't you make calls as we planned? Your mother and Angel were very worried."

Words Can Kill

The waiter interrupted the briefing with no attention to the seriousness of their conversation.

"What you going to have?" the substitute waiter, cook, and greasy spoon maître d' said.

"You better order and finish up your long awaited meal Mike." Keith said as he ordered another coffee and a donut. "I need to check back into the station right after I drop you off."

"Well ole buddie, I feel like I could eat everything on the menu if it wasn't burned."

Mike scanned the menu one more time feeling pressure for a quick order from the fidgety waiter who did a rhythm drumming with his pencil on the order pad.

"Just give me some eggs over medium, potatoes, and bacon, and fill the coffee cups again."

When the waiter went back to the kitchen Mike continued sharing information about his truck adventure in Mexico.

George W. Clever

"I couldn't call you or mom. A big Mexican by the name of Franco was with me from the time I hit Altamira until crossing at the World Trade Bridge. At that point a Department of Homeland Security uniform took over and drove the rig to the distribution point. I was never alone."

"Well you had better check in with your secretary and mother when we finish here."

"Anything new in the Casey case since I left?"

"Quite a bit. As you know, it is not possible to determine the DNA of a person cremated, however, if the cremation is not complete at a temperature over eighteen hundred degrees, the body may not be totally changed to ashes. Fragments of teeth and bone may provide material for the DNA test.

Keith took a bite from the donut he ordered. He tried to justify to himself the sweet thing was necessary. He was working overtime, and needed a blood sugar lift.

"The body found in your Charger car trunk was not totally cremated. We know this about the victim. It was a woman,

Words Can Kill

most likely a semi-identical twin. Identical twins have the same DNA. Semi-identical twins have seventy-five percent of the same DNA. Given that information, we may find the twin to match the DNA and determine who was stuffed into your car trunk. Oh, we also found partially melted gold from a ring, but no diamonds.

Mike finished his meal wiping the egg left on his plate with a muffin. He took another sip of coffee using the break in his report to run his memory for any information not yet shared.

"In the morning, I will have the pleasure of waking Harlan Casey for another challenging talk. Mike, I think it is time for him to tell us where his wife is now, that is, if he knows. If Mr. Casey does not know where Helen is now it will be necessary for him to file a missing person report with my department. That will certainly make the front pages and TV news when reporters tie the missing report he files to his campaign for Governor.":

Keith finished off the donut, took another sip of coffee, and pushed himself away from the table. He was ready to leave.

"Oh, one more thing. We need to meet again with Lieutenant Meagan after she gets a look at these pictures you provided. She's having a hard time tagging Harlan Casey with this child smuggling ring. We'll meet at the same place. I will let you know when."

Farrell picked up the check on their table and headed toward the counter to pay. He didn't expect a check paying protest from his 'economically challenged", and tired friend.

"Let's go Mike."

*****

Chapter 31

Pregnant Surprise

Mike was pleased to see everything in his office was in order as he opened the door. No unknown visitors had trashed the place this time. He caught a smell of lemons. Angel must have been dusting the desk and file cabinets. There was a note on his desk from her which read, Myrna is pregnant!

This bizarre thought drifted into Fred's mind and jumped onto the laptop screen. His mind reeled with the realization he had let another one of those damn brain farts enter his thinking, breaking his writing focus. Fred knew the screen would make sure Myrna was with child. *The flat screen blinked and printed out* **Myrna is with child.** *How could that be?* He pondered. *Myrna and I had no sex life, none since her mother came to live with us. On many occasions when I was feeling a bit frisky Myrna would say, 'Fred, stop that! You know Mother will hear us.' How many times had she* told *me, 'No sniveling brats in my house.'*

George W. Clever

Her verbal distaste for children was displayed in public too many times for Fred. He remembered the time when Myrna was standing in a twenty items or less line at Wally World when she saw a woman in front of her struggling with three children under five and a baby in the shopping basket. Myrna told the mother in a loud voice to stop cranking out kids and save the world from over population.

This particular embarrassment was enough to flip the switch to off on Fred's sex control second brain. *This pregnancy thought must be a mistake! Please let it be one that will soon be corrected by another 'inverse mental butterfly'.* Fred thoughtfully pleaded. No butterfly came.

"Sir…sir please, I would like to register for a room."

The insistent voice dragged him back from the world of his novel to the daily demands of desk clerking.

"Why certainly sir, I am truly sorry. Sometimes the computer demands too much of one's attention. Let me help you. Please fill out the registration card."

Words Can Kill

Fred prepared a room key card and ran the credit card offered by the customer. The card was valid, and the card holder was growing more impatient by the moment.

"Your room is right through the lobby hall to the elevator on your left. Take the elevator to the second floor. Your room number is 212 on the right as you exit the elevator. Here is your pass card, sir."

The disapproving customer lifted his bag and started toward the elevator. Fred wasted no time getting back to his laptop computer, hoping an inverse thought would appear to erase Myrna's computer generated pregnancy. None came to his mind. No words appeared on the screen by themselves.

"Come on! Come on!" he shouted quietly to himself. *"Give me a way to terminate this pregnancy announcement."* Nothing appeared on the computer laptop screen. *Oh hell! Maybe I am imagining this birthing announcement*, Fred considered. *"If I write a little more, the pregnancy inverse will show up.*

George W. Clever

Let me see now…. Mike is waiting for Angel at his office. I had better hammer out a few more lines before the late hotel arrival bed hoppers show up. Why is Mike afraid of a commitment to his Angel? Surely he cannot blame it on his wartime flashbacks. I know she is a stronger woman who can handle his PTSD lows. If my Angelina asked me to run away to Tahiti and marry her I would be out of here in a blink. **Angelina asked you to run away to Tahiti** *appeared on his screen. What is this nonsense? Focus, focus. I must finish this chapter, and think clearly before I confront Myrna when she returns from work.*

*****

The moment Mike read Angel's note to call her on his return from the truck run, his office door opened. Angel rushed in with squeals, arms flailing like a wacky, inflatable, air dancer at a gas station opening. She crushed him in a long lasting hug.

"Thank God you're back. Sergeant Keith called me."

Words Can Kill

Angel leaped up on him, wrapping her arms and legs, legs with no end, around him like a Koala Bear clinging to a eucalyptus tree.

"We were so worried when you didn't call. Are you ok?"

"I'm fine, Angel. This first trip was my midterm test by the child smugglers. If I had made any calls I am sure I would have flunked."

"You're not going on the road again are you?"

"Not sure right now sweetie. I will have to wait for their call to decide if another haul would be of value."

"Oh your mother was so worried when you didn't call her or Sergeant Keith. She asked over and over why you were doing this trucking business. I think she hoped you were leaving the dangers of PI work for a little less dangerous trucking gig. You must see her."

"I will after a good night's sleep. Will you grab a few blankets and a pillow out of the closet for me? This old leather couch will do nicely after two days in the Peterbilt truck."

George W. Clever

Angel gave him another kiss, released her long legs from his body, and walked, teasingly as only she could, to the closet. She found the bedding, and spread the sheets and blankets on the couch.

"Are you hungry, Mike? I could get something at the all night deli on Stevens Street for you?"

"No honey, I will be fine. Any business in the office I should know about?"

"No, it has been quiet as a Queen's fart here. You did have one call from a woman in Indiana needing help to find her missing twin granddaughters. I left her phone numbers on your desk with all the information."

"I'm beat and need a year of shut eye, Angel. Do you think you could pick me up tomorrow morning about ten o'clock, and take me to my apartment to retrieve the Vette? We could have a late breakfast, and a quick stop at Mom's before you have classes."

"Sure, I'll be here at ten."

Words Can Kill

Angel pulled a cover over Mike on the office couch, leaned down, and kissed each of his shut eyelids. Her kiss lingered at his lips with a promise of something more. He was asleep. She shook her head with a disappointment smile, but understanding his weariness. Angel picked up her purse, opened the office door, stepped into the hall, and locked the office door quietly.

Mike was in a deep sleep when he was interrupted by one too many cups of coffee and message from his kidneys to make a sleeping pit stop. He rolled from the couch leaving a pile of covers and pillows in a big lump. He staggered out of the office, sleepwalk weaving down the hall to the only restroom on the third floor of the office building.

It was not the first time he made this trip since returning from Iraq. He could make the john with his eyes closed. There was another war going on between his brain and his body this night. His brain was ordering his eyes to stay closed avoiding any light. His body demanded his eyes be open so it would not be hurt if they were to stumble over *objects and furniture on their way to kidney relief. Eyes took its orders from the body. They opened the moment Mike's feet hit the cold restroom tile floor.*

Seated on the john in a meditative state, new orders were issued to his eyes to close. That order was overruled when several gun shots followed by a burst of an automatic weapon firing echoed down the hall.

"Damn, I must be getting senile breaking rule number one. Never leave home without your heater. The Browning pistol is in my desk drawer. Time for rule number two. Hide!" Mike reasoned.

Pulling his pants up with a yank on his belt buckle, and sliding it into a well-worn notch. He climbed on top of the john tank so his legs and feet would not be seen under the stall if someone was looking for him. No one entered the men's restroom. After several minutes, Mike opened the lavatory door a crack, and looked down the hall. One dim sixty-watt bulb was hanging from a converted gas light fixture. The dirty bulb did not offer much illumination for him to see beyond the next office.

Words Can Kill

There was a flash of a shadow near his office door followed by swearing, and a slam rattling the Private Detective stenciled door glass. Mike waited a moment listening to the sharp noise of footsteps on tile going down the hall to the back stairs. When he was sure the unexpected visitor was gone, he pressed his body tightly against the shadows lining the wall leading to his office door. Entering his office, Mike surveyed the room for places where another perp might be hiding.

Flipping on the office light, Mike dove for the safety of the only bunker in the room, his oak desk. He could see the target of the previous gunfire in the office room. It was his old, revered, leather couch. The divan had history. It provided comfort after nights of heavy partying, usefulness for an occasional roll in the hay with some cutie, or a nap after a long boring day on a P.I. stakeout. Now the chesterfield was filled with holes. Its stuffing showed white colors for surrender. The heap of blankets where he slept was riddled to shreds.

George W. Clever

He retrieved his nine-millimeter Browning handgun from the desk drawer. Pulling on his shoes, he remembered one of his grandfather's sayings. 'In an emergency, always put on your shoes first. You can run far naked with shoes on, but not far without the protection of good leather soles.'

Mike hit the light switch again, crossing the room to the windows overlooking the street. Car lights and yellow streetlight beams bounced off the rain soaked cars parked along the near curb. Puddles became mirrors in the night after an all-night shower. No one exited the building's front door. No parked cars moved away from the curb. Whoever did the shooting knew the building well enough to exit out one of the many side doors, or even a basement door leading to the back lot.

He knew nothing could be done until morning. It made no sense to call the police. If they showed up, their interrogation would just burn away what was left of his sleep time. Mike concluded the person using his blankets for target practice would not return. He was sure the swearing heard was an indication the shooter knew no one

Words Can Kill

was sleeping on the couch, and their target was probably not anywhere in the building.

The black desk chair did recline. It would have to do for what sleep he could grab this night. Angel would arrive early in the morning. Together, they could find a replacement couch after breakfast. She never liked the old brown leather anyway. Angel told him often to hire an office decorator to make the place more suitable for upscale clients.

*****

Myrna was asleep as usual when Fred opened their bedroom door. Just how was he to ask her if she was pregnant? There was no good way to do so without her thinking he was saying she was getting fat. He climbed into their warm bed without any indication Myrna knew her husband was even there.

From his side of the bed, he wrapped his mind around the writer's block website curse. With luck, what appeared on the screen would not become real. Fred considered the possibility of having a child come into his life at this time. Each of his thoughts fed an increase in feelings of panic. *I know if I say anything about the possibility she is pregnant it will only complicate our relationship which is not good on the best of days. Writing time would be more difficult to find with her on a rant. And what if she was pregnant? Who was the father? We haven't had sex for months before her mother died. Yes, who could be the father?*

There seemed no good way for his sleepy brain to deliver an answer on how a pregnancy discussion could be started with Myrna. It would have to come from her own initiative in the morning. With eyes staring at the dark bedroom ceiling, Fred's need for sleep slammed his eyelids shut. But only after one last thought. *What if she denies her pregnancy? The computer website has not been wrong before.*

Morning breakfast came early for Fred the next day. Normally he would just sleep in, and let his wife leave for work without any notice. He wanted time now for Myrna to break the family news to him. Their baby conversation

Words Can Kill

would have to be in the morning before she left for work. Fred was making coffee when she entered the kitchen.

"Good morning. Nice day for new beginnings. What do you have planned for the day?" Fred enquired.

He turned his back to her avoiding Myrna's unusual ability to read his face.

"Just another day at the candy factory packaging my quota of forty-seven variety packs of chocolates. The company is so fussy about quotas. They make sure there are exactly forty-seven all different, bite size pieces in each pack. I will be forever working at a job I hate."

"Why don't you have coffee with me this morning? We haven't had much time together to just talk," Fred offered.

"Is something wrong with you, Fred? You never are up this early."

"No, nothing is wrong. I was just wondering how you are doing since your mother died?"

"Do you have to bring that up? I'm fine. Don't tell me you are hearing that voice coming from the cellar stairs now?"

George W. Clever

"No, I still don't hear any voices from the basement. Are you going back to the Voice Hearers meeting next week Myrna?"

"Yes, I will be there."

"Do you want me to go with you?"

"No you just don't get it."

"I try Myrna. I try."

"Maybe you tried too hard last time. Maybe you should think about that."

Myrna picked up her purse and opened the door to the garage. When she left, Fred thought about the meaning of her last words. Was he 'trying too hard'? What did Myrna mean by that statement? He could only guess. Being awake with hours before his pre-work routine, Fred could feel the pull toward his computer and the novel yet to be finished. He wondered, *will it ever be finished? I am sick of it now. Even if I wanted it finished, what then? Perhaps the Never Ending website would be the answer I am seeking about my latest brain fart.*

Words Can Kill

Fred settled into his black computer chair and clicked the desktop icon file labeled 'story'. He realized it was a lame working title. Yes, the working title would have to be changed. Finding a good appropriate title for his novel would be his morning's work. Mike Dunmore adventures deserved better than just 'story' for a title.

*****

The early morning sun was a better alarm than Mike's radio box with its irritating sound. Sunlight forced its way through the dirt and dust covered office window slipping between half open blinds. It settled its rays directly on to Mike's closed eyelids. Eyes and brain were saying 'Wake up! Wake up!' A very weary body was saying 'Leave me alone I need more sleep.' The eyes, brain, body struggle ended when Mike heard the office door lock snap open followed by the door scraping across the vinyl floor. After the couch was couch killed in the night by machine pistol bullets, his combat instincts kicked. Mike responded to the sound by jumping out of the chair with his Browning nine in hand.

George W. Clever

"It's me Mike. Don't shoot me!" It was Angel screaming. "What happened to the couch? Are you ok?"

Wiping the sleep from his eyes, Mike said, "Some interior decorator with an automatic Mac 10 machine pistol hated the office couch more than you do."

Mike put the Browning back in his back holster, and looked for his shoes. He found his pants hanging over the desk chair and his flannel shirt on the floor.

"Give me a minute, Angel. I need to wash the cobwebs out of my eyes before we go to breakfast. Yes, I will tell you about last night's fracas over coffee. Maybe we can find time to shop for a new couch this morning."

Mike had met some tough customers in his time, but none tougher than Angel when it came to choosing a new couch. He was all for another leather one capable of opening into a bed. She insisted on choosing a sofa with a nice bright flowery pattern to soften up the atmosphere of the office. Angel won the couch argument of course. Winning the "buying the sofa" contest was not enough for

Words Can Kill

Angel. She picked out two end tables, a coffee table, and matching lamps.

It was a mistake for Mike to ask "Is that all we should buy?" It was not. Angel had to add a framed print of a Parisian street scene to be hung over the sofa. When the furniture delivery arrived, she offered to help Mike push the bullet-riddled couch into the elevator. Together, they pressed the elevator's down button, sending the couch to the basement, hoping someone would take it away. As they watched the elevator doors close both realized it was a very close call for Mike.

Angel said, "Well lucky, I'm off to class. How about dinner at my place this evening? You could use a little R and R."

"Sure, I'll see you there after seven. Right now I have to call the woman in Indiana with the missing twins. We could use a few extra dollars since you tapped out my checking account with the office re-decoration. See you tonight."

After Angel was gone, Mike settled into his desk chair and dialed the Indiana number she left for him. He wondered where the energy would come from for him to take on another case. The need for cash to pay Angel for her office work was a good energizer.

"Hello, this is Mike Dunmore Private Investigator. I understand you have missing grandchildren you would like me to find."

There were several important questions to ask before he would take the case.

"Yes, there are many reasons children run away. Were they in any trouble? How were things at school? Do they use drugs? Do you think the twins ran away to punish their parents or grandparents? Yes, I know these are hard questions for you to answer. You may not know the answers. Why do you think they would head this way? Oh, a boyfriend lives here. Do you have his name and address? I'll do some checking here, and call you by Friday."

He took down all the information offered about the runaways. Mike asked for photos to be sent to him by email attachment as soon as possible. One point three million kids run away each year. It would not be an easy find, but Mike hoped he might get lucky for the kids, their parents,

Words Can Kill

and grandparents. The moment he hung up his office phone the cell phone in his pocket rang. It was Detective Keith.

"We need to meet with Lieutenant Meagan. Same place about four o'clock, ok?"

"I'll be there, Keith." The cell phone was hot in his hand as he closed it. Another call rang in.

"Mike Torcher? This is the dispatcher at Casey Trucking. You're scheduled for another truck haul on Saturday, six in the morning. Don't be late."

"I'll be there."

*****

32

More than Editing

Fred worked at his computer all morning looking for the right working title to his mystery novel. He rejected several promising ones including *Mike Dunmore Private Eye; the Case of the Flaming Charger*, *Your Kid is My Kid*, *Murder He Wrote*, and *More Than One Angel*. Nothing seemed right even for a working title. Finally, he settled on *Child For Sale*. The title would do until at least the first editing.

A gentle knock on the basement door interrupted his thoughts on the meeting between Mike Dunmore, Lieutenant Meagan and Detective Sergeant Keith. Fred opened the door cautiously as it was unusual to have someone knock on the cellar door. It was Angelina.

"I tried your front door, but you didn't answer. I thought you might be working here in your computer basement room. Do you have a few chapters of your book ready for me to edit?"

George W. Clever

Fred turned on his selective hearing as Angelina spoke. He was more interested in what she was wearing than what she was saying. Her tight short red skirt waistband almost met the bottom of a white blouse. The blouse was unbuttoned enough to for him to see large firm breasts gathered in a deep cleavage. Angelina's long black hair hung loosely to her waist with a camellia flower tied at the side of her forehead with a short braid.

"Yaaa-yes, I ca-can give you th-three chapters today," he stuttered. "I do appreciate it when you only come here for the editing work. Let me get the copies for you."

He returned to his desk computer. With a quick touch of the computer mouse, the Child For Sale file appeared on the screen. Fred hit the print icon for chapters five, six and seven. Angelina moved close to the printer catching each paper copy as it dropped into the tray. All the copies began to rush past the tray stop falling to the floor. Angelina bent over quickly to pick up the papers. Fred's eyes focused on how tight Angelina's skirt was as it pressed so firmly against her hips. Her skirt rose up

Words Can Kill

enough so he could see her thighs spreading apart each time she bent to pick up another paper.

Fred felt something within his chest like a hydraulic vise compressing his rib bones toward his spine. It felt the same way in the past when Myrna was sending signals for their monthly bedroom boogie. Angelina shifted her weight from one hip and buttock to the other. It was an action like the hula dance he had seen on the travel channel. His eyes locked to her arousing, erotic spot. Fred knew in that moment he had to have her now.

Picking up the last errant copy from the floor, she turned on bended knees toward Fred. "See anything there you like?"

"Oh yes there is much to admire."

Angelina moved closer to Fred as she gathered the sheaf of papers into a file, holding them tightly to her chest. She could feel his eyes locked on her as she rose from the floor. One of the lectures in her biology classes was about human sex pheromones. Yes, pheromones yet to be thoroughly understood by scientists. It was a lesson she now understood very well standing beside Fred at his desk. There was lust in the way he looked into her eyes and a boat load of exciting pheromones to exchange.

"Are these the papers you want me to caress, I mean address. You know editing is like a good kiss. It starts off SLOW, but the editor has to have a PASSION for finishing it."

Fred focused on Angelina's hands as they tightly gripped the papers. Without hesitation, they both moved toward each other. He reached for the copies with clumsy hands missing their mark. His hands ending up somewhere close to the open space between her blouse and skirt. Fred grasped Angelina's waist with both hands drawing her closer to him. He kissed her closed eyes and lips. His hand moved to unbutton the few remaining pearl buttons on her blouse.

She responded, pressing her body hard against his thighs. One of those wild mental butterflies found an opening taking attention and focus away from his smaller

Words Can Kill

*brain. It announced his prayer for an Angelina wardrobe malfunction. The desktop computer screen hammered out the words **Wardrobe Malfunction** as the chapter copies she clutched slipped between her blouse and Fred's hands.*

All her blouse buttons opened on command. He slipped the garment from her shoulders to the floor. The move revealed her bra filled with two well-shaped firm breasts with pink nipples, nipples only those who are yet to be a mother could ever display. He lifted his hands to her face placing one on each side, finding the soft full lips she offered. Fred gave in to the butterfly thought as her kisses landed lightly on his lips. She softly moaned words he needed to hear.

"I have waited months for this moment with you."

Her words of expected pleasure were followed by longer moments Fred would describe as mouth eating unmatched by the sweetness of an overripe plum. Both of their eyes closed as they should be, closed in wonder and fear, fear that the moment would be over when their eyes opened.

George W. Clever

Eager hands groped for snaps, zippers, belt buckles and buttons until most of their clothing fell in a pile, only to be kicked away. Fred, stood wearing only his shirt, and lifted Angelina above his head like a ballerina in dance before slowly letting her near nakedness slide down his sweating body. She kissed his hands, placing them in hers.

Slowly, Angelina drew him to the carpeted floor directing his Mr. Wiggle into her life. Rug burns be damned! Fred was on automatic pilot as she wrapped her long legs around his waist drawing him tightly into her body. She unbuttoned his shirt to feel his skin against hers. Fred, frustrated with the back clasp of her bra, pulled it off her shoulders, and began suckling one breast then another, then both together.

Angelina reached down between his legs, rubbing softly with her cool hands. She discovered he was ready for her. Fred ripped off her remaining panties, kicking their pile of clothes even further away. She whispered in his ear again. "Fred I have waited so long to feel you inside me.

Words Can Kill

Together we are one person, one love. I am the woman you always needed."

Fred's heartbeat went faster than the speed of sound as he plunged into Angelina. In that instant they became the one she described passing her energy to him and his to her. Each moment of the coupling drew more strength away from their passion. Her screams trailed into moans, moans into sighs until they lay wrapped in each other's arms exhausted, spent, unable to move.

The cold of the basement settled in. Their bodies demanded a more comfortable place than a cement floor to press on with their lovemaking. Settling on a velour, Colonial scene print sofa, each stroked the other's body. Angelina kissed his head, chest, and face.

She whispered once again in his ear, "I want you. Come away with me. I won a two-week vacation to Tahiti at a college raffle."

Fred sighed regretfully. Her offer sounded like paradise. He knew a wrong answer to her proposal could mean the end to the most intense sex he ever had. On a scale of one to ten, Myrna was a two and Angelina was a google-plex beyond infinity.

"I want to, but I can't. I have been told Myrna is pregnant. By what man I do not know."

"Did she say you are the father?"

"No, she has not told me anything about her pregnancy."

"What does it matter? Come with me."

And he did her again and again, but not yet in Tahiti.

No sooner than Angelina located her slacks and panties, she and Fred heard the sound of a garage door opening as the grinding noise filtered through walls into Fred's cellar office. Myrna was home early.

"Hurry Angelina, here are the chapters I want you to edit. You must go."

"When will I see you again, Fred?"

"Soon! Now go!"

Words Can Kill

"All right, but I want an answer by tomorrow. If you are not going to go with me to Tahiti I will find one of the horny football players at our college to be my trip partner. I'm not kidding, Fred. If you thought this afternoon was a fulfillment of your most erotic fantasy, just imagine what I can do for you on a Tahiti white sand beach."

"All right, I will work it out with Myrna. Now go!" Fred replied in a hoarse whisper.

Angelina dress like a striptease in reverse. She looked at Fred one more time before blowing him a kiss, and slipping out the basement side door. He was sure they would never meet again because of the way he fumbled her Tahiti offer. His mind raced through a flood of thoughts. I must finish with Myrna if I am ever to have a moment of happiness in my life, he reasoned. This novel is the key to any new life. I will write the second meeting between Meagan, Keith and Mike now. Myrna and her baby can wait. I need the money from this novel now!

*****

33

One More Haul

Sergeant Keith parked his car in the far corners of the library parking lot as a precaution. Everyone who looked at the dark blue Ford LTD knew it was a cop car with those little cheap moon wheel covers and antennae. As he entered the library, Keith knew people sitting at the long reading tables recognized a plain clothes cop when they saw one.

He was wearing the plain clothes uniform, cheap Sears suit, white shirt, navy tie, and brown shoes worn at the heals. When he made detective during orientation the surprise information on the handout material said, 'Detectives buy their own civilian uniforms.' The small increase in pay did little for his clothes budget. He stood out like a penguin in a pool parlor among young students in the library. After a brief knock on the meeting room door, he entered.

"Keith, good to see you again. Please close the sound room door, and have a chair." Mike said.

George W. Clever

"Have you been waiting long, Mike?" Detective Farrell asked.

"No just long enough to balance my checkbook. It cost me a bundle this morning to redecorate my office after some goons shot the hell out of my couch last night."

Mike put his check book into his hoodie pouch looking up to see Lieutenant Meagan Glade enter the library listening room. Somehow she made the clothes of a working girl into fashion model chic. He was sure Harlan Casey would find this employee irresistible.

"Good to see you again, Lieutenant."

"Can't say the same myself after you walked into the Casey office last week, Mike. You trying your best to blow my cover? Do you realize the danger you put me in?"

Lieutenant Glade took a breath, trying to get a grip on her anger. She had committed to the first meeting with Detective Farrell and his rogue P.I. friend with huge reservations. Their second meeting was primarily in her

Words Can Kill

mind, just an opportunity to ream Mike the P.I. out for his clumsy interference in her case.

She continued with a modicum of self-control, "I do however appreciate the photos you took. Sergeant Keith shared them with me."

"Sorry if my truck driving job interview at Casey's upset you. I was just stirring the Harlan Casey pot a little. It is making for an interesting stew. What's happening with my burned Charger case, Keith?"

"Well, we worked very hard to tie the two cases together, the child smuggling one, and your car fire with the dead woman.," Keith replied with a stone like grin. "Yes, everything in the undercover work Meagan has done seems to point to the Casey's Trucking firm's involvement in child smuggling.

Sergeant Farrell shuffled the photos Mike provided back into a pile and continued.

"From your trucking adventure pictures and Meagan's information, we have identified several workers at Casey

George W. Clever

Trucking involved in the child smuggling ring. Mike, please tell us what you learned about how the transport side of the Casey Trucking smuggling enterprise seems to work," Keith added. "What can you share with us?"

Mike filled them in on the child smuggling operation he uncovered. He explained how the dispatcher sends special freight halls to Mexico about every third week. The night shift dock PIC and a few of his handlers unload the truck carrying the illegals who are crammed in specially marked boxes stamped with Medical Equipment labels. Lieutenant Meagan added her findings.

"Only those boxes are opened. The people hidden in them, mostly children and young girls, are taken by yellow short bus to several warehouses in the city. Here the children are sorted out into two groups, the sweat shop slaves, and the more attractive young working girls. All the boxes these young people come in, their waste, and other survival items, are burned in an illegal furnace outside the Casey Trucking office building. The remainder of the cargo load

Words Can Kill

is moved on for local distribution to legit businesses by a new driver."

Mike pulled his chair closer to the table looking again at the ocean blue eyes of Meagan. He could not, and did not want to break their eye connection. She blinked freeing Mike to ask Keith a question about the human cargo disposition.

"Keith, do you have any idea what happens to the kids after they leave Casey Trucking?"

"Yes, our snitches tell us the young girls and a few boys are divided up by organizational pimps and moved to safe houses scattered in the city. Some are sold to operatives in other major cities like Las Vegas, Nevada. We have rescued several of the runaways and illegal street working young women who filled in the nasty details for us. They are sexually assaulted, beaten by the pimps, drugged, and forced to work the street business. Craigslist is used to make contact with the johns.

George W. Clever

Keith took a minute to think about his briefing. Was there anything he had forgotten to share? Then he remembered the run-aways.

"If the kids smuggled into the U.S. run away or try to do so, they are killed. Their remains are run through a leaf shredder as a lesson for the prostitutes who are forced to watch. Black bags of body parts are dumped in the river to feed the fishes. Fishermen have turned up some grisly floating bags caught on their lines. The boys in blue in unmarked cars are keeping an eye on the warehouses, tailing cars coming and going to and from those locations. We think we have a good idea of all the places they use as drop houses now. The biggest problem we have is knowing exactly when a haul of new illegals will take place."

Now it was Mike's turn. He had a plan for setting a trap that might bring in the big smuggling fish.

"You both should know I have been asked to make another Mexico run early Saturday morning. I am trying to decide if making that haul would be of any value. What do you

Words Can Kill

think? I can't find it in my heart to contribute more kids to their witch's brew," Mike said.

"We can't tell you to go or not to go, but we are ready to close the loop shutting down this part of the child smuggling system," Meagan replied.

"Well, Lieutenant Meagan, your task force may be in for a shock when they examine the pictures I took more carefully. The truck transport action at the border was staffed with Department of Homeland Security uniforms. The feds may throw a few road blocks in front of your Human Trafficking Taskforce."

"How did you know I was working with the HTT?"

"Come on Meagan, I can use a computer. It's all there."

Detective Farrell rocked back in his chair, twisted his tie knot, and waited for Meagan to recover from her HTT work connection bomb Mike had dropped. He realized it was his call on the decision to send his friend on a dangerous second haul to Mexico. He was sure the ole Marine could take care of himself if anything got sticky.

George W. Clever

"Make the truck haul, Mike, but for God's sake you must let us know when you are returning to the Casey Trucking dock. I want to know exactly when you make the drop. This information will be key to our plans. No screw-ups like the last time when you did not call your mom. Promise?" Sergeant Keith ordered.

"Ok. Let's hope I have a little more unobserved travel time this trip. Now if you will excuse me I have to call a woman who has runaway granddaughters. She will pay big bucks for me to find them. The P.I. business has not been cost effective of late. From my last look at my checking account balance, I need a cash transfusion. I should be back from the Mexico haul by Monday."

As Mike left the room, Meagan turned to Keith and said, *"We still do not know who the boss is in this local child distribution. Nothing seems to point to Harlan Casey, at least not what I have found in his personal backyard. Do you think we will get sandbagged by the F.B.I. on orders from their real national political bosses?"*

Words Can Kill

"I don't think we have to fight that ambush quite yet. I have a federal political connection I can trust. Maybe a call to him now will give us an upfront alert we need. Tell your handlers to keep HHT's next move very tight to their chest. When Mike returns, we will move to close this local shop down even if we are blocked from netting the federal kingpins. Turn every rock you can for help in uncovering the local boss of this child slave and prostitution ring. When we find that person, I believe we will also have a line on who torched Mike's car, and positively identify the person who killed the woman burned in his trunk."

"Ok Keith, my department will jerk the noose the moment Mike calls about his arrival time. We both better share this information with as few people on the force as possible. You know there is a lot of money in this game. Some cops are easily bought."

It was Lieutenant Meagan Glade and Mike's turn to slip out of the library listening room leaving Sergeant Keith to his own private thoughts. How could Harlan Casey not know the child smuggling ring was operating out of his trucking company? Could it be that he did know, but had bigger fish to fry in his quest for power as governor? If not Harlan, just who was running the child slavery show? It had to be someone Harlan could trust, someone who knew the dark side of the business from truck high jacking to running a string of lot lizards. That someone also had to be connected to the Feds.

Sergeant Keith took the case file from the sound room table. He realized in that moment none of the privacy checks were done before this meeting, not even a bug scan. No one even carried a book or listening earphones in to the sound room like library users would normally do.

"I must be getting sloppy in my old age." He considered. "Maybe I am also a bit paranoid after what Mike told us about the border smuggling assistance from Homeland Security operatives. There could be a big hammer out there waiting for Mike Dunmore if he makes any mistake on the haul Saturday."

*****

34

Voice from the Cellar Tells

When Angelina closed the basement door Fred could hear Myrna crossing the kitchen floor above. His heart beat against his dirty shirt when she opened the cellar door.

"Fred are you down there? I have something I must tell you. Please come up."

Fred did a quick check of his rumpled clothes for any evidence of the greatest sexual encounter of his life, and climbed the stairs to the kitchen. Maybe this would be the opportune time to confront his wife about her pregnancy.

"What is it, Myrna?"

"I think you should sit down."

Moving to the Keurig coffee maker, he made his usual cup of coffee, no sugar, no cream. Myrna stared at him impatiently with a frown for not responding to her suggestion to sit down. Finally, he placed the coffee cup on the kitchen table in front of his chair, and sat down.

"There is no easy way to do this, so I will just make it quick. I'm leaving you. I just can't continue to live in a loveless marriage. We hardly spend any time together with you always buried in writing your book. When I have a problem like the voice I hear coming from the cellar stairs you seem to mock me, and belittle every effort I make to understand what the voice is telling me."

Hearing Myrna announce she was leaving was like setting Fred free from a sweat stained, prison chain gang. Each sentence of her explanation of why she was leaving felt like another hammer stroke of freedom smashing at his leg irons. He would be free to be with Angelina, travel to Tahiti, and finish writing his book uninterrupted. He made the mistake of opening his mouth with a question.

"Are you leaving because you are pregnant?"

"How do you know I am pregnant? It has only been six weeks since I had my appointment with Doctor Branson. How did you know?" she demanded.

Words Can Kill

"I just know. You would not believe me if I told you how I learned about it."

"Was it someone in the Hearing Voices group who told you?"

"Why should they know?" Fred replied. "Who is the father, Myra? Is it someone from the HVG? I know it can't be me. You haven't let me touch you since before your mother died. Who is it! Is it someone from the group? Is it someone I know? Tell me who it is!"

Fred worked his anger up in the same manner he had seen betrayed men play it in all the TV soaps and movies. She was not going to be let off the hook easily without him inflicting some pain on her psyche. It was payback time for all the mental abuse Myrna and her mother had dumped on him over the years. He felt a smile forming in the corner of his mouth and squeezed it shut. It felt good to be angry.

"All I will tell you is the father works with me at the candy factory." Myrna murmured.

George W. Clever

"How could you do this after telling me you hated children? You told me many times no sniveling brat was coming into this house. Did you really mean you hated me so much my fathering your child would be repulsive?" Fred asked.

Once the words were out of his mouth, Fred's mind began to be overwhelmed with thoughts of her actually rejecting him as a sperm donor. She was rejecting him once more in the most hurtful way. His rejection began to be replaced by stronger feelings of revenge, a feeling taking on a life of its own. He had experienced a lifetime of being rejected and ignored. The freedom he would gain in a new life with Angelina did not seem enough. In place of being thrilled with his future dream life, a monster person of revenge and retribution took over. Fred the angry deranged man had arrived. He was a man feeling more pain from his wife's choice of sexual mating than any previous slight or ridicules his self-concept had ever endured.

Fred's anger began to feed voraciously on years of denial, mistrust, belittlement, and abuse from Myrna and

Words Can Kill

her mother. He had kept a closet full of those memories. No, it was more like an enormous pile of tinder scattered on the forest floor. Fred's anger ignited the tinder, busting his actions into a fire storm.

"Are you still hearing voices from the cellar? Do you hear voices coming from there now telling you to leave? No? Maybe we should go to the cellar door, and listen to be sure."

Fred grabbed Myrna by the arm, knocking over his kitchen chair. He dragged her toward the cellar door. She offered little resistance. Her shock from hearing Fred spew a tsunami of accusations, a verbal tide wave carrying all the flotsam and jetsam from the earliest days of their marriage, froze her in the cellar doorway. Myrna's eyes rolled their lids up behind ever enlarging eyeballs as Fred threw open the cellar door.

He shouted, "Do you hear any voice now. Do you hear what the voice is saying? It says your mother did not accidently fall down the stairs. Can you hear it? It says she was pushed like this!"

George W. Clever

Myrna felt his push as it twisted her around until she could no longer see the cellar stairs. Fred shoved her body with the strength available in times of great stress, times when a person's response to extreme threats gives them power like the Hulk. Releasing his grip on her dress, she danced down the cellar stairs with the same choreography her mother had used.

Myrna was bouncing, tumbling, floating, and slamming her body from one side of the stairs to the other as she fell toward the cellar cement floor. No one heard her screams during in her fall. Fred hear her screams stop when she became a motionless heap of twisted body parts spread in an awkward shape on the cellar floor.

He waited at the top of the stairs, empty of compassion and concern, staring at her twitching legs. Fred hoped she was dead. She wasn't. A soft moan filtered out of Myrna's smashed mouth. Her body twitched spasmodically as the moan accelerated into a twisted unending scream. Words and blood flowed through her

Words Can Kill

broken teeth as she begged for help with an ever increasing volume.

"Help me...HELP ME!"

Several moments passed as Fred stood transfixed at the top of the stairs. He thought of the choices made by Myrna and himself. Perhaps those choices were not totally theirs to own. The icon on the computer screen was to blame for the ways he solved problems with Myrna and her mother. He could call 9-11 which would certainly present the opportunity for Myrna, injured as she was, to tell them he had pushed her down the stairs. Prison for him was not an option. He could leave her, giving her time to die, and return later after building an alibi somewhere.

The police might not buy a second accidental fall down the cellar stairs as quickly as they did for her mother. No, this time he had but one choice. He would be sure she was not going to talk. It was the only way he would ever feel free to leave the house. Fred walked down the cellar stairs, stepped over Myrna's twisted body, and picked up his short gardening spade. A few practice swings preceded his well-aimed shovel hits to her head. Myrna would not be saying anything. She would just be another voice coming from the cellar stairs.

It would be a few hours before Angelina finished her afternoon college classes. That would be enough time for him to pack and buy two airline tickets to Tahiti. Fred's thoughts returned to the unfinished novel. *I might even have enough time to finish writing another chapter in my book. They say Tahiti is an artist's dream for creativity. Paul Gauguin did his best work there.*

His mind wandered to daydream about beach living with Angelina while finishing his first in a series detective stories. *I could write more of these thrillers to keep Angelina in coconuts. She could snail mail or send by webmail my great novel to an agent and publisher. We would never return to America again. Tahiti did not have an extradition treaty with the USA. Angelina and I could live free in our own tropical paradise. We will need an income.* He had to finish the novel, and now.

Fred leaned the bloody shovel against the cellar wall. Myrna's quivering body mess was blocking his way to the computer desk chair. He reached for her ankles dragging his dead wife toward the cellar door. *Should I clean up this mess and dispose of her body?* Fred considered. *No, first things first. It will take some time to clean the blood from the stairs and floor. Maybe I can wrap her up in this rug for now. They say Jimmy Hoffa's remains were dumped in cement poured for the new Jets stadium. Eastern Western Hotel is resurfacing their parking lot. She could go there.*

I will tell Angelina it would be necessary for me to work one more night shift at the hotel so I can collect my check before we leave for Tahiti. He returned to his computer. *Now, where did I leave off in my novel Child For Sale?*

*****

35

Q Bugged

"Boss, I did what you asked, planting the Q bugs yesterday in the library listening rooms A, B and C. You know those bugs are the tiny ones activated with a cell phone. As I told you I was waiting for my daughter to check out a book for her school project a few weeks ago when I saw the company secretary Meagan and that truck driver Mike Torcher go into the library. It seemed odd, so I watched from the parking lot, and saw a cop also enter the library. He was a police detective I had met before in unpleasant circumstances. I followed him inside. He went into one of those listening rooms meeting with Mike and Meagan. Well, I thought something was fishy about that. Here is the tape from their second meeting in the same room."

"Good work, Bruno. What should I know about that meeting?"

"Well, I heard they are working on something together. It sounds like they are intent on busting our kid smuggling

business. I think they will try to make their arrests when Mike finishes his second haul from Mexico."

"Ok, I want you to make Meagan disappear. Do it now when she is here working. Tomorrow morning you are to ride with Mr. Torcher. There must be a thousand places on that Mexican route where he could have a serious personal accident. Policía Federales will not be troubled enough to look for the killer of another nameless corpse found on some farm. You and I know dead bodies are commonly found in mexicana chili fields, or in deserted roadside ditchs."

Taking another cheap throw-away cell phone from the desk, the boss placed it in a pocket, turned out the office light, locked the door, and followed Bruno out into the parking lot.

"See you Saturday night, Bruno. I think the call I am going to make will solve our problem with Mr. Torcher, if that is really his name. I need to walk a few blocks before making this call. You know all our cell phone calls are being monitored by the Feds."

Words Can Kill

"Ok boss, see you Saturday night."

It was another hot day in Port Altamira with no ocean breeze, no cloud cover and no shade where Franco was working. His 'special' phone rang to add more heat to his discomfort. Calls on that cell phone were never good new.

"Hello Franco, Tenemos un problema y hay que cambiar algo, qué hacemos? (We got a problem, what can we do). Mike Torcher, the driver scheduled for Saturday, is a cop plant. I don't know local cops or feds. Ok, just do it before he reaches the border after his haul is picked up. Bruno will be riding with him. He will bring the rig back after Torcher is no longer in the picture. No shooting into the container. I need that delivery without holes. Waste the tractor if necessary, but have another tractor and driver ready to pick up the haul. Make it look like a hijack. No screw ups. My customers are not very perdonar. They will find you."

Once Franco had received his instructions it was time to be rid of any phone that might tie the boss to the

George W. Clever

Torcher solution. Dropping the cell phone in the sewer grate, it slipped into the watery abyss below. Like the satisfaction of sliding a paid bill envelope in a post office mail slot, the disappearing phone produced a crooked scar of a smile on the face of the caller.

This was just one more management issue, like many in the past, solved without getting the hands dirty. There was to be a big payoff anticipated for Monday night. This solution to the current crisis was the kind of management in politics that would make being connected to a governor's office very profitable.

*****

Computer keys clicked at an increasing intensity as the Child For Sale mystery gather speed rushing toward the story end. Writer Fred had already charted the novel ending on his story board. He was intent on finishing the book before his Tahiti rendezvous with Angelina.

The open door alert buzzed as Mike entered the pawn shop. He looked around the shop for a few moments before moving to the diamond ring display. Mike studied

Words Can Kill

the case of diamond rings sparkling from the lights in the showcase. His interest in that kind of jewelry peaked the pawn shop owner's interest. Passing off a guitar pawn customer to one of his clerks, Carmichael moved to the counter in front of Mike.

"Hey Carmichael."

"Michael how's it hanging?"

"Progress my friend progress, but I need a little assistance."

"What kind of assistance?"

"Well, I need something with a little more power. The last motor you got for me is what car guys would call "stock and a bit low on horsepower". I need something made in Israel. You know, something that oozes power."

"Oh, something with a supercharger, but it will cost you a bundle."

"Car, you know I am between gigs. How about a loan on my new Vette? I won't be using it for a while."

George W. Clever

"Sure Mike I can work that out. When do you need it?"

"How about now?"

"Sorry, Mike, I let my miracle worker go when things got slow here at Paupers Pawn. I'll have it ready tomorrow morning at the earliest, if that works for you."

"Ok, see you before noon."

Mike turning to leave, stopped before the door and returned to the diamond ring counter looking embarrassed.

"Carm, do any of these rings have a Wal-Mart return policy? I don't know a thing about size."

"Sure, Mike, I can work that out. You had better wait until you pick up your new motor, and finish that race before you think about the future. Who is the unlucky lady?"

"If I tell you, I would have to kill you. It's a national government secret you know. He winked and said, "See you tomorrow." It was no surprise to Carm, but Angel would be surprised

*****

Words Can Kill

The loading dock at Casey Trucking was quiet at four in the morning, the kind of quiet Mike remembered in the streets of Fallujah before an ambush or an I.E.D blast. He punched in his driver card at the time clock, lifted a set of keys for the assigned Peterbilt from its hook on the wall hanger, and picked up his manifest for the trip he had been assigned. The smell of coffee drifted through the building. It was being made somewhere behind a closed office door. Another time he would have followed the smell trail with his nose to the brewing location for a cup of hot, eye opening, morning joe. There was no time for that. He wanted to get his ride moving south before the regulars showed up on the dock.

Mike had one of those hinky feelings that often came to him in Iraq when his senses were telling him something was not as it should be. Back then, it was a raghead ducking into an open door, a street without kids, or the wreck of a truck parked where it should not be. Maybe a warning flash from some rooftop told him he was soon to be a target. This morning it was nothing visual as he studied the lot, but the danger sense was still there. Mike located truck 534 in the row of trucks. It was the same red Peterbilt he drove on his first haul. He carried his old Corps gym bag and a brown bag of goodies across the tarmac to stash them in the cab for his trip to Altamira. This time the brown bag was stuffed with munchies to satisfy his driving needs in case no other dining stop was in the works.

He took another quick survey of the staging lot to be sure he was not being watched. The cover on the truck's air cleaner could be pulled on his pre-drive inspection of the rig. The truck lot always had someone watching the security cameras. The air cleaner would not be his hiding place of choice this time. Mike wanted the Browning pistol and UZI to be a little bit closer. Yes, this trip they would be inside the truck cab. He opened the truck's driver door and climbed in. After stashing his lunch munchies in the refrigerator, he examined the sleeper cab for a safe place to hide the UZI submachine gun hidden under his coat. His examination of the sleeper cab did not provide a safe place to hide the Uzi automatic weapon Carmichael had given him in exchange for pawning the Corvette.

Words Can Kill

Mike couldn't locate the Vette title. Car titles were usually redeemable at Pauper's Pawn for a fee. Carm took the car on a faith pawn hoping Mike would manage to return from the haul to Mexico.

The Uzi and the Browning pistol would be of no value if Mike had to dig them out in a hurry from their hiding place. He could only hope the trip would provide a moment to place both weapons by his side before there was any need to use them. Hiding the weapons close to his driver seat would be chancy, and open to discovery by U.S. Border Patrol, the Mexican Border Mafia, or DHS guys like 'Just Jim'. There was no other choice.

The sleeper had a refrigerator with a freezer within reach of Mike as he was driving. With luck, the UZI would fit alongside the Browning in the freezer. It was not likely anyone would check there. Having fire power just behind the driver seat was comforting. Mike made no excuses for the K-Bar knife he strapped to his side hanging from his belt. This honed steel was Marine Corps issue from his latest tour. It was a gift from his dad who carried it in the

George W. Clever

Korean War, a war initially described by President Harry Truman as a 'police action', but just as hot and costly in human lives as any war. Mike thought about his word 'hot'. Maybe the 'police action' was not hot for those Jarheads who wound up at Chosin in the winter.

Marine Corps League detachment members, who lived through that battle, never complained about the cold after suffering what Chesty Puller called an advance to the rear. Mike remembered ole Chesty's famous quote. 'We've been looking for the enemy for some time now. We've finally found him. We're surrounded. That simplifies our problem of getting to these people and killing them.' Mike felt just as surrounded as the Chosin Marines when he thought about the run to Mexico. It was a different war on the streets for him not unlike his time in Fallujah, Iraq.

He fired up the honking diesel after a quick "pre-flight" around the truck, checking the trailer to exclude the possibility of leftover freight or sleeping vagrants who might be given a free ride out of country. The sun was just offering yellowy white slivers of light into its dark sky as he

Words Can Kill

climbed into the cab, and drove to the Casey compound gate. A guard stepped out of the gatehouse with a coffee cup in one hand. His other hand was resting on a holstered pistol.

"Where's you going?"

The coffee aroma was too much for Mike a second time.

"You wouldn't by any chance have an extra cup of joe in your shack would you?" he asked the guard.

"Yes sir, there is an extra cup I can give you from my thermos. Let me see your manifest for this trip."

Mike handed down the manifest papers. The guard snapped them on to his clipboard, and walked back into the guard shed.

"I see you have a non-stop run to Mexico today," the guard shouted out the shack window. "Let me see if I can find an extra Styrofoam cup around here. You can take an eye-opener with you."

The cup felt warm in Mike's hand as the guard delivered the checked manifest and the promised coffee.

George W. Clever

There was an unexpected smirk on his face when he said, "Have a nice day."

"Thanks," Mike replied, driving out of the gate.

Glancing at the truck side mirror as he passed through the gate, he saw a familiar person standing on the truck loading dock. It was a hundred yards back to the dock, but Mike was sure the person standing there was someone he had seen before. But where? And what motivated the guard's smirk after 'Have a nice day'?

Three miles away from Casey Trucking he remembered. The blue Impala by the library, it was the man sitting in the blue Impala. It was Bruno standing on the dock yelling something at the guard. Maybe the guard took his pot of coffee?

"Boss, he's gone! He left early just as I got to the loading dock."

"I told you never to call me on this phone, Bruno. This had better be important or you will be swimming with cement shoes in someone's piranha tank."

Words Can Kill

"It is, boss, Torcher came in early and took the dead haul to Altamira alone. You should also know Glade called in sick this morning."

"Find Glade Bruno. I never want to hear that name again. Do you understand? We must get that shipment in as planned. You make her disappear, and their plans will be screwed up. It may deter them long enough for our delivery. After that we will shut down for a while. Find someplace for your vacation. Do not disappoint me a second time, Bruno. I know your car is not fireproof."

"What about Torcher?"

"Make a call to Franco. He will take care of Mr. Torcher."

It would be necessary to call Franco again on one of the throwaway cell phone found in the office desk. No one was in the office so early in the day as he opened the desk drawer, and took out the flip phone. It was getting to be a costly habit.

"Franco, ¿Cómo estás hoy? (How are you today.)"

"Muy bien. (Very good.)"

"Torcher is making the run alone. I missed his departure. This is a heads up call. Be ready."

"¡Sí, yo estoy listo! (I am ready.) We will take care of Torcher."

"The boss wants that shipment. Do you understand? No slipups!"

*****

36

Port Altamira Return

The trip to Altamira, Mexico was another nine hours of routine travel run after Mike's truck cleared the World Trade Bridge in Laredo, Texas. Traffic south moved through the border check point quickly with moderate delays. He could see northbound traffic would again be another story. His computer told him over a million and a half trucks moved out of Mexico at this check point every year. Mike could expect a long delay on his return, a delay he could not afford. No problem at the border, and no sleeper inspections caused him any problem. Maybe an empty cargo container was not worth an inspection effort going into Mexico. Mike reasoned a full trailer on return could be a different story if the Border agents had not been sufficiently greased by those at the Fed level involved in the kid smuggling.

The gate guard at Altamira Harbor took the manifest Mike offered without a word, gave it a glance, and handed back though the cab window.

George W. Clever

"Second row turn right. Third row turn left. Park on the end and wait for Franco."

Mike pulled through the gate and followed the instructions given. This trip would be different from his last. He had a surprise for Franco. Maybe Franco had a surprise up his sleeve for him. Mike could not afford to be lulled into a stupor of easy travel like the day he fell asleep at the fifty on top of their Hummer as it rolled through the streets of Fallujah. He remembered that day from the hum and smell of diesel fuel filling the port loading area. He remembered the desert sun cooking his sleepless brain under his helmet, forcing his eyelids shut driving him deep into slumber city. It was a snooze costing Mike to pay a heavy price.

Not now! He reminded himself, not now, as he parked the Peterbilt on the end of the truck row. Mike considered his cover may have been blown. Franco would be the first of many hit men they would use to take him out. One way or the other, he would have to deal with Franco on the return trip. Mike reached into the small dorm room

Words Can Kill

sized refrigerator freezer and removed the ice cold UZI and frosty Browning pistol. He slipped the Browning 9mm into his belt at the back of his shirt. The UZI, he slid into the large map pocket in the driver's door. If Franco tried any funny stuff it would be on the Mexican side of the border. After he used his security pieces they would have to go back in the refrigerator before Mike crossed the border.

Fatigue again hammered his eyelids rolling them down like an electric garage door opener. His brain sent immediate signals. Danger...danger...danger messages were received by all parts of his body trying to keep him awake and alert. It seemed to be an hour wait, but in only five minutes there was a pounding on the passenger side door.

"Franco! Oup! Oup! Open up!"

Mike looked out the window. He had to be sure it was Franco. Yes, it was the same pockmarked face with unkempt beard staring back at him Mike remembered from the first run. Franco stood on the running board in his grungy, dirt caked, orange jump suit wearing a battered *yellow hard hat. Tempted to reach for the Uzi with his left hand off the wheel, Mike hit the unlock door switch instead.*

"You bring me more Church's Chicken dinner Franco?"

"No we go now! We go pronto! Turn right to end of containers. Diesel pumps on the left."

There would be no other greetings or instructions. Franco slid into the passenger seat and closed the door. Mike rubbed the sleep from his eyes and fired up the Peterbilt. His driving instructions from Franco were the same route he remembered from his first visit to the Altamira docks. Attendants at the pumps filled the truck tanks full. Mike opened the door to stretch his legs. His check of the truck tires and the engine was interrupted when he heard Franco shout.

"You stay in cab!"

A 1950s military green Jeep pulled alongside the truck cab. Four armed men dressed in black surrounded the truck. There was a sense of urgency in their moments he had not felt before.

Words Can Kill

"Follow this road to the crane."

A tall straddle carry gantry crane was waiting with a container in its sling as Mike's Peterbilt rolled its trailer under the box. The container box was secured with come-along straps and chains before Mike was given the order by Franco to move out.

"Drive left four lanes now. Fill diesel now."

The truck tanks were filled up in a manner similar to a NASCAR pit stop with the truck engine running.

"Now turn right dos row then left. Pull into el numero tres warehouse."

Mike drove away from the straddle gantry crane as instructed driving to the front of the third warehouse. The Jeep filled with men in ninja garb followed close behind.

"Torcher, stay in the cab."

Franco left the passenger door open as he climbed out and walked to the rear of the container. The armed men followed him setting a perimeter around the truck cargo box. Mike could hear the container doors open and sensed some of the cargo was being unloaded. A few minutes later he heard forklifts moving new cargo boxes into the container. From the side rear view truck-mirror, he could see similar boxes with large printed labels which read in English, Medical Equipment: Caution Do Not Expose to Radiation. Mike pressed his back against the seat feeling the cold steel of his automatic pistol. It gave him some assurance anything Franco threw his way could be handled.

The trailer container's doors closed and Franco returned to his perch on the truck's passenger seat.

"Out the Gate now same roads you came just as before."

Mike needed to find out where this cargo was going. He hoped it was to be a direct hall to the Casey Trucking Warehouse.

"Where to Franco?"

"Just drive. I will tell you when you need to know."

Words Can Kill

Franco placed the clipboard manifest on the center console, and adjusted the GPS. The dock security guard opened the gate without checking the manifest as he waved the red Peterbilt on. Mike hope this would be the last time he would be seeing the Altamira Harbor in a Casey truck.

Glancing at the GPS on the truck dash, Mike could see his route north to the border was changed from his dead haul in. After a short travel on several different four lane roads, he was instructed to turn off on to a two lane blue highway. The eighteen wheeler found its comfortable mechanical groove as it rumbled through remote rural areas always heading north toward the border. He could not be sure if they were headed to the crossing at the World Trade Bridge.

Miles of gray highway asphalt seldom showed any side line white road markers. Deep ditches rolled away from the edge of the roads and in places took part of the road berm with them. An occasional street light flashed like strobe lights into the interior of the red truck's cab. Blue incandescent lighting from a few adobe house windows gave a cold cast to the landscape on an otherwise warm evening. These same lights from scattered farm homes pierced the night like lighthouse beacons reminding Mike of the desert dangers he had left in Iraq.

A quick check in his rear view side mirror told Mike they were not traveling alone on this deserted highway. Two sets of car headlights trailed the truck at a distance. He always considered the best defense was a good offense. The phrase was a truism Mike learned first on the football field, and later in battle. Now was time to lighten the load in the Peterbilt cab.

He flipped the high beams and fog lights on high, scanning the road edge for a large enough area to pull the rig to a stop. It had to be a place where he could unload the unwanted cargo sitting in the passenger seat without rolling the truck and trailer into a ditch. This would be no easy maneuver as his truck was traveling in excess of 60 mph. Mike had to put some distance between his rig and the cars following. Franco repeatedly moved his head closer to the steering wheel to read the speedometer. A simple plan

Words Can Kill

was rolling through Mike's mind as he stomped the gas pedal. The Peterbilt truck responded in a roar of increasing speed. He had plan A at least.

First: Stick the Browning 9mm into Franco's face while driving into a roadside pull off.

Second: Get Franco to put his cell phone and any weapons on the truck dash board and console.

And Third: Release the door lock button on the driver door to Kick Franko out of the cab, willing or not.

Now that is what Angel calls multi-tasking at trucking moving down the road at speed. There it was, a wide turn around big enough to bring ten tons of truck to a stop. His truck could still do a quick exit before the unknown travelers in the cars following arrived on scene. Out of the corner of his eye he could see Franco watching the car lights following the Peterbilt. Mike lifted his left hand off the wheel, reached behind his back to draw out the Browning pistol. He pulled hard on the wheel, and hit the brakes as the truck and cargo container slammed into the dirt surface of the turn-around.

George W. Clever

"Don't move a muscle," Mike yelled at Franco.

The rough surface sent the two of them bouncing off the seat held only in place by their seatbelts. Finally, the truck stopped as a cloud of tan dirt lifted off the ground and surrounded the headlight beams.

"Now Franco, very slowly place any weapon you are carrying on the dash board. Slide them over to me. If you expect all parts of you to exit this truck cab be very careful. Do what I tell you quickly."

With some hesitation, Franco reached into his jacket pocket and removed a knife and a revolver. Gathering them both in one hand, he slid them across the dash to Mike.

"Now Franco I want your cell phones, every one."

Franco stared at Mike waiting for an opportunity to take change and kill him. He pulled two cell phones out of his deep pants pockets, and slid them clattering into his revolver.

Words Can Kill

"I should shoot you now Franco as you would certainly have killed me, but your amigos are not far behind so I am in a bit of a hurry. Out of the truck and run into the night until I cannot see you or I will kill you. Believe me when I tell you I can make that shot."

Franco's face was a mixture of blood drained fear and killer anger as he pulled open the passenger side truck door. He stepped down from the cab, and fled into the shadows. As soon as he was out of sight, Mike rammed the truck in gear, and mashed the gas pedal as the truck threw dirt in all directions before it reached the blacktop highway.

Mike could see the car lights behind him pulling off the highway at the turn-around. Apparently, they had to see what happened to Franco, or at least receive some instruction from him or someone else. Their detour delay saved Mike's bacon. It would not take them long to pick up Franco, and resume the chase. The red Peterbilt was fast, but there was the question of how fast Mike could drive if there were children in the boxes stacked in the trailer.

George W. Clever

There was no way his Peterbilt would be able to safely outrun the cars. It was just a matter of time before they would initiate an adjusted round two of their attack. It might make a difference if he could make it to a more traveled four-lane highway. Maybe this GPS system would respond to voice command, he thought.

"Find a faster route to I-35."

"Finding a faster route to I-35." The voice responded.

The GPS responding voice sounded English. Mike made a mental note if he got out of this jam his GPS computer voice would be called Bridget. He made a left turn at the next intersection as "Bridget" directed, and jammed his foot hard against the gas pedal. He could still see the intersection in his mirrors when two sets of car lights appeared at the corner. Well it didn't take long to find Franco and pick him up, he thought.

Mike knew it would be just a few miles before he would have to deal with the two hostile vehicles following him. Blue and red lights were flashing from the cars behind. He could see the two cars were SUV black ops

Words Can Kill

vehicles. His truck speedo read 90 when the flashing lights of the first car pulled alongside his cab. The car passed him and slowed in front of the truck. The second car followed behind the trailer at a respectable, albeit short distance. Any attempt Mike made to pass the front car was met with it moving into the second lane and slowing again. Now the second car was alongside with its strobe light and color bar flashing.

An amplified voice shouted, "Pull over now or we will shoot."

Having delivered their message, the second car returned to its position behind Mike's trailer. He had a sense they would not shoot in fear the cargo of kids he was pulling would be damaged. Eventually, they would shoot the tires or him if he kept the truck running hoping his cargo would be recoverable from a crash. The best defensive plan Mike knew was an offensive one they would not expect. Reaching for a cigar and a lighter in his shirt pocket, he bit off the end and lighted it while steering with his knees. Drawing several puffs of smoke, he looked for and found a wide spot at the side of the road, pulled to the side, jamming on the airbrakes. His red Peterbilt truck came to a sliding stop half on and off the asphalt road.

The lead car locked up its brakes in front of the Peterbilt. A rainbow of flashing lights and Mike's truck high beams headlights illuminated the distance between the front car and his cab. Four men boiled out of the vehicle with AK-47s on the ready. The second vehicle stopped several car lengths behind the truck's cargo container. From his side mirrors he could see no one exited that vehicle. Its spotlight and racing lights made it difficult for Mike to use his truck side mirrors, and to survey the rear scene. Police light bars bathed the trailer in red and blue lights. Now he was sure the bad guys in the second car would not fire on the cargo container.

Mike was no longer in Mexico. He was back on the dirty streets in Fallujah. His headaches had returned. The Mexican road and countryside waved like a desert mirage as flaming 50 cal. tracers arched across the river as the Wolf Pack hit targets with MIAI tanks and Bradley

Words Can Kill

Fighting Vehicles spraying the enemy with 25mm and 105 mm cannons. He was spread eagle on his stomach peering between sandbags from a sandbagged, flat rooftop on the Euphrates river bank. He could hear mortar rounds zipping overhead. He hears the Major shouting on the radio, "Mike, Mike! Wake up! Find the mortar bad guys and take them out."

His spotting scope framed six insurgents manning a 120 mm. mortar at about 900 yards. Two black shirts stood up. Mike fires two quick rounds. They both fold and fall down. Four more ragheads ran away from the mortar weapon. I need to climb down from this roof and catch up with my team. My task force crew in a LAV-L are receiving small arms and automatic weapons fire from a house on their left.

"Got to take out that house. I see the guy with the RPG running. I'll get the sonabitch! Clear the house!" Mike shouted, as his Peterbilt rig roared toward the flashing lights of the Mexican Police car.

George W. Clever

"Ok, Ok, I see my team entering the building. A blast? NO! NO! NO!"

Wait! I'm not there! This is no time for thought stroking old ghosts. Got to remember what VA Counselor Tanya said. 'One good outcome!' I can save the children. I can do this! This is not Fallujah! Breathe damn it breathe! The only time he had was reaction time, time based on years of Marine training.

Mike hit the button for the driver side window, lifted the UZI from the map holder door pocket, he held it outside the window with the short barrel resting on the truck mirror. Mike sprayed a full clip in the direction of the front vehicle, jammed the gearbox into reverse and drove the trailer's Jane Mansfield bar and dock bumper guards into the front end and radiator of the rear car. The force of the crash eliminated most of the SUV's front end. It would not be going anywhere without an AAA tow.

He kept his finger frozen on the trigger until the full clip was emptied. He slammed a second clip in to the UZI when the first was emptied. Again in full auto fire, he sent

Words Can Kill

rounds into the car at his front. Dropping the UZI back into the driver door pocket, he shifted into low with the air actuated gears. Gripped the shift knob's two switches, he accelerated through gears Lo-to 4. Listening to the revs of the truck motor before each shift, Mike kept his eyes on the bullet riddled car in front of his truck. He toggled between low to high gear settings as the truck speed increased. Several AK rounds were fired by the black ops guys hiding behind their bullet riddled car. The rounds hit the truck cab walking a spider line of concentric holes across the truck windshield toward Mike.

He slammed down the gas pedal hard, all the way to the metal truck cab floor. The big diesel engine roared alive. Smoke belched out of both stacks above the cab. The big cowcatcher guard at the front of the Peterbilt truck smashed into the rear left quarter of the black car as its occupants scrambled for the ditch. With a grinding noise, the driver side rear quarter panel lifted high into the air as the SUV rolled on its side off the road. Gasoline poured along the path of the twisting wreck as it rolled into the deep, water filled ditch. Mike shifted gears again flipping the high/low switch up into high. He continued to accelerate through the upper highway drive gears as the truck pulled back on the highway.

A pool of gas formed a trail from the road shoulder making a small lake behind the wrecked SUV. Hitting the passenger side window switch with his elbow, Mike took a puff on the lighted cigar pitching it out the window like one of the darts he often threw in Kelly's Bar. It was a perfect hit. The gasoline exploded just as the cargo container trailer passed.

He could see the flaming scene lighting up the sky reflecting in his rearview mirrors. The semi- tractor trailer was a country block from the burning wreckage when Mike heard the zip and rattle of rounds ricocheting off his truck as frustrated shooters fired into the night. He was once again on automatic pilot headed for the border.

A third set of lights could be seen in the tractor mirrors far back at the blaze. Its flashing yellow lights told the story. A replacement tractor had arrived expecting to pick up the high jacked cargo. The tractor stayed at the

Words Can Kill

carnage, and did not pursue. Mike wondered how long it would be before the survivors he left behind would be calling ahead for someone else to have a shot at killing him. It seemed a good bet they would not try anything at the border crossing now only a few miles ahead. These guys don't take on much self- initiative, Mike thought. It was not likely they would alert their comrades in the Mexican Border Patrol. They would call, but it would be to the boss at Casey Trucking who would solve the problem of Mike Torcher. He knew his next hurtle would be after crossing the border with the stop to pick up the Homeland Security driver.

It was Mike's guess the Casey boss would not want to alert the Federal arm of their smuggling system to the problem he created. They would not want feds to find out about the Casey Trucking local screw up. Mike knew he must get the D.H.S. driver onboard and away from the border. Slipping a new clip back in the UZI was not an easy trick while steering and shifting the Peterbilt.

George W. Clever

It was time to put his equalizers back in the cooler before the border checks. A quick phone call brought a windshield repair service to his truck at a truck stop before the border. With luck, the Border Patrol, on both sides would not find any other bullet holes in the ole Peterbilt. If they did find a few holes, he would complain about being required to drive trucks from Chicago's Northeast rust belt where salt on the road made rust looking bullet holes and gangbangers did the rest.

Lights were reflected in the cloudless night sky from the distant border crossing check point. Heavy truck traffic picked up as Mike slid his rig in line with a string of others heading north. It was Mexican Border check time. Bright lights flooded the inspection gates making the landscape view resemble a piece of ground the daylight sun had left behind. The lines were reasonably short at the World Trade Bridge. Six lanes of trucks exited the inspection booths like eager horses at the Belmont Stakes race track. Mike realized his luck was running thin when the Mexican Border Guard took his manifest.

Words Can Kill

"Buenos noches." He said. "I see you have not entered your log since leaving Altamira. I am sure you do not want me to hold you here, nor have the Americans do so. Please attend to this before you pick up the D.H.S. driver on the other side."

Personnel outreach of the kid smuggling system never ceased to amaze Mike with its network of contributors. Here was one more official on the take as he guarded the border.

Mike responded, "Gracias Amigo."

Lifting a pencil from the glove box, he filled in the required numbers, handing the log book back to the border guard through the open cab window. Without even a glance at the log additions, the guard shoved the book back through the window into Mike's open hand.

"Ponerse en marcha! Move on!"

The American Border check was a wave through with a signal to stop at the D.H.S. pull through. Several trucks were waiting in diagonal parking under bright

George W. Clever

Sulphur yellow lights. As luck would have it ole silent Jim showed up at the driver side door. No friendly hello, just his order.

"Slide over Torcher."

"Hey 'Only Jim'. How the hell are you? Long time no see."

"Shut up motor mouth. I am not your lost friend. Just sit quietly, and we will have a short ride to a place you know well. I have been told to be sure you get there. Seems the big boss wants to have a chat with you."

"Ok Jim let's roll."

With diesel smell rolling through the windows from the border crossing congestion, Mike found the excuse he was seeking for a visit to the tiny cooler.

"Hey Jim. You want a cold coke? I'm nearly choking with dry throat sitting at the border crossing with all those diesel fumes."

"No coke."

"You don't mind if I get one do you?"

Words Can Kill

"No. Make it quick."

Mike climbed into the sleeper, opened the refrigerator, and lifted the cold Browning pistol into his right hand. With his left hand he pulled the curtain away from the D.H.S. driver pressing the barrel of the 9 mm to 'Just Jim's' temple.

"Nothing fancy now Jim. Yes, sir, this is not the cold end of a coke. It is Mr. Frig Browning you feel. Keep both hands on the wheel. We will find a nice spot along the side of this interstate wide enough for you to pull this rig off safely. I have a little change of plan for you."

A service area for the interstate road repair crew appeared in the truck high beams. Tucked behind a mound three stories high asphalt material was a road grader and grass cutting tractor. This would be a perfect place for Just Jim to spend some time.

"Pull in there behind that pile."

The Peterbilt ground to stop lifting a dusty gray cloud to billow over the rig. Mike reached over and flipped the gear shifter into park. He slid out of the sleeper into the passenger seat making certain Just Jim could see the pistol he was holding.

"Ahh...that's fine. Now very slowly take any weapon you have out of your nice hiding places, and put them on the dash board. Thank you Jim. Oh yes, put your cell phone and the radio on your belt there also. You and I will be going for a short walk. Get out. Oh yes Jim I have seen the movie where the guy slammed the truck door on another guy who had the pistol. I think you should leave that move to the movies. I will shoot you if you try."

Mike reached for his athletic bag in the sleeper and climbed down from the cab with Jim. The Peterbilt truck lights illuminated an area behind the asphalt spoil pile. Mike shoved the barrel of his pistol into the back of the D.H.S. driver pushing him onward the well-lighted area in front of the cab.

"Oh this is so much better now that I can see you Jim. It is sort of like an Improv Comedy stage for us," Mike said as he grabbed Jim's arm with enough force to lift him off the

Words Can Kill

ground. *"I think you will find the things I ask you to do here are really very funny."*

The force from Mike's six foot four frame reminded 'Just Jim' he had better pay attention, and do what he was being told.

"Now strip. I want your cap, jacket, and shirt. Put them in a pile on the deck."

Jim removed his clothes as directed and turned to face Mike.

"What are you going to do now, kill me? That would be a big mistake you know. Kill a Federal officer and you will always be a hunted man."

"No, I'm not going to kill you, Jim. I just want to keep you in this garden spot for a few hours. Now kneel, and put your arms behind your back."

Mike stuck his pistol behind his belt buckle, opened a lock back knife, and took a roll of Duct Tape and a set of handcuffs from his bag.

"Ok Jim, on the ground with your arms behind your back."

George W. Clever

After snapping the cuffs on Jim's wrists, Mike pushed Jim to one side, taped his ankles together, and checked around the nearly naked D.H.S. guard's body to be sure he was not hiding any radio or weapon.

"Now I know Jim you will want to enjoy the quiet of this night in your road maintenance garden. A little tape across your mouth will help you avoid any urge to yell and spoil the quiet."

Jim twisted his body, swinging his face side to side in a silent plea. His eyes reflected his fear of being left to die behind the spoil pile unable too free himself or call for help.

"Oh no, Just Jim, I will not leave you here to die. See this lock back knife? It is my gift to you. Yes, a gift, but one that must be earned. I will leave it stuck in the ground before I get back into the cab. I am sure the D.H.S. training you received will provide you with a way to reach the knife, and free yourself."

Mike, a man of his word, stuck the blade in the ground twenty feet from the truck cab before dressing in the

Words Can Kill

D.H.S. uniform. It was a bit snug, but it would help him pass as a regular D.H.S. driver when he stopped at the transfer compound using ole Jim's I.D. It was a risky stop, but he had to be sure his cargo was something other than the Medical Equipment stamped on every box.

Climbing the steps back into the cab, he took one more look at "Just Jim" squirming on the ground awash in the truck headlights. Unless there was a glitch in his plan it should be several hours before ole Jim freed himself with the knife he left, and walk in his underwear to the D.H.S. compound for help. With luck, there would be only a short stop at Homeland Security's illegal smuggling camp to check his cargo before moving on to the Casey Trucking docks. It was time for a call to Sergeant Keith.

*****

37

Nearly Missed Again

It was not a call Franco wanted to make. He searched through the wreckage of the two SUVs until he found a working cell phone, and dialed a forbidden number with his trembling fingers.

"Buena's noche Me puede comunicar con boss? Diga English. It is Franco. Torcher has escaped with the cargo. Two cars destroyed and burning. Several compadres soldados killed. Can he be stopped at the Mexican border? No...No es possible."

"You have failed me, Franco. I warned you of the consequences of this screw up."

Franco's face turned as white as the sheets being placed over the bodies in the ditch by the EMT clean-up crew. He heard the click on the other end of the phone call.

"Ni modo," he said under his breath.

George W. Clever

He realized it was time to find another line of business, maybe on one of those ships in the Altamira Harbor, and pronto.

Another cell phone joined the myth of alligators in the city sewers as the disturbing news from Franco was processed. Two calls to this emergency number were two too many. There was no time to spare now. Mike Torcher, or whatever his name really was, would be making no calls from his cab, and no calls from fifty feet around it thanks to the technical protection made to every truck used in the smuggling operation. Any call he made would go directly to the cell phone the boss carried providing for just such a problem.

The money a driver alone could make with the smuggled cargo was a great temptation. A driver might decide to go rogue for his own profit, or trade the container guests for a new witness protection identity provided by the police. The bug provided by Bruno was enough to learn when the police would raid Casey Trucking. The cops would receive a call setting the time of the raid to match

Words Can Kill

Mr. Torcher's return to the Casey loading dock. With Ms. Glade out of the picture, thanks to Bruno, and no call from Torcher, it just might be possible to receive and process the load without the arrival of cops. But how?

Looking in the mirror by the desk, forehead lines of a frown or stressful thought appeared. The lines were becoming more permanent of late. That would have to change. Thankfully in a short moment a smile erased the frown lines as a plan for dealing with the rogue driver was formed. Ok Mr. Torcher, we will see you at the Casey dock. You will meet with a very sad conclusion to your last haul. There will be no reunion with your police friends. After we drag you out of the cab, one of our drivers will move the truck and its load to our child training center warehouse on Second Street. It is a safe place where our illegal children study ways to become good slaves or prostitutes. We can unload right inside the building, and move other cargo by bus from there. One more call and we will be ready for Mr. Torcher.

George W. Clever

"Carlo, there is a change of plans for the shipment tonight. When Torcher arrives I want your boys to meet him with enough firepower to help him out of the truck cab. Have one of your drivers immediately drive the rig over to the 235 warehouse off the I-35 just past General Dodson Street. Park it inside for unloading out of sight. Mr. Torcher should join our re-cycling program for a nice trip to the cardboard shredder. This will be the last haul for a while. You and all the boys are to take a long vacation. Tell them I will let them know when we have a Grand Opening for the new business. Got it! Do you understand if you fail we all will be on a State paid vacation?"

"Si, boss. It will be done."

*****

Sergeant Keith did not answer Mike's call. Neither did he get a connection with Lieutenant Meagan, Angel, or his mother in Temple, Texas. He tried a text message. His phone screen read 'searching' with no connection. Using any cell phone, it was necessary to consider the possibility of driving into a dead zone, a place where satellite radio

Words Can Kill

and cell phones do not work. He would try again in a few minutes. It was imperative for him to get an arrival time to either Keith or Meagan. Mike felt his irritation with the call was building into a crippling anxiety bringing on the PTSD jitters.

Panic built to overflow as he thought about the reception he could expect when entering the transfer D.H.S. Compound. Even if he got by the transfer station a hot reception would be expected later at the Casey Trucking loading dock. What difference did it make who received his delivery of the poor souls in the cargo container? If he turned them over to the police they would pass them on to U.S. Immigration, who would turn them over to D.H.S. These fine folk would pass them on to the same people who were paying Casey Trucking for delivery. This was one load in a system bringing tens of thousands of children into the country from Mexico and Central America.

As the miles on the interstate clicked off before the turn to the desert processing center, Mike continued to *examine his options. If the truck trailer he was hauling was indeed filled with medical equipment as stamped on the boxes, and not children the police raid expected, it would be a great embarrassment. With action like that he could lose his P.I. license, and expect a hefty lawsuit from Harlan Casey. Mike could feel a blanket of depression covering every thought he could muster.*

It was then he remembered the time he had spent with counselor Tanya after being up on a reprimand by his police precinct commander for excessive violence with a perp. Tanya was a lifesaver counselor at the VA who helped him avoid a riptide of destruction in his life from PTSD. Mike did not volunteer to meet with the VA counselor. He was required to do so on a referral from the precinct supervisor. No Marine was going to spill his war guts to some VA counselor, especially if the counselor turned out to be a woman. He would do the appointment, and keep his mouth shut. There was nothing wrong with him. Yes, this was his plan until he met Tanya.

Words Can Kill

"Semper Fi Marine. Welcome to my house," she greeted him at her office door.

Counselor Tanya was also a retired Marine who in a few words let him know she was in-charge of his visit. They discussed their time in the Corps, and got down to the business of dealing with their mission together. The mission ahead would put Mike in control of his PTSD. The first session was over too quickly for Mike. Perhaps it was because Tanya was a no nonsense, mature woman, and so very easy on the eyes. She certainly did not fit his expectations of some bureaucrat screwing up the VA's delivery of care to veterans.

As the Peterbilt cab rumbled through the night, Mike knew he must focus on the lessons learned from Tanya, or his sanity would revert to anger and disinterest in how this kid smuggling haul might turn out. During his first counseling session with Tanya, she asked if there was a bottle in his pocket. Yes, whiskey made all the nightmares go away, and a certain detachment from life threats in police work. She helped him see his emotional numbness, a

George W. Clever

numbness his secretary Angel found distressing when he would not, or could not commit to a serious relationship with her.

His Marine transition from the Corps to the Cops was supposed to be easy. It was not. A certain smell or a sound would trigger a flash back at the wrong time during a routine traffic stop or 911 call. What sleep he got at night was possible only with a home defense twelve-gauge shotgun securely resting across his chest. Tanya changed all that destructive behavior, but not before he was cashiered from the police force for diving under a precinct desk when a jug of cooler water was accidently dropped.

Another time, he got into a yelling argument with his precinct captain over a coffee shop he had almost destroyed with his patrol car while chasing a robbery suspect. Now he had to remember what she taught him to do when unwanted behaviors are triggered, behaviors like he experienced when Franco and friends tried to kill him in Mexico. He could not release his finger from the UZI trigger in that fight until the clip was empty. Now free from

Words Can Kill

Mexico, his heart rate was running away like a freight train with no engineer.

Tanya often said, 'Mike you must breathe deeply. Focus on one good outcome from the danger you are facing at that moment.' Her suggestion was similar to a book he had once read titled 'Inner Skiing'. The idea proposed was to always in-vision a successful ski turn and path down the mountain without falling. After reading the book, Mike would run a picture through his mind before and during every mission in Iraq.

He repeated Doctor Tanya's words as his mind dealt with the trucking haul.

He said to himself, "Mike, you are the only one who can save the children in the trailer You can do it."

Tanya's words came to him like she was sitting in the passenger seat doing a moment to moment commentary as the truck rolled the last few miles to the interstate exit. 'Mike focus and breathe deeply' she would say.

George W. Clever

Yes, Tanya had helped him avoid military movies and TV adventure stories motivating his nightmares. She had him describe in detail why he felt guilty all the time when any one of a number of events from Iraq showed up on his memory screen. It was better now, he was better now, but PTSD never really goes away.

Well, when you get right down to it, every decision is either pre-determined or a crapshoot, Mike considered. If it is pre-determined, the cargo of children he was hauling was just part of a larger plan of which Mike had no control to alter. If on the other hand decisions in life are a choice, it would be up to him to see the people in this cargo received good results from his involvement. But what was the best plan now? A good Ops Marine always knows once the battle commits all previous plans go in the crapper. Jarheads have to be flexible, open to a plan B change, and invent plan C if necessary.

If he could not get a message to Sergeant Keith, then his return travel should be put on hold. He needed to know what was in his trailer. Mike downshifted and pulled

Words Can Kill

off on the highway exit headed to the transfer compound. Now if I can only remember all the twists and turns Ole Jim made when we were here on the first haul, he mused.

*****

38

In the Heart of the D.H.S. Beast

It is a much easier process to remember directions from a past trip to the compound as a driver, but more difficult as a passenger. As a passenger on the first trip, Mike was sure all dirt back roads in the maze surrounding the compound were under surveillance. One wrong turn and his cover would be blown. One mistake in his memory would bring on a posse of heavily armed black ops Hummers to intercept his lost truck.

Reflected light in the night sky once again re-enforced his direction choices of road turns. The guard at the compound gate waved him in to avoid being covered with the cloud of sand and dust billowing from Mike's rig. So far so good. Looks like they did not get any alert from D.H.S driver since I left him behind the asphalt pile, he thought. They probably received no alarm from Franco or I would have been met with an armed 'welcome home' committee, Mike concluded.

George W. Clever

Two uniforms stood near the loading platform to the left of the bunker. They were waving what looked like lights used by ground crew directing aircraft to their gates. Mike followed their direction and keyed up behind two other eighteen wheelers that arrived shortly before his entrance. One, two, three trucks in a convoy. With luck, my rig will be waved on to its delivery route after a short stop. He deduced.

He parked behind the other two trucks rolling down his driver side window as one of the D.H.S. uniforms approached.

"Manifest."

Mike handed it through the open window.

"Where's your other driver?"

The uniform flashed his light into the red cab.

"He got sick at the border. Brought this one in alone. The boss said I should change out of this uniform and take it on to the next stop." Mike replied.

Words Can Kill

"Let me see your I.D."

His request raised a flag in Mike's mind. Was security at the compound tipped off? Relax, got to be focused, he reminded himself.

"Ok. Line up along the loading dock. Don't leave your cab. You are not going to be here long."

"What's the rush? I was looking for some down time for a meal."

"Don't know. We got some kind of order to clear the compound tonight."

The security guard waved him forward as two other trucks joined the line. Mike stayed in the cab turning the cab headlight off so he could see what was happening on the loading platform. He watched and waited. It was business as usual with forklifts moving cartons from the back of trailers as buses lined up behind the building. Empty cartons piled up around the dumpster. One by one the trucks in front of the red Peterbilt moved off to park in the lot near the main building. Mike expected to be waved on his way when one of the uniforms inspecting the trucks approached with a clipboard in hand. As he stepped up on the first stair of the cab. Mike opened the driver side window.

"What's up? Time for me to roll?"

"No, not yet. Step out of the truck."

That sentence did not sound like a request. It didn't sound routine to Mike either. He opened the door and gave his back a little reassuring pat to be sure his pistol was still there.

"Ok. Now what?"

The uniform walked toward the back of the truck and waved Mike to follow him.

"We're short one box. Some kind of screw-up when they ship a box with no holes."

"Something wrong with the cargo in the box then?"

"Better you don't ask those kind of questions," the guard said. "Someone will think you're a cop." He laughed. "It

Words Can Kill

will only take a minute and you can be on your way. I need you here to verify the load change before we seal it."

Mike watched as the seal was broken and the trailer door opened. A forklift came and lifted the first carton at the back near the door onto the ground before moving it behind the unloading building. He could see the carton they removed had no set of holes around the top. Mike was sure he heard a moaning sound coming from the carton as it was jostled and dropped twice during the load. Those sounds were enough for him to know his load to the Casey Trucking Company was probably filled with illegal human cargo.

"Ok driver, sign here. You had better get out of that uniform if you expect to clear the gate when you leave. You do have other clothes in the sleeper?"

"Oh yes, I came prepared. You know the 'Boy Scout Motto, always be prepared'," Mike said with a smile climbing back into his cab.

The guards with fairy light wands became more irritated the longer it took for Mike to shed the D.H.S.

uniform and fire up the Peterbilt. They were waving their flashlights, and shouting what he discerned to be a string of swear words as the big red truck moved toward the gate.

The gate guard house was empty as he rolled past. The dirt road outside the gate was not. Mike's truck headlights picked up a lone figure in white, government issue, whitey tighties shorts, hobbling toward the compound. It was 'Just Jim'.

"Looks like ole Jim was a faster escape artist than I expected," Mike said to himself. "Only a few minutes for me to make the interstate highway before he sets off an alarm at the compound."

Once he had successfully driven in to the transfer station it was a piece of cake to find the roads leading out. Pulling on to the Interstate, Mike began to form a plan that would get him to Casey Trucking without being intercepted by some unwitting police the D.H.S. would dupe into stopping him.

"No cell phone connection again," Mike mumbled. "I wonder if there is some kind of hidden technology blocking

Words Can Kill

calls from inside this truck? If that is so, Keith and Meagan will never know when I will be arriving with this haul. Oh well, there is always plan B or C."

Plan C was for S.N.A.F.U. When everything hits the fan Marines go in with guns blazing making a lot of noise. With enough noise the local law enforcement might run to the sound of battle. Ten more miles and Mike's Altamira Express would be on arrival at the Casey Trucking gate. The best military plan always involved offense moving forward at speed. Mike knew any stop he made now would only give the bad guys waiting at Casey Trucking and the D.H.S. creeps more time to plan a reversal of their setbacks. He must keep moving.

On both of his Altamira, Mexico hauls there was little time to think about the fate unfolding for the children in the cargo containers, and the illegal adults who may be an even greater threat to America than Osama Bin Laden. His first run had been closely monitored all the way to and from the Mexican dock with little opportunity to change course delivering the hidden contents to U.S. Immigration.

George W. Clever

This haul was different from the moment he took on the smuggling system based at Casey Trucking. Safety of the children in those boxes was most certainly more important than finding out who torched his car. The absence of bullet holes in his red truck box provided Mike some confidence there were people in the crates back in the cargo container. He could only hope they were not harmed by those who tried to kill him at the road block.

It was seriously troublesome when he met Homeland Security Jim in a D.H.S. uniform at the U.S. border, the same 'Just Jim' who drove him to the smuggling compound in the Texas desert. Just how far was the federal government involved in illegal smuggling of children and adults? He had solved the problem at the compound. Now, Mike had to bring in his last haul for Casey Trucking to a happy conclusion for all the human cargo boxed in the back.

As his rig rolled the miles north, a file of questions flooded his thinking. What happened to the thousands of illegal children bussed into the U.S. as reported by the

Words Can Kill

news propaganda media? Maybe a few were delivered to their illegal parents in the U.S.A., but what happened to the others in camps across the Mexican/US border? Were the children dropped off in a variety of U.S. cities to fend for themselves. Maybe they were ultimately delivered to sweat shops as slaves, or to pimps for prostitution? The media and government were very quiet on disposition of these children.

Some of the kids were as young as three years old. He could drive the rig up to the front door of INS, and turn his baby cargo over to their authority. What if there were no hidden people in the packing crates on this load? Worse yet, if those children and adults were handed over only to INS would they be herded on to yellow short busses to be delivered to slave markets or terrorist cells? He had to have a better plan. This was not a time for PTSD numbness. There were choices and decisions to be made the last few miles into Temple, Texas.

A soft rain began to fall into thousands of street light reflecting puddles as the Peterbilt splashed its way

George W. Clever

along I-35 and onto exit ramp 299. Highway overhead lights pierced the cab with an illusion of a never ending day of sunlight for the people of Temple, Texas. Three A.M. was a time when most residents were drawing whatever rest they could from the last hours of deep sleep. The truck windshield wipers beat a slow sweep in the light rain as Mike turned on to Dodgen Avenue, merged on to the 363 loop, and turned again at the Wendland Road intersection into the Temple Industrial Park. The gates in front of the Casey Trucking Company were open. No guard was in sight. Alarm bells rang in his head as he pulled the rig through the gates.

Where was the guard? There was always a guard on duty in the shack unless the gate was locked. Heavier rain passed in front of the floodlights turning the asphalt parking lot into a black sea. Mike made a wide circular sweep in front of two semi-trucks that were backed into the dock. Like bookends, there was an eighteen wheeler at each end of the warehouse dock. The two trucks were not stationed at the ends of the dock by accident. Mike realized they were placed there to usher the next truck into the

Words Can Kill

middle of the dock. The next truck the PI boss knew would be Mike's.

It was a perfect ambush set up. None of the trucks were being loaded or unloaded. Several other Casey semis were parked some distance from the platform at the far end of the yard. It seemed odd to him none of the night shift personnel were anywhere to be seen as he backed the cargo container trailer into the middle position parallel with the unlighted trucks. Rolling the driver side window down, he could hear only the sound of his own truck. Another alarm went off in his head. Seldom are trucks at the dock shut down. It was a trap. He had driven right into an ambush.

His mind began to dislocate. He was again in his last battle on the streets of Fallujah, Al Anbar, Iraq. An ambush was set. What were we trained to do after being ambushed? His brain received the question and began its instant recall of Corps training. Rush toward the sound of guns, maneuver, and exploit the terrain looking for the high ground. How can I surprise the enemy doing the

George W. Clever

unexpected? He wondered. Oh, yes, act fast and get the hell out of there if at all possible. Was there a plan C?

*****

39

Ambush at the Dock

A single person appeared out of the shadows on the dock platform and motioned for Mike to back the truck to a station between the end trucks for unloading. The PIC waved and directed Mike's cargo container toward the platform. He held up his hands up to stop the container a few feet from the dock. Another alarm went off in Mike's head for the trailer was too far from the dock for unloading.

He reached for his Browning automatic pistol placing it on the seat by his side. His other hand lifted the UZI out of the door pocket. Mike was unsure of what was going on with the Casey PIC. Nothing normal had happened since he pulled into the compound past the guard gate.

"Come-mierda huelebicho interj! Interj! Camion porta contenedores Out! Out!"

George W. Clever

Two armed men with machine pistols appeared on either side of Mike's truck. They had been hiding beside the parked trucks at the dock. Two others with automatic weapons appeared in his mirrors as they stood on the dock. Mike's first reaction was to unload the UZI and stomp the diesel to pull away, but what about those box people in the trailer if bullets began to fly. Two men on the tarmac jumped on the truck's running boards. They smashed the cab's side windows and pointed their weapons at him.

There was no time for the heroics and firepower of Plan B. They had the drop on him, and he was covered with shards of glass. It was time for plan C whatever that was going to be. One of the men jerked the driver side door open and shoved his pistol in Mike's ribs. There was a time to be a bold aggressive Marine, but in this case, not if Mike intended to get old.

"Hands up...up! Oup! Oup! Now you! Out! Put hands up against the trailer. Here!" Another of the goons shouted as he pointed to the side of the truck. Another armed man with a machine pistol moved into the passenger side of the cab

Words Can Kill

*pushing Mike out the driver door. Together, the thugs
dragged him to the back of the trailer, and stood Mike
against the trailer doors patting him down. They found and
removed his Browning pistol.*

*"I hope you move so I can kill you now," one of the men
said to Mike.*

*It was a voice Mike knew from the moment he left
the Casey loading dock. It was the guard at the gate who
offered a coffee to Mike as he was leaving for Mexico. The
dock door to the office opened, and someone else joined the
party. Mike could not see who it was, but he recognized the
voice.*

*"You would have been better off sticking to the business of
snooping on delinquent husbands, Mr. Dunmore.
Homeboy, get this truck out of here now! Take it downtown
to the storage building."*

"Yes, boss."

*The man opened the cab door, threw his machine
piston on the passenger seat, brushed away the broken*

window glass on the driver side, and started the red truck moving toward the open gate.

"Kill Mr. Torcher and throw his body into the cardboard shredder dumpster."

Two shots rang out like the word 'dumpster' was a synonym for ready, aim, fire. The sounds were not the sound from small machine pistols, but a 'whump' sound from a police Remington 700, SPS tactical .308, SWAT sniper rifle. Two gutter punks folded up around their shoes like clothes falling off a hanger. Their automatic pistols clanged on the asphalt spinning around like tops.

At the far end of the compound, a rainbow of blue and red strobe lights appeared with two rollers, panda cars, police cruisers blocking the road. Their spotlights blinded the coyote driving the Peterbilt truck who immediately locked up the air brakes. The truck shuddered to a halt, giving off the smell of burning tire rubber. The driver raised both his hands, shoving them out the shattered driver side window. He was familiar with the drill.

Words Can Kill

Mike turned to face the voice he had recognized, looking at his own Browning pistol in the perp's hand.

Another familiar voice from behind the trailer said, "Put the pistol down, NOW! I wouldn't try anything funny. Our S.W.A.T. snipers on the top of those trucks at the back of the compound have you in their scope cross hairs. If you look carefully there is a red dot on your forehead. One move and there will be a .308 bullet hole where the dot used to be."

It was Lieutenant Meagan Glade. Glade stood there in the sodium vapor light of the loading dock with her own 9 burner aimed directly at the woman holding Mike's Browning handgun. A yellow aura silhouetted Glade's form like a visitor from another world.

"It can't be you. You're dead. Bruno killed you!" the woman screeched.

Mike moved close to the woman on the dock. He put his hand around her wrist pointing the pistol she was holding toward the wall. Prying it from her hand, he returned his Browning 9 to its rightful place in the back of his belt. Sergeant Keith joined the party at just the right moment to provide an answer to Lieutenant Meagan's re-incarnation.

"Sorry to disappoint you, lady, but I am sure you are not as disappointed as Bruno when he made the mistake of calling Meagan's name in her apartment before shooting her. Lieutenant Glade is not only an expert shot with her Glock 9 pistol, but she is also the fastest draw in our police department as poor dead Bruno found out. His gun never made it out of his jacket pocket."

"Do you know this woman, Mike?" Lieutenant Glade asked.

"Well, yes, I think I do. If you would be so kind to take a look at her right shoulder. I think you will find a small candy cane tattoo there."

"Don't move, sister. Show me your right shoulder or I will rip your clothes right off your body."

Words Can Kill

"Oooh! Meagan, what's got you so steamed? I never heard you speak like a Lieutenant before," Keith said with a smile.

"Listen, Sergeant Keith, I get really steamed, as you say, when some candy cane ass puts out a hit on me. Cuff her, Sergeant. It's here all right, Mike. She has the candy cane tattoo on her shoulder."

"Well, Sergeant Keith, say hello to Stephanie Kelly, Orville Kelly's wife, the former pole dancer Candy Sparkles, and Helen Casey's twin sister," Mike said. "Stephanie, you are violating your Bible Baptist dress code this evening with that hot pink leather dress? It must have been tiring making all those wardrobe changes after killing your sister and adding her to the bonfire you made out of my classic '69 Dodge Charger."

"You can't pin that on me. I had nothing to do with the disappearance of my sister."

"Well I think we can," Sergeant Keith replied. "We made a surprise visit to Kelly's Bar with a search warrant. In a panel behind the parking lot security monitor TV we found

a video tape very similar to the one you studied, Mike, but with a few differences. This one showed a family gathering alongside Dunmore's old Charger. Yes, it was very clear you, Stephanie, and your husband were arguing with each other and with Helen Casey before you struck her with the ball bat you found in the passenger side of Mike's car. Forensics found burned wood residue in the car trunk ashes."

"Kelly must have made an edited copy of the tape he gave to me on my request. He used the copy to throw me off the trail of the person who torched my car," Mike added. "I think he kept the original as insurance Stephanie would not say he murdered Helen Casey. Nice touch throwing my bat into the fire to be rid of the murder weapon, Stephie."

Meagan reached over toward Mike, and picked several pieces of truck window glass from his neck and face. He reached into his open shirt retrieving several larger, sharp pieces.

"Why did she kill her sister?" Lieutenant Meagan asked.

Words Can Kill

"Well we know Helen Casey was interested in divorcing her husband Harlan. She needed a lever to get the money she wanted from him. That is where I entered the picture and provided the file she sought. Unfortunately, I gave information about her child smuggling ring based in the Casey Trucking firm which really couldn't help her divorce case. I did not know at the time she was the ring leader. She and Kelly were having an affair, an affair Stephanie photographed during one of their heavy dates in the old camper. You may remember it was Helen who secured the loan from Harlan for the purchase of the bar for Kelly, and she was a regular at the bar way before Kelly bought the restaurant," Mike replied.

"John the barkeep saved the small pieces of photo Stephanie pasted to the bottom of Kelly's daily morning eye opener shot glasses. It was the method his wife chose to inform him she knew about his affair with Helen. He gave us the pieces of the photo when we did the warrant search of the bar. The picture showed Kelly and Helen doing

"bing-a-bang-a bong" in the motor home hideaway at the back parking lot," Sergeant Keith offered.

Detective Farrell snapped the cuffs on Stephanie and directed several boys in blue to assist the coroner with body clean up after his detective staff took all the evidence and made appropriate photos.

"After chicken frying your sister, you went to Harlan Casey and showed him the RV pictures. He could not afford a divorce scandal in the governor's race. He needed the money from kid smuggling for his governor campaign. Stephanie, you cooked up a deal with him. You would be Helen to continue the smuggling game as your sister for a share of the take. Sometimes you changed from the Baptist dress to a Victoria Secret wardrobe on the run to manage the kid smuggling racket."

Lieutenant Meagan stepped closer to Stephanie and padded her down for any hidden weapons in womanly places.

"There were even occasions when you did photo ops with Harlan so the police would think his wife was no longer

Words Can Kill

missing. You did a 'Helen impersonation' very well as the smuggling system 'boss'. Even those dock working creeps did not know you were not Helen. I suppose sister's share a lot including private information and husbands. You were a very busy woman returning to Kelly's Bar as Stephanie to keep an eye your husband Orville." Meagan said.

"It is a very interesting story you spin, Lieutenant, but you can't prove any of that. You've got me for the human trafficking, smuggling and nothing else," Stephanie screamed.

"Oh yes, child smuggling and so much more." Meagan continued. "The F.B.I. picked up Harlan Casey on money laundering for his campaign war chest. He copped as a witness in the murder case of his wife for a reduced sentence. Harlan said you told him you had taken care of his problem wife, and offered to temporarily replace her until he was elected. After becoming Governor, he was to offer you and Kelly pardons if you were ever convicted, plus of course, a continuing split of the illegal human trafficking and smuggling revenue. His motivation for the

deal he made with you? He needed the campaign cash from the kid smuggling. His wife's street sex history and current craziness had become a liability in the campaign. The plan you all made for explaining Helen's disappearance after the election was brilliant, but flawed. Helen was to learn to fly small aircraft, having an unfortunate accident over the Gulf never to be seen again. Just who was going to fly the plane into the water?"

"Oh yes, I failed to mention our wonderful forensic lab found unburned teeth in Mike's burned Charger for dental confirmation with enough DNA to identify your sister Helen as the crispy critter in Mike's car trunk. Helen was very proud of her dental work she had done on Harlan's money," Sergeant Keith said as he turned to the two uniform cops standing behind Stephanie.

"Either of you guys named Dan?"

"No sir."

"Damn! Too bad. I always wanted to say, 'Book her Dan O.' Guess it is time to give Stephanie another wardrobe *change into one of our orange jumpsuits. Take her downtown, officers."*

Turning to Lieutenant Meagan he said, "I am leaving to pick up Kelly at his bar. Do you or Mike want to come along?"

"Not me, Keith. I am hoping to resolve the disposition of those children in the little yellow short bus over there when your team gets them all out of the boxes," Mike answered.

"Probably will turn them over to Border Patrol agents at U.S. Immigration," Keith replied.

"If you do that, Keith, some of these kids may be delivered to relatives who are here illegally, or all of them will be returned to Mexico for re-cycling. If my hunch was right after meeting 'Just Jim' the DHS agent, the re-cycling of these children will bring them right back into the child prostitution and slave worker market as originally planned," Mike responded.

"We could hold them for a few hours at the precinct during an interview to gain information necessary for our case,

and delay our call to INS Immigration. I don't have the staff this shift to deal with all these kids and the other illegal adults. And then what would we do with them?" Keith offered.

"I know an advocate for illegal aliens I can call," Meagan said. "Sister Riley of the Maryknoll Order has many volunteers who are trained to assist refugees and illegal immigrants. She will help us get enough Spanish speaking helpers to do a one on one with everyone on the bus, even the ones who speak Farsi or any other language."

"But what do we do then?" Mike grunted. "They will still have to be sent back through the system."

Lieutenant Meagan looked at Mikes sad face. She knew the frustration of making so little difference in police work when in drug cases so many of the criminals are bailed out with the very profits of their shady business. She had to think of some way to help him resolve this dilemma.

"Maybe not. We need to let Sister Riley do her magic. If there are dangerous people in the group, we can ship them immediately to INS. Just leave this up to your Lieutenant

Words Can Kill

Meagan. I am very good at sorting out the terrorists in illegal alien groups. You can be sure I will get the best outcome for the kids possible. Now you need to go pick up Kelly at the bar, Sergeant Keith. And Mike you need to see your mom and Angel. They are at your mom's home waiting for your promised calls, and worrying about you."

"Before I check in at Mom's I want to know one thing. This was just one tiny child smuggling operation. Like a cold sore, we covered it with a bandage when the patient was suffering a gunshot wound. Tomorrow another kid smuggling racket will take the place of the one at Casey Trucking. Does anyone really care?"

"All any of us can do, Mike, is to clean and paint one little room in this world. It is frustrating, but that is what cop work is all about. We keep on sweeping and painting to keep evil away from the door. Like the Sorcerer's Apprentice, evil keeps on coming until we can't deal with it anymore. We always are hoping another young cop will be our relief. That is why I stay on the force," Sergeant Keith said. "If we quit, the ocean of evil will sweep us all away.

George W. Clever

You painted your room, Mike. Come to me, your old cop cruiser partner when you are ready to return to the force. Oh, and it was a good thing I got your call in time to set up a P.D. swat reception. How did you manage a call?"

"I realized the truck was wired to prevent any phone calls Made a quick stop at a rest area and called you from a pay phone there. Marines always have a plan C." I will consider your offer for a return to the force. Not sure it will fit into my plan if things go well with Angel when I see her. Anyone care to give me a lift to my mom's home?"

"I'll take you, Mike. Then I am going to find Sister Riley," Meagan said.

*****

40

The Proposal

Lieutenant Meagan pulled her unmarked police car to the curb in front of Terza Dunmore's home. She could see all the windows were dark.

"Mike do you think your mother and Angel went to bed? It is quite late."

The walkway at the side of the house was outlined by light from a small window casting shadows on the sidewalk. A circus of insects buzzed and smashed their little bodies against the window.

"Those women are probably drinking coffee and waiting in the kitchen. If not, I will find my way to my old bedroom, and try not to wake anyone. I am, well, I was going to say 'dead tired'. Never could understand how that could happen. Thanks for the lift, Meagan. You did a superior job on this case. Maybe we can work together again sometime."

George W. Clever

"Maybe when you are back on the force." She smiled. "Call me for coffee or lunch when you are."

Mike closed the car door gently like he did in the past when sneaking into the house after a long party night. The back door was not locked, but he did not expect it would be as Terza was a very trusting soul. He remembered she always said, "Locks just take bad guys a bit longer to break into your house. German Shepard dogs are much better locks." Her dog Hildegard did not move from his place by the stove when Mike opened the door. The door made a grinding sound as its wooden bottom slid over the linoleum floor. It rattled the door glass with a bang as it hit the edge of the kitchen counter.

"Come in, we have been waiting for you."

Mothers seem to have an instinct about where their sons are, what they are doing, and when they are coming home. Angel sat at the chrome-legged kitchen table with hot tea in a favorite German china cup, the one with a Neuschwanstein Castle picture ringed with roses. There

Words Can Kill

was a moment when all, including Hildegard the German Shepard dog, seemed stuck in time.

They were all released from the 1950s when Mike was able to say with his boyish grin, "What you all doing up so late?"

Angel and Terza sprang from their chairs like they heard the cannon shot for the Oklahoma land rush. Mike was caught in a double squeeze as the women threw their arms around him almost tipping over the kitchen table. Hildegard was pushing her way between legs to get into the 'Welcome Home' celebration.

"Whoa…easy now… I have not been gone that long."

"Too long for us, Mike. We want you to promise this will be the last time you will have us wait here in the kitchen to find out if you are still alive."

"I'm fine, Mom. The trip was a piece of cake. With the help of Sergeant Keith and Lieutenant Meagan, we found out who torched my classic Dodge Charger, and who was stuffed in the car trunk burned to a crispy critter."

George W. Clever

Both of the women blurted out the same expected question to Mike as the petted his mom's dog.

"Who set your car on fire? Was it Mrs. Casey in the trunk?"

"Yes, it was Helen Casey in the trunk. Her sister Stephanie and her husband Kelly set fire to the car after she whacked Helen with the ball bat they found in the passenger side of my car. They stuffed her in the trunk, and Stephanie took her place as boss of the child smuggling ring after she struck a deal with Harlan Casey. She made appearances as his wife for political candid P.R. shots and to end the police missing person search. Harlan Casey needed money for his Governor campaign which his wife had been providing by smuggling children into our country. Stephanie was an identical twin to Helen. She looked enough like her to fool everyone."

"Sit down and tell us what happened on your trip to Mexico. I saved a nice warm piece of apple pie for you.

Words Can Kill

Would you like a sandwich?" His mother said pushing him into one of the kitchen chairs.

"No thanks, Mom, I have one more very important thing to do before I get to enjoy your great pie."

Mike patted his chest pocket to see if the small box Carmichael had given him was still there. It was. He grasped the little black velvet box with two fingers and enclosed it in his palm, out of sight. His knee joints cracked as he bent down on one knee.

"Angel, I know we have unfinished business put off for some time by me after I realized the wounds I carried from Iraq, though not visible, had not healed. I could not keep my job on the police force, and acted out with anger many times at you, all undeserved. Our sleep together was anything but peaceful on those nights when my dreams took me back to Fallujah. I could see the fear in your eyes after one of my episodes. Well, I think the PTSD will not go away ever for me, but it can be controlled. The fire fight I went through when the smugglers tried to hit me on the Mexican highway triggered the Marine I had been taught to be, but I

didn't lose control of my anger. When it was over I was still driving a truck load of children out of Mexico. I did not see the familiar, but threatening streets of my past Marine experiences. I can control what returns as a flash back. I can be as near normal as most Marines ever are. I can be someone who gives love as well as receives it. You were with me Angel, all the way through my PTSD struggles."

He opened the box and offered it to Angel. A single full karat diamond was set in a tiny white gold band. Carmichael had good taste in jewelry as well as the weapons he had given to Mike.

"Angel, will you marry me?"

Terza Dunmore's face had a full smile as she looked at the couple. This was the moment she had hoped to see for so long. Mike needed a partner, someone who could love him with his wounds, and someone who would look after him when his mom took her dirt nap. No, not someone, only Angel would do.

Words Can Kill

Tears, starting as a trickle from the bottom of Angel's beautiful dark eyes. Soon they became a torrent flowing down her soft cheeks. Angel's cheeks now turned red on a tortured face as words formed in her mouth, found replacements, formed again, fought to replace her sobs until at last she was able bring some control to her emotions.

She turned to Mike looking him directly in his eyes to say, "No Mike. I can't marry you."

Terza and Mike were sure they had not heard the word 'No.' After all this time and Angel's dedication to keeping Mike's Private Investigation business solvent; and after all the conversations Angel and Terza held about their future together once Mike proposed, the word 'No' was impossible.

Mike was the first to speak. "Did you say no? I will quit the P.I. work, and find some nice steady safe job. I can meet with VA counselors and get this demon PTSD in my control."

George W. Clever

"No Mike, I will always be afraid of you as I wait for another night when you leap from the bed and chamber a round into the shotgun you keep by the nightstand. I will be waiting for a time when a truck backfire sends you under a restaurant table. Perhaps it will be another dream time when you think I am some threatening rag head, and put your hands around my neck. You will always be a thrill junkie. Now, you are like a genie in a bottle waiting for someone or something to flip your Marine switch. No Mike, I cannot marry you.

Angel drew a Kleenex from the box Terza had on the kitchen counter, and wiped away her tears. She placed her hand and on Mike's arm looking at his bewildered face.

"My friend Shawn, from college, you know the street gambler with medical service plans, has asked me to marry him. I said yes. Shawn is to graduate this spring with a degree in Radiology. He is safe and dependable. We have been seeing each other during all those times when you were gone to find the danger you need. No Mike I will not marry you."

Words Can Kill

Terza and Mike stared at Angel like people frozen in a cryogenic chamber as she handed the ring box back to Mike. Each of the staring faces of disbelief covered different thoughts. Terza was struggling with a broken heart, and dashed dreams of the grandchildren these two people might bring to her home, beautiful, handsome, intelligent grandchildren. She grew to love Angel, and trusted her, believing Angel loved her son. The work she put into steering Mike into proposing to Angel now seemed purposeless. There would be no marriage. There would be no grandchildren.

Mike was not accustomed to being rejected, or failing in anything he set out to do. His unemotional face mask hid the shock of this unexpected result. He was sure Angel wanted to marry him. All the time she spent helping him with his P.I. work went way beyond what little he could pay for a part-time secretary. Her patience with his outrageous quirks from the PTSD, and his need for a danger fix, seemed to re-enforce his expectation they would solve his nightmare problem, and eventually marry. She came to the hospital when I was hurt. What did that mean? Angel seemed like a marriage partner-in-waiting.

Her rejection of his proposal reminded him of the school dances he attended where the girls were on one side of the gym and the boys on the other. How many times had he crossed the gym no man's land to ask a girl to dance only to be rejected? He was too short and too geeky before his late growth spirt brought him to a six-foot height. The feeling of rejections at school dances, and his long retreat back from the girl's side of the gym to face a snickering pack of guys, had developed his control of peer ridicule. It even developed into a swagger and his devil may care smile.

It was a smile he could not put on in front of his mother. He did care. This rejection by Angel hurt. None of his thoughts could be laid out in front of Angel and his mother. It was not a thing Marines do. All he could force from his mouth was one pathetically practical thought.

"How am I going to run the P.I. office without you?" Mike asked.

Words Can Kill

"I know someone from the college library looking for part-time secretarial work. If you like, I can ask her to call you?"

"Yeeah, I guess that would be fine. What's her name?"

"Her name is Angelina."

Mike pushed off from his proposal kneeling position and stood by the table. Snapped the cover of the diamond ring box, and returned it to his pocket.

"You know, I was never able to shoot well from the kneeling position in the Corps. Time for me to see Carmichael at Paupers Pawn, and return the toys, along with this black box he loaned to me. I hope he will return my Vette to me. Good luck to you and Shawn, Angel."

He pulled the kitchen door open with a little extra force. It slammed against the sink counter. Terza followed him out into the side yard. Standing together in the dark, she stroked his cheek.

"Are you all right?" she asked.

George W. Clever

"I'm fine. Life is full of surprises and disappointments. Then Christmas comes around. Are you ok?"

"Yes, I am ok, just a little disappointed. I had visions of bridal shower plans in my head for Angel, and beautiful grandchildren to fuss over, but I do understand her decision. I hope you do also."

"Sure. You remember old Uncle Harold's saying, 'Cute women are like buses. Another one will come by in ten minutes.' See you tomorrow, Mom."

"Oh, I have one more disappointment for you before you go. Your mom was the admirer who paid the car rental company to switch the KIA Rio for the white Vette. That little Rio just wasn't what a good P.I. should be driving. The Corvette wasn't a gift, only a rental. I thought you needed a sports car. I hope Carmichael has not dented it. Never could sign for rental car extra insurance. The company called me today, and the rental lease is up. They want the car back tomorrow. Do give my best to Carmichael.

Words Can Kill

Mike kissed his mom on her cheek, did an about face from close order drill, and started the long walk back to Paupers Pawn shop on Main street.

As he closed the gate behind him mom yelled, "Bring Carmichael around Sunday for dinner. My good pot roast may sooth his unhappiness when you take back the Corvette."

*****

41

Tahiti Bound

That was a wrap for Fred Fonsworth's first novel, *Mike Dunmore Private Eye: The Case of the Lizard Lot Sisters.* The title was a bit long compared to the working one *Child For Sale.* He knew the publishers might change it. This book was sure to be the beginning of his spectacular career as a mystery writing author. There would be plenty more thriller stories just as the computer icon promised. Maybe there would even be a series of sequels featuring Mike Dunmore, Private Eye.

As soon as they were in the islands, Fred speculated, *Angelina would get them a new mailing address. It would be easy to mail his manuscript to Harper and Row Publishing. Several pen names were considered and most rejected. Fred decided he would need a name with strength and character. He could be Mike Dunmore. Well why not? After all he did create the famous private investigator.*

George W. Clever

Well ok. I know it was my laptop giving me all the character names in this story, but I was a partner with the computer in writing the story. Maybe it was destined that I would become Mike Dell (from my computer) Dunmore. Fred Fonsworth was a name for a loser. Yes, choosing the P.I.s name as a non-de-plume will make my laptop computer very happy. Publishers can fight over my masterpiece, and send big best seller checks to Mike and Angelina Dunmore, care of a post office box in Papeete, Tahiti.

"Hurry, Angelina, we will miss our flight," Fred shouted. "Do you have the tickets I gave you?"

"Yes, Fred. See in my hand, two tickets for Tahiti. Our hotel reservations for a free vacation are also with them. Put them in your carry-on please. Did you bring my luggage?"

"Yes, here is your pink personal items bag. I checked its matching suitcase with my gray one."

Words Can Kill

"It's a long line to the scanner. Will we make it in time? Do you think I will have to take off my shoes?"

"Yes, I think so."

As they approached the first TSA check point Fred dug into his brief case carry-on for the documents he would have to show.

"Ticket and I.D. Sir, may I have your airline ticket and your photo identification?" The TSA agent directed.

"Yes sir, I have them for myself and my wife Angelina."

"Where is your wife sir?"

"Well right beside me of course."

"Sir, there is no one beside you or behind you except a man with a beard."

"You must be mistaken. Can't you see she is right here? My wife, Angelina, is taking off her shoes to place them in a plastic bin with mine this very minute. See she is by that box right there!" Fred said pointing to an empty box containing only his shoes as it rolled into the scanner.

George W. Clever

The TSA screener looked to Fred's right and then his left. His super serious face took on a more intense stare as he looked at the brief case Fred carried. *Could it be a bomb from someone who is claiming an invisible wife?* He considered.

"Will you please step aside and wait just a moment, sir?"

The TSA agent touched his radio mic. "Security, code blue, traveler in distress."

Two armed uniforms quickly approached taking a position on either side of Fred. The TSA agent checking carry-ons moved up in support the forming triangle of detention around the strange passenger.

"Sir please follow me. We need to ask you a few questions. It's a simple security check."

"May I bring my wife Angelina with me?"

"Yes, of course sir, right this way."

Fred, carrying his shoes and carry-ons, was taken to a holding room within sight of the screener's desk. The

Words Can Kill

sterile room contained a single metal desk, half a dozen plastic chairs and a door with the sign 'detention room.

"Sit here dear." Fred directed Angelina toward one of the orange chairs by the door. "This will only take a minute. I am sure there is just a simple misunderstanding resulting in this special security check. They can't be too careful now days."

The TSA officer offered Fred to a chair by his desk.

"Please take a seat Mr. Fonsworth. This will only take a short amount of time."

The agent turned to the uniformed police woman standing by the door and spoke in a harsh whisper.

"Call County Public Mental Health. Get two of their sheriff deputies and the on call psychiatrist to come here immediately. This man is delusional. He thinks he's traveling with an invisible wife."

*****

42

The Interview

It was a nice room, nicer in many ways than Fred's basement writing den. It had windows. Sunlight painted the walls with yellow shades in a checker board pattern, a pattern made by iron mesh over each window. Hoping to find some fresh air from outside the building to cleanse the smell of pine solvent, medicine, and a hint of urine from his room, he tried to open two windows, but failed. A yellow pad and a stub of pencil were alone on the metal desk where he sat looking out at the gray clouds forming above the hospital pushing away the blue sky. His red Dell laptop was resting on a woolen blanket covering the bed. Sharply folded military corners of the bed linens were comforting and orderly.

The bed was made at 8:15 A.M. exactly each morning by a bearded man dressed in hospital green scrubs. The orderly had dragon tattoos lining both of his muscular arms. The dragon's tails flexed as he made the bed. This was not a man Fred wanted to annoy. No words were ever exchanged when he was in the room.

Fred could only ask himself the questions, where am I? How did I get here? Picking up the pencil stub, he looked through the window to the busy street below. He was fascinated with the picture as miniature people moving in and out of cars and shops. The people crossed streets at the corner to a musical background of horns with a base of vehicle rumbles.

Am I dead? Could I be with God so high above in this room? Is this a hotel I'm in? The hotel desk clerk asked so many questions when I registered. She never even asked for my credit card and photo I.D. I must write down the questions she asked. He considered. *Yes, I remember the doctor's first question. Was she a doctor? Not sure. She could have been a hotel manager. Her first question was about Angelina when she said…*

"Fred, my name is Doris. I'm going to use this little tape recorder so I don't forget anything important you might tell me. Do you mind?"

Words Can Kill

I saw my answer to her first question really didn't matter as she pressed the record button on the machine.

"When did you hire Ms. Angelina?" she asked.

Yes, I remember telling her Angelina was hired, no that is not right, she did my editing for free as a college English intern. She came to my office right after I thought it would be nice to have someone help me with my work, someone like the part-time secretary Mike Dunmore had working for him. I needed Angelina to do my editing.

Then Doris asked me, "Do you mean like the secretary character in the novel you're writing?"

"Oh yes," I said. "Just like in my novel, but words to hire her did appear on my computer screen before Angelina showed up in my basement office."

Yes, of course, I know now the woman asking me all those questions was probably a doctor. She wore a white coat, and around her neck was one of those things they use to hear your heart beat. Why did she want to know about my computer research? I bet she was trying to steal novel.

George W. Clever

She asked me if my thoughts often appear on my computer screen.

I knew this could be a loaded question, but I carefully explained, "Well, not often. I tried not to have what I call 'butterfly thoughts'. You might call them 'brain farts'. I have to keep focused on writing my novel you know."

After I said that, the doctor rubbed her head with the pencil she was holding. What was she thinking? Was the pencil a hearing device for someone outside of the room?

Her next question was very odd. She said, "When the words appeared on your computer screen was it because you typed them?"

Oh that was certainly a silly question. I explained I had absolutely nothing to do with typing any of those messages. It was all the work of the computer responding to my butterfly thoughts. I did wonder why she asked me that question. Was it because the judge who sent me here

Words Can Kill

told her to do so? She seemed bent in one direction of her questioning. I was asked if my butterfly thoughts ever got me in trouble.

"Oh yes," I told her. "They did cause me a great deal of trouble. There was one time when I thought it would be better if Myrna's mother died so my wife and I could get back to a better relationship. I had hoped we would love each other more and have greater sex."

Like a bulldog she asked me a very personal question. "Was that when her mother fell down the cellar stairs?"

I told her it was a very terrible accident. Yes, I remember the doctor reaching over the table and placing her hand on mine. She stared at me asking about Myrna's mother falling down the cellar stairs. Her next question was a lulu. She asked me if I pushed Myrna's mother down the stairs. I was shocked she would even consider asking such a question.

"Oh for heaven sakes no, I did not push her down the stairs. I wasn't even there. I was at work after shopping in the early afternoon." I replied.

George W. Clever

Then she asked, "Did Myrna's mother Bertha grab for your shirt to keep from falling?"

How did she know that? Maybe I pulled the shirt away to get a better hold on her before she fell. Could it be I did give her an accidental push in adjusting my grip? No, I wasn't even home. I don't remember.

Fred turned from the window with the woven wire guard and stared at his room door wondering if it was locked. He ran the meeting with Doctor Doris through his mind like a DVD with a big scratch playing the same song over and over. *Did the doctor lady really think I killed my mother-in-law? Why would she think that? I'm not some kind of monster. Computers make people do lots of bad things. They can make people take money from naïve folks. TV news had a program on how perverts use computer chat lines to steal children. Maybe computers can even do worse things on their own. No, I didn't really want Bertha Scones to die. Then my interrogation by Doris took a turn I knew could be dangerous for me.*

Words Can Kill

She asked, "Fred, will you tell me about the times when those, what do you call them, butterfly thoughts got you in trouble?"

Doctor Doris, if she is a doctor, never believed what I said to her. I told her about the time I was so hungry I said out loud, 'I can eat a horse.' A dead mustang was delivered to my home for me to eat. I sent it back to the butcher. Not all these messages were bad. Why I was glad to get rid of Myrna's damn dog Killer, the big Poodle/Golden Retriever. One of my brain farts replaced Killer with a little Poodle/Chihuahua. Then there was the time when I got my new laptop, and a job at the hotel so I could do more writing.

All through my interview I could hear a humming sound with an occasional squeak made by the small wheels of her cassette recorder turning on the table before us. The doctor seemed to count three squeaks each time before asking her next question. It was like waiting for the sound chalk made on a school room board. She wanted to know if I had a good loving relationship with my wife, Myrna.

George W. Clever

Doris repeated the question a second time adding, "after her mother died." Yes, I really thought it would get better, but Myrna found someone else for her sex partner. They made a baby together. I don't know why she never wanted children with me.

I remember the doctor looked up from her notes, and asked me the question I really did not want to answer. It was so embarrassing. What man wants to admit he can't satisfy his wife? Doctor Doris wanted all the horrid details. She even asked me how I found out Myrna was pregnant. Doris would never believe I received the information from one of those brain farts appearing on my laptop screen. I couldn't tell her the computer told me Myrna was pregnant!

You know, as I think about this message it was totally confusing to me. We hadn't had sex for months before and after her mother died, but I never considered someone else could be the father of her baby. I would like to find out who was the father of Myrna's baby. Don't know

Words Can Kill

who it was, but she said it was someone from her work at the candy factory. She wouldn't tell me his name.

Why would Doctor Doris ask me how I learned of Myrna's pregnancy? Well, she probably was one of those 'shrink' doctors. It felt like her eyes were entering a worm hole in my head, and I couldn't stop my answers. I wanted to fill my ears with cotton stuffing from the lumpy bed mattress in the room. I knew there was no way to end this third degree interrogation by Doctor Doris short of killing her. A brain fart to solve that problem would have been most welcome at this point. Maybe that is what they mean by mercy killing... or maybe...

I think Doris put this mercy killing thing in my head when she said, "Is that the reason you pushed Myrna and her mother down the cellar stairs? Did you think it would be considered a mercy killing?"

"How can you say such a thing?" I told her. "No, Myrna was the one hearing voices. She was the crazy one, you know. She heard the voice from the cellar before she fell. I

George W. Clever

even went to a support group meeting with her. The Hearing Voices seminar was held at St. Drogo's church. Nothing seemed to help her. She still heard a voice coming from the basement stairs in our home after all the meetings she attended."

"You sound defensive Fred." Doris said.

"Listen Doctor Doris, I do not hear voices coming from the cellar stairs, nor from anywhere other than people who speak with me." I really told her off.

I know I should have stopped answering any more of the doctor's questions right then. She will use them to keep me from joining Angelina in Tahiti now. I sent my lovely secretary ahead when the TSA officer made such a fuss about us traveling together.

If I see Doris again I will tell her once more, "Doctor Doris, I do not hear strange voices. Not in the cellar. Not anywhere." Then I will say, "You are a doctor, right?"

"I am a psychiatrist, Fred."

"Oh, I didn't hear you come in the room."

Words Can Kill

"I never left the room, Fred."

"You a head shrinker? I guess I was thinking out loud when you came in. Oh, yes, I forgot you were already here. You probably will use what I said against me. I do have the right to remain silent. I always try to be silent, but it was so hard. Why are you here again?"

"I have a few more questions to ask you."

"Well, Doctor, I don't hear voices now, and I didn't hear them then. Maybe Myrna heard the voices because she was pregnant. You know pregnant women do funny things."

From the frown on the doctor's face I could see my comment on the funny things pregos do was not very P.C. I really am sick of all the P.C. stuff. People should honor the First amendment and be able to accept anything others say. Well, in most cases. Maybe not yelling fire in a crowded theater or saying someone should be killed. Maybe pregos don't do funny things, but I see it in the movies a lot. People just have lost their sense of humor.

"Did you ask Myrna if she was pregnant, Fred?"

George W. Clever

"Not at first, I thought it would embarrass her if she was just gaining weight, and not pregnant. She never brought up the subject, but after a few months I noticed her body changing."

"Is that when you asked Myrna to name the father of her child?"

"No, I did not. But one morning she told me the voice coming from the cellar stairs was asking her to come and listen. The voice had something to tell her. I probably never should have said what I did at that moment. I told her the voice was saying, SHUT UP. I also told her something else that really made her mad."

I can tell this interview was dragging my ass into a landmine field as Doris readies her next question. She even poked me with her pencil just now when I started to doze off.

Doris leaned forward, almost in Fred's face and said, "Did you ask her if she was pregnant when she stood at the top of the cellar stairs listening to the voice you couldn't hear?"

Words Can Kill

"Well, Doc, I said this to Myrna. "Maybe the voice is from the man who made you pregnant."

When I did ask who was the father of the child she was carrying she really reacted in a strange way. A frightened look spread across her face like a surprise wave crashing down on the beach. I opened the cellar door, grabbed her by the arm, and told her to look down the stairs. There is no one in the cellar! No one was calling her

"Did she look?"

"I had to push her to the door so she would listen."

"Did she fall down the stairs then?"

"NO! She just screamed at me. I heard her say the voice told her I had pushed her mother to her death."

Oh my, why is it I am just now remembering those famous words. 'I have the right to remain silent.' What will this woman do with the information she is recording? I could be in serious trouble here.

"What happened after she heard the voice, Fred?"

George W. Clever

"She pulled away from my hand, and fell down the stairs."

"Was that the cause of her death?"

"No, she hit her head on a shovel."

"Did she hit her head during the fall?"

"Absolutely not! She hit her head many times after the fall"

I shouldn't have said that, but I did. That doctor didn't fool me. I will give her no more answers. She will not be able to pry a thing out of me, not ever.

"How did she hit her head with a shovel many times?"

"I don't remember."

"Did you do it, Fred? Did you hit her in the head with the shovel?"

"No, I didn't. I can't remember. Maybe the voice did it."

Like a broken record, more like a cop than a doctor, she keeps hammering me with these questions. Now I know how the police get confessions, and how political brainwashing happens.

Words Can Kill

"But you never heard the voice did you?"

"No! You are making me hear a voice in my head. It is saying 'Shut up Fred, Shut up."

Doc Doris had to know it was not me doing any of those bad things. I tried to explain again, but she did not seem to listen. You can tell when someone makes up their mind never to change it. I slipped again telling Doris about the special writer's icon on the computer.

"No, for the third time, I do not hear voices. It was my laptop screen that told me Myrna was going to be killed. When words appear on my computer screen you know what they say will really happen."

"Ok Fred, I guess that will be all today.

I heard the door handle turn with a loud click. Someone was coming to rescue me from Doctor Doris and this place. All this fuss over my wife's accident made no sense to me.

A young woman, about twenty, dressed in one of those 'dress for success' gray suits with lace from a see-

George W. Clever

through blouse showing above the top jacket button, pushed the door open. She placed a door stop under it and turned toward us when Doctor Doris spoke.

"Fred, this is Clara Barter. Ms. Barter will show you to our recreation room. Clara, will you be sure to include Fred in our focus group this afternoon? You will like this gathering, Fred. There will be many writers in the group: Ms. Emily Dickenson, Mr. Swift, Mr. Shakespeare, Mr. Dickens, Mr. Goethe, and a couple of members from the Sinclairville Library Write Circle writers group, just to name a few."

I knew all those writers would be very intimidating to me. Where was my laptop? Oh, there it is on the bed. It would be needed if they asked me about my writing. I have to ask the doctor about my laptop.

"Will it be all right if I bring my laptop computer? I can use it to write my next novel."

"We have P. C.s, you know, Personal Computers, in the recreation room you can use. But I think using your own

Words Can Kill

laptop might be permitted. I will have to find out if it is ok. Clara will let you know."

"Oh, that will be wonderful. I will start on my next Mike Dunmore P.I sequel novel tomorrow. My editor is waiting for it."

The last thing she said to me before Ms. Barter took my arm and led me out of the room was very threating. I shiver when I think about it. She looked directly at me speaking in an alarming tone of voice.

"I think you will find your stay at Shady Elms most pleasant. You will be our guest for quite a while."

"Well, maybe not" the butterfly thought replied.

S

Made in the USA
Columbia, SC
21 February 2018